D1644120

BEACH BODIES

"In Delaware, the beaches are free (no tags, no fees) and summer feels like a religious rite, with the beach as altar and the parking meter a kind of collection plate."
—Charles Strum
The New York Times

CHAPTER 1

On the day he was murdered, Frank Wilson's morning got off to a bad start, which was saying something, considering that he lived and worked in Rehoboth Beach. Even the worst morning in Rehoboth was pretty good, simply because you were at the beach, and not commuting to work on the beltway or stuck in a cubicle somewhere.

People scrimped and saved—or put a major dent in their credit card balance—just so they could spend a week at the beach each summer. Frank woke up every day and tried to sell a piece of that dream to those happy hordes.

Along with working on their tans, fishing or whale watching on the *Keena Dale* out of Lewes, eating Grotto Pizza and strolling the boardwalk, a favorite activity of any normal adult who visited the beach was looking at real estate. Most vacationers just gawked at the for sale signs and whistled at the prices, but Frank's job as the marketing director at a real estate firm was to get them to do more than kick the tires. He wanted people to think about floor plans, balloon mortgages and location, location, location.

Normally, it wasn't really a bad job because he was helping people actualize their dreams of living at the beach. The people were pleasant and he was nice to them. Happy, happy. But on this morning he overslept and had to skip his cup of coffee, so he was groggy when he got to the office. Fighting the summer beach traffic had not improved his mood.

One of the surreal things about working at the beach was that everyone else was on vacation, wearing swimsuits and flip-flops, but Frank was in a wrinkled shirt and tie, heading to the office. Once he got there, the hotshot new manager who was ten years younger than Frank—and still had all his hair, goddamn him—stopped by Frank's desk to bust his balls just because he could, considering that he was the nephew of the firm's owner.

The kid wanted Frank's marketing plan for the new development they were selling at an old farm a good ten miles north of Lewes and five miles off Route 1. Everything about the place was on the wrong side of location, location, location, so they were having a hard time pitching it as beach-oriented. If you enjoyed chicken farms and soybean fields you'd love the view, but you were more likely to smell manure than salt spray from your deck.

Frank was well aware that ninety-nine percent of selling the project would have to do with the name. They'd been kicking around Delmarva Acres and The Peach Orchard, because the farm had once been home to fields of fruit trees before the big peach blight wrecked the boom times back in 1890 ... well, that had been a while ago, but in Frank's experience you could never go wrong with names invoking history, trees, fruit or orchards. However, the ball-busting nephew kept pushing Ocean Acres as a likely name. Frank thought that just seemed like too much lipstick on the pig.

Frank did not have the marketing report ready. It was at the bottom of a pile of papers on his desk because he figured nobody would need it for a couple of weeks.

"Oh, *that* report," Frank said. "I just need to polish it up a little."

He spent the rest of the day scrambling to finish the report and had it on the nephew's desk by five o'clock, where he was sure it would sit for the next couple of weeks, untouched, while the kid dreamed up more great names: Mariner's

Cove, Oyster Ridge, Seaweed Estates ... well, that last one was a stretch even for the kid.

Frank left the office and met Tom Brody, who managed vacation rentals, for a couple of beers and nachos. They settled into a booth and hunkered over their India Pale Ales.

"Twitter stock," Brody said, shaking his head and smiling as he hefted a fresh draft. "Who would have thought? It went through the roof. Hell, with what I made off that I can pay the college tuition for all three of my kids."

Frank ordered another beer and tried to smile. He was glad for his buddy, but his own most recent dabbling in the stock market had been a terrible mistake. A solar energy company, seemingly undervalued, had proven just how valueless it was by going bankrupt. He hoped his kid would be smart enough to get a scholarship somewhere. Right now, Del Tech was looking good.

He left the bar with three beers under his belt. Frank rarely drank so much.

He didn't even see the red light.

His car slammed into the side of a brand new pickup truck. Two burly construction workers got out of the damaged pickup and started toward him. They looked seriously unhappy.

He tried to get out, but the collision had crumpled the hood of his car, jamming the door shut. As he struggled with the door, Frank got a look at himself in the rear view mirror. He was covered in blood. *Holy crap. I'm dying!* That was weird when he thought about it, because he felt good, more like you'd expect with a few brews in you and less like the Grim Reaper had one arm around your shoulders. He took a closer look and saw his nose was bleeding. Bleeding *a lot*, but it didn't hurt that much. He sort of remembered banging his face on the steering wheel. His heart quit trying to punch a hole through his chest. Not dying. So far so good.

Somebody rapped on his window and Frank looked up to see one of the construction workers peering into the car. He tapped at the glass again with a finger thick as a sausage.

"You okay, buddy?"

"Yeah," Frank said. "I just can't get my door open."

The man grabbed hold of the handle and tugged. With a wrenching sound, the door fell away and clattered to the street.

"I hope you got good insurance," the construction worker said. "I just bought that goddamn truck. Cost me forty-five grand, dude. Custom paint and everything."

Frank didn't say a word. He knew from watching those lawyer infomercials on late-night TV that you weren't supposed to admit you were at fault in an accident, even if you knew you were. And Frank was sure he was.

Two Rehoboth Beach Police cars arrived, lights flashing. Officers lit flares and started directing traffic through the intersection. Horns honked. Rubberneckers crept past to see the wreckage. Frank shrank lower in the driver's seat.

"Are you all right, sir?" asked an officer who materialized at the side of the car.

"Just banged my nose."

"Let me get traffic going here and then I'll have some questions for you."

Frank nodded. And then he remembered the beers he'd had. Uh oh.

"Z, Y, X," he started reciting to himself, practicing for a sobriety test. "Z, Y, X, T, U, V — damn."

An ambulance pulled up and two medics dressed in blue coveralls approached. One fat, one thin.

"How do you feel?" the skinny one asked. He was tall and bony, with jet-black hair that stood out from his head in clumpy, stiff corkscrews. A silver hoop earring flashed in his right ear and there was a stud centered under his lower lip, like a rivet. His eyes looked mismatched, one slightly greener than the other. Spooky.

Frank's fashion knowledge didn't extend much beyond penny loafers and golf shirts, but he could tell this kid was a goth. He also looked awfully young to be an EMT.

"All I've got is a bloody nose," Frank said.

The fat medic helped Frank position a gauze pad on his nose, which was beginning to ache. Frank couldn't help noticing the fat one's hands were sticky. What the hell was on them? Blood? Then he got a whiff of chocolate. And wasn't the guy supposed to be wearing latex gloves? He'll probably give me AIDS or something, Frank thought.

"Why don't you come along and get in the back of the ambulance, mister," suggested the skinny medic.

"Fine," Frank said. "We're going to the hospital, right?"

The skinny medic and the fat guy looked at each other.

"That's usually where ambulances go," the kid said slowly, glancing at the fat medic. *Ha, ha, funny.*

"All right, you don't have to be a smart ass about it." Frank looked over at the cops. They were almost finished untangling the traffic jam, and in a minute they'd turn their attention to him and his BAC. "What I mean is, shouldn't we go right away? I don't feel so hot."

"Sure. Hop in."

Frank climbed in and sat on the stretcher in back as the medics shut the door behind him and locked it. He felt relieved. If he waited around the hospital for a while, his liver would metabolize some of the alcohol out of his system before the cops arrived to question him and give him a blood-alcohol test.

"Z, Y, X," Frank chanted to himself as the ambulance drove away.

• • •

A minute later another ambulance pulled up at the accident scene.

"Where's the patient?" the driver asked one of the cops directing traffic. "We were dispatched for a ten-fifty P.I."

"You guys are a little late," the cop said.

"Huh? You got a DOA for us out of this fender bender?"

The cop shook his head. "Hell, no. An ambulance already took him to the hospital. He wasn't hurt too bad. Bumped his nose. Worse than that he'll get DUI, judging by the beer I smelled on his breath."

"Geez, another drunk. Welcome to summer at the beach. But what ambulance?" the driver asked. "We were the only unit dispatched."

"Beats me." The cop shrugged. "It was an ambulance. Red and white. Lights on top."

"I know what an ambulance looks like," the driver snapped. "Whose ambulance was it? Lewes? Don't tell me dispatch sent someone from way the hell up in Milford."

"How am I supposed to know?" the cop asked, getting annoyed. "I guess one of those private services saw the accident and stopped. They'll do anything for a buck."

"Huh," the ambulance driver said. He shut off the emergency lights and eased back into traffic.

• • •

In the back of that private ambulance, Frank was thinking that he shouldn't have had those beers. He didn't even see the red light. Now his insurance would go sky high, and that was even if the police didn't get him on some kind of drinking and driving charge.

Frank tried to relax. At least he wasn't hurt too badly. Even the ambulance crew must have thought he was in good shape, considering they weren't using lights and sirens.

Well, it did seem ridiculous to use lights and sirens for a bloody nose. But what if it was broken? The ambulance driver, the one who looked like an Alice Cooper wannabe, was taking his time through the congested resort town streets.

Wasn't one of them supposed to ride back here with him? A bloody nose was one thing, Frank thought, but what if he had a heart attack or a hemorrhage or something? There didn't seem to be any way of getting the attention of the two medics up front.

The more he thought about it, the shabbier

the ambulance began to look. The interior was dingy and some of the metal surfaces had a coating of rust. There wasn't much equipment on the shelves overhead, and even the various cardboard boxes of bandages looked slightly yellowed. A couple boxes were obviously empty. What if someone needed—he strained to read the writing on an empty box—*toilet tissue, hospital grade*. What did they need that for on an ambulance? Clearly, the vehicle should have been better equipped. He knew that all the beach towns had a very strong property tax base. His tax dollars were supposed to take care of this kind of thing. God knows he paid enough in taxes.

Finally, the ambulance slowed and he felt it turn a corner. His nose was throbbing. Through the back windows he could tell they were in a parking lot.

They stopped, and the two medics walked around and opened the ambulance doors. The fat one was blowing a bubblegum bubble between his thick lips. It popped and he peeled a skim of gum off his face and jammed it back into his mouth.

"We're here," the goth medic said. "Welcome to the hospital."

The fat one grinned.

"Great," Frank said, starting to get up.

"Uh, no," the goth-looking attendant said,

jumping up into the ambulance. Being so tall and thin, you expected him to be gawky and awkward as Ichabod Crane, but this guy moved like a cat. "What I mean, mister, is that you have to lie down. We have to take you into the hospital on the stretcher."

"But I'm fine," Frank insisted.

"Sorry, mister. It's the rules."

Frank lay back on the stretcher. He started to protest when the fat guy strapped down his legs. The skinny EMT did his arms. "Hey —"

"Regulations," the skinny one said, pulling a strap tight. "We've had some people get in there and just go nuts. It's for your own protection."

They unloaded the stretcher and wheeled him through a gray door into a dimly lit area that must have been the hospital's basement. Heating pipes, electrical conduit and assorted wires were woven together overhead as they rolled Frank down a hallway.

"Looks kind of rough," Frank said, starting to wonder which hospital this was. He had been to Southern Delaware General before, and this didn't look like it. "I've never seen an emergency room like this."

"Uh, we're in the basement," the goth explained. "They're doing some work on the ER so we have to go in this way."

They arrived in a windowless, cinderblock room. Bright lights shined down. Frank's medical knowledge consisted of what he had picked up from late-night reruns of *ER*, but to him this looked like some kind of crude operating room. Medical gadgets lined the walls. He noticed a Styrofoam cooler in the corner that had "Human Organ" stenciled on the side. Whoa.

The goth jammed a needle into Frank's arm.

"Ouch! Jesus, what's that for?"

"It'll help you relax."

The fat one poised some kind of mask over Frank's face. To Frank, it looked like a gas mask. He started to sweat. All this for a bloody nose?

Then a doctor walked in. He wore a green surgical gown, his face covered with a mask. The green-clad figure didn't even look human except for the eyes, which were magnified behind the man's thick glasses. The doctor's freshly scrubbed hands were held in front of him and the goth kid slipped surgical gloves over them. Then the goth cut away Frank's shirt, exposing his abdomen.

His heart was pounding. What the hell was going on?

"Bloody nose," he tried to say, his syllables slurred. What had that shot been? He tugged weakly against the straps holding him to the stretcher. "All I have is a bl—"

"Shut up," the goth said.

The surgeon began painting lines on Frank's abdomen with an orange-red solution.

Frank saw the scalpel coming down.

The fat medic smothered Frank's scream with the mask.

CHAPTER 2

The phone was ringing. Nick Logan fumbled for it in the dark and managed to knock the cell phone off the bedside table and under the bed. *Great.*. The ringing stopped and he rolled over.

He was just drifting off again when the ringing started back up. What time was it? *Two a.m.* Nobody ever got a call they wanted at this time of night. It was bound to be bad news or an old friend who'd gotten drunk and wanted to talk. He dug around in the dust bunnies under the bed, dragged out the phone, glanced at the number.

Beverly. His sister wasn't in the habit of drinking heavily or staying up late. Bad news, then.

"Sis," he grunted into the phone. "What's

wrong?"

"Nick, Nick, thank God you answered."

He felt something cold grip at his heart. Was it mom? Dad? In his career as a cop he had delivered his share of bad news late at night, so maybe now it was his turn to be on the receiving end.

"It's Katie," his sister said. The vise around Nick's heart tightened. Katie was his twenty-year-old niece, a junior at Towson University who was spending the summer working at the beach. "She's missing, Nick. I'm so worried."

Beverly's next words came at him in a gush. Katie hadn't returned to her beach house the night before and her worried roommates called her mother on the off chance that Katie had headed home and forgotten to tell them. She wasn't answering her phone or texts. Her roommates hadn't seen her now in nearly twenty-four hours. Nick spent a lot of time saying, "Uh, huh" and just hearing his sister out. When she started repeating herself he broke in.

"You know, she is twenty years old, sis. Remember how we were at that age? Maybe she met a lifeguard—"

"I know that, Nick! But not to call anybody? Not even her friends? You've got to find her, Nick. The police down there were just humoring me when I called. You know the chief there. We talked about that, remember? He used to be your partner, for God's sake."

"Yeah, well. That was a long time ago."

"Please find her, Nick!"

He promised.

When he got off the phone, he started to pack. He took two pairs of neatly folded jeans out of his dresser, along with four T-shirts. He thought a moment, and added a couple pairs of shorts that were in the very bottom drawer. He was going to the beach, after all. Since moving to the mountains he'd been more of a boots and jeans kind of guy. Come to think of it, the shorts probably wouldn't fit because he'd lost a lot of weight over the last few months. He spent most of his time now cutting firewood and splitting the chunks of oak and maple and cherry the old school way with a maul and wedge.

One thing you soon realized when you moved out to Garrett County was that it got goddamn cold in the winter, not like in Baltimore. They measured the snow out here in feet, not inches. And it got *really* goddamn cold when you lived in an old farmhouse that relied on a wood stove to keep the pipes—and your ass—from freezing. So Nick's hands were now leathery and calloused. At six-foot-two Nick was a big, square-shouldered guy, and his muscles were now a lot like those stubborn knots in the firewood that he'd been busting up for months. If some asshole lifeguard had been mistreating his niece, that boy was sure as shit going to get his ass kicked. The last item he put in the duffel bag was a Beretta Storm .45, just in case something more sinister than horny lifeguards was involved.

He locked up, tossed the duffel bag on the seat of his pickup truck, and started up the bumpy old driveway that wound toward the paved road. The overgrown farm had been in the family for decades, but until Nick showed up nobody had lived there for years. The house was almost half a mile off the road, deep in the woods, and last winter Nick had been snowed in for a week before the farmer next door came with a tractor to plow him out. Nick gave him a cord of wood.

The mountains were still dark, but dawn tinged the sky pink. He had come to love these mountains, and sometimes in this new place he caught himself thinking of something he had seen or done that he was excited to tell Karen about. Then he remembered. *Aw, Jesus.*

The quiet out here had been a salve for his soul. Away from the city, he even found he could pray. Nick wasn't all that religious and he didn't go to church, but being in the mountains made him come to appreciate the possibility that there was some kind of God up there, a higher being.

Mostly, he prayed for Karen and wondered if, just maybe, there was something else that awaited them all. If not heaven, then another kind of dimension or plane of existence. He sure as hell hoped there was a place like that.

He pushed the thought from his mind. It would be a rosy kind of summer morning, with a little mist between the trees. Lights starting to come on in the houses he passed. There was an all-night gas station with decent coffee just before the interstate, so he'd stop there to get a dose of caffeine. Nick wasn't a morning person.

He turned on the radio and fiddled a bit, but could only get country music. He was living the country life, but he drew the line at listening to some dude in a cowboy hat and high-heeled boots that made him walk funny. Nick forgot about the radio and thought about his niece. Deep down, he had a feeling that she was all right. During twenty years as a Baltimore City cop, Nick had learned to trust his instincts. But he'd make the six-hour drive to the ocean just to put his sister's mind at ease. And then he'd head back to the mountains, hunker down, and split more firewood.

• • •

As the morning sun crept over Delaware Bay and the Atlantic Ocean beyond, Grubb steered the van down a dirt road that weaved through the coastal marshes. He brushed a shock of jet black hair out of his eyes and hit the low beams so he could see the pot holes in the road. This area near

Bowers Beach had been flooded during the last big hurricane, and the road was still a mess.

"I'm not so sure this is a good place to dump a body. It's the first place the police are going to look," Fat Boy said. His real name was Johnny Kraftheimer, but Grubb could never think of him as anything other than Fat Boy. Johnny? Nah. And he definitely wasn't *Krafty*. Not by a long shot. The name Fat Boy fit him like an oversized T shirt.

Nobody knew Grubb's first name. He was just Grubb.

"What do you think they do, Fatty, have body-finding patrols through here? It's perfect."

Unsuitable even for the nearby chicken farms, the marshy ground had become a haven for illegal dumping and dirt bike aficionados. Grubb drove past rusting washing machines, torn couches, rotting heaps of brush. He'd heard rumors that pirates used to bury their treasure in this no man's land, which wouldn't surprise him at all. He stopped the van near the black water of a tributary that ran out into the bay.

"Here's good," Grubb said. He got out and slid open the side door of the battered van. Fat Boy helped him drag the naked body out.

"He's heavy," Fat Boy said.

They hoisted the body and carried it toward the dark water.

"Wait a minute," Grubb said.

"What?"

"Put him down." Grubb nodded at an old couch. "Just sit him down on that thing."

"Grubb, man, we can't leave him *here*."

"Just do it, Fat Boy."

They dropped Frank Wilson's remains on the old sofa and Grubb plopped down next to him and put his arm around the dead man's shoulders.

"You got your phone handy? Take my picture."

Fat Boy shook his head but pulled out his phone. The thing about Grubb was that he was seriously messed up, as in *mental*. All that goth crap gave him an obsession with death and destruction.

When Fat Boy was done, Grubb insisted on seeing the photo. Fat Boy handed him the phone and then found a warm candy bar in his pocket. He gulped it down and then licked his sticky fingers while Grubb texted the photo to himself.

"Please don't put that on Facebook."

"Do you think I'm that stupid? This is more of a personal keepsake." He cackled, the sound of his laughter making Fat Boy shiver. Then Grubb got up. "Grab the legs."

Grubb took the corpse by the arms, Fat Boy grabbed the feet, and on the count of three the body splashed into the brackish water and sank.

CHAPTER 3

Dr. Karl Kreeger worked through the night. Time was everything in the organ business. As soon as the kidneys left the body an invisible clock began ticking off the minutes. The kidneys Kreeger had extracted from the accident victim had a value in the six figures and he had just two days to place them.

Kreeger was a local boy, having grown up in lower, slower Delaware. It was a fact he wasn't particularly proud of, considering that he was still here all these years later, medical degree or not. While there were those who loved their Delmarva roots, reveling in their boyhoods on the farm and swapping muskrat recipes, Kreeger thought it was something best kept hidden, like a bad tattoo left over from a drunken night on the Dover strip.

His grandfather used to have a produce farm near Harrington, Delaware, and his business plan could be summed up by the simple words he used to mutter while looking over the mounds of ripe tomatoes and cantaloupes and sweet corn: "Sell it or smell it, boy. Sell it or smell it."

Those words made Kreeger smile as he worked tonight. His grandfather's melons weren't all that different from a set of kidneys.

The heart, liver and pancreas would have brought a good price but these organs lasted only a few hours outside the body. Considering they were in the midst of the Washington-Philadelphia-New York-Boston metroplex, he easily could have found a patient nearby, but Kreeger didn't want Southern Delaware General Hospital to get a reputation for serving up quickie hearts and livers. Others might become suspicious.

The man's kidneys were far more marketable. Hooked to the perfusion machine that pumped fluids through the kidneys and kept them viable, the organs could last up to seventy-two hours outside the body. Time enough to fly them anywhere in the country. While it was true that some medical centers would not accept kidneys more than forty-two hours old, there would still be plenty of takers.

So Kreeger had pulled an all nighter, just like in med school.

The thought of a new Aston Martin kept him going. It was the world's most beautiful sports car right down to its hand-sewn leather seats, but it was unattainable even on a surgeon's salary, particularly if that surgeon had steep student loans for med school and worked at a second-rate regional hospital. His grandfather had been rich enough to pay for med school, but the old man had as much family feeling as a dried-up leather boot. He hadn't offered Kreeger a dime of that produce money. Years later, Kreeger had mountains in student debt.

Kreeger figured he had never gotten a break in his career, never made the right connections. The parade had passed him by when it came to promotions and the best jobs. He had dreamed of New York or Chicago or San Diego. Others may have been satisfied riding out the rest of their careers as a cut-and-paste surgeon at the beach, but he wanted something more. Something better. An Aston Martin was a good start. So was finally paying off those student loans.

Focus, he told himself.

In order to make the kidneys available on the United Network for Organ Sharing, Kreeger had to identify the man's antigens. Tissue types, like blood types, are distinct. They are identified by specific proteins found in the body's cells. These proteins, called antigens, are part of the complex mechanism that helps the body fight disease by distinguishing what belongs and what is an intruder.

Donors that had the most matching antigens had bodies that were most likely to accept the donor kidneys. The best possible match was for a patient to have all four of the donor's antigens. Kreeger laughed to himself as he set up the centrifuge. Donor. Kreeger didn't think of himself as a monster, but the look of horror in the man's eyes had been delicious.

Kreeger had even thought up a little joke which he planned to use the next time a victim was wheeled into the makeshift operating room, strapped down and trussed like a roast from the butcher.

"So, you're here to donate your kidneys?"

That would get them screaming. Then down would come the gas and it was all over for them. Nighty night. Forever.

Kreeger put a tube of the man's blood in the centrifuge and pushed a button. The machine began to spin, its motion separating the blood, leaving the heavier red cells at the bottom of the test tube and the whitish layer of pure lymphocytes at the top.

Other surgeons never had to perform these tests themselves. This was work for lab technicians. But he had decided that the fewer who knew about this chop shop operation, the better.

Kreeger stopped the machine and opened the tube of separated blood. He used a pipette to suck off the lymphocytes that contained the antigens and put them on a plate. It still took several hours to identify the antigens themselves.

Kreeger had made a pot of coffee, and he stopped to refill his mug before going to work on the microscope. He enjoyed the quiet of the hospital at night as he worked alone in the lab. Nurses were making their rounds and a sleepy resident shuffled down the hall to check on the more difficult patients, but for the most part he was left alone.

Somebody knocked on the door and Kreeger jumped, spilling some of the coffee on his lab coat.

"Damn," he muttered, swiping at the stain with a paper towel. "Come in."

"Oh, Dr. Kreeger," said the maintenance man. "I saw the light under the door. I didn't know you were working."

"Yes, unfortunately," Kreeger said. He sighed. "We've got a snakebite victim up on the third floor."

"Snakebite?"

"Yes, some poor woman was bitten by a water moccasin." Kreeger nodded at the equipment in front of him. "I'm just preparing the antivenom."

"A snake?"

"One of the deadliest on the Delmarva Peninsula, at that."

"Geez, Doc, I'd better let you get back to work."

"That sounds like a good idea."

The maintenance man shut the door quietly behind him. Kreeger was a kidder; he enjoyed yanking everybody's chain, even if his sense of humor was warped as a sail in a hurricane. He put his eye to the microscope.

By three a.m. he had identified all the antigens. Then he logged onto the UNOS network and entered the man's age, race, blood type and tissue type.

The computer processed the information and came back with a list of names having type A blood, same as the involuntary donor's. The names were listed in order of urgency. He found a man in Cincinnati who needed a kidney and had three matching antigens. Three out of four ain't bad. Another man in Nashville was a perfect four-antigen match, although his case was not as urgent.

Kreeger made some calls. Both hospitals said they would take the kidneys.

He took out two sterile, industrial-grade Styrofoam chests, one for each organ. He placed each kidney in a sterile bag, half filled the chest with chipped ice, put the bag in, and buried it in more ice. It was extraordinary in a way that for all the medical technology that existed, it was good ol' ice in a cooler that kept the kidneys viable. Might as well be a chest full of rockfish.

Then he texted Grubb. Next stop for the organs would be Philadelphia International, where they would be put on a plane to their destinations. Grubb texted back that he'd take care of it. The goth kid was nuttier than a Snickers bar, but he was reliable.

In the afternoon, after he slept in, Kreeger would drive across the Chesapeake Bay Bridge to the Aston Martin dealership in Tyson's Corner, Virginia, and make a down payment on the car he had test driven last week. It was all he could do as he sat at his desk sending emails with final arrangements regarding the organs not to make engine noises, pretending he was shifting through the gears on his new sports car.

CHAPTER 4

It was nearly lunchtime when Nick walked into the Rehoboth Beach Police Department and asked to see Chief Hawley.

When Hawley got the message who it was that wanted to see him, he came out grinning. "Nick, it's great to see you."

"I've got to admit, it's been a long time since anyone has told me that."

His old friend and partner, Michael Hawley, was looking good, and Nick told him so. Hawley was little heavier, it was true, but more relaxed. Being the chief of police for the City of Rehoboth Beach, Delaware, must have agreed with him. Leave it to Hawley to land the job as police chief for the nation's summer capitol. He'd always been political, kissing up to the right people. Nick should have been a little jealous, maybe, that his old partner had done so well while he was on the farm splitting firewood, but Hawley seemed so glad to see him that any such thoughts evaporated.

They talked about old times for a few minutes, and then Nick explained what he was doing at the beach. He had debated bothering Hawley with it, but it was common courtesy to give the local police a heads up if you were going to be doing a little detecting on your own. In Nick's experience, it helped prevent misunderstandings and bad feelings down the road.

"Anything you need, you let me know," Hawley said.

"I appreciate that, Mike. I really do. I'm just going to ask around, but I'll give you a call if it goes to the next level." By next level, Nick meant that an actual crime had been committed or that his niece was seriously missing.

"Keep me posted on what you find out," Hawley said. Both men got up—Hawley struggling a little with the extra weight as he moved out from behind the desk—and shook hands. To Nick's surprise, Hawley didn't let go. "Jesus, Nick, what have you been doing out there in the mountains? You've got hands like a lumberjack. Listen, I know this is out of the blue, but why don't you stick around? We could really use someone like you for the summer."

Nick laughed. Beach towns were notorious for bringing in seasonal officers, who were a lot like adjunct professors at a community college. Low pay and little respect, in other words, although they worked just as hard as the full timers. "What, like a rent-a-cop?"

"No, not someone like you, who knows what the hell he's doing. We've got a solid group of good people here with nineteen fulltime officers. With your experience you'd be a detective, not out writing parking tickets. You see, we've had a little trouble down here with muggings on the Junction and Breakwater Trail and I need somebody who can go under cover and kick ass. We've got a new officer I want to put on it, and you'd be perfect working with her."

"I'm a little rusty."

"Perfect, because she's new metal. She can help you knock off some of that rust and you can show her the difference between her ass and a hole in the ground. Look, you should at least meet her." He punched a button on his desk phone. "Hey, is Sarah available? Ask her to come in here a minute, will you?

Nick was thinking that Hawley hadn't countered that he didn't *look* rusty, which must have meant he *did*. He'd be the first to admit he was a little off his game. More than a little. Maybe he did need to get off the farm—

That's where Nick's thought process ended, because the woman who walked into Chief Hawley's office won his full attention. She was not what Nick had imagined she would be. She was tall, about five-nine, with long blond hair and a sinewy, athletic body. She looked to be in her early thirties, a few years younger than Nick. She glanced from Hawley to Nick, plainly curious. "What's up?"

"See what happens to cops at the beach? All discipline goes by the wayside. Imagine saying 'What's up' instead of 'Yes, sir' to the captain back in the day in Baltimore when you got called into his office. You would have walked out carrying your head in your hands. Nick, I want you to meet Sarah Monahan. Uh, *Detective* Monahan. Nick is thinking about joining the force for the summer, maybe helping out with that trouble we've been having on the Junction and Breakwater Trail."

"Oh?" The detective looked a little taken aback. Nick felt like Hawley was putting her on the spot.

Sarah Monahan managed to settle lightly and gracefully into her chair.

"Before you even start, uh, *sir*, I know this patrol is a public relations move by the mayor's office," the detective said. The chief's dig about discipline had not gone unnoticed.

"Yes," Hawley said. "But it's still serious

business."

"How come everyone knows about this but me?" Nick asked.

"Just so you don't feel left out, Nick, I'll explain," Hawley said. "In a nutshell, the mayor wants us patrolling the Junction and Breakwater Trail. We'll probably expand into Cape Henlopen State Park as well to supplement the patrols there. Mayor Gates thinks there have been too many muggings and attacks lately. He takes it very personally, considering that the trail is one of the jewels in what he's promoting as the city's so-called triple crown."

"Triple crown?" Nick asked.

Hawley counted them off on his fingers. "Beach. Boardwalk. Breakwater trail. Rehoboth's Triple Crown, according to the mayor, which is why we can't have all those vacationers getting knocked in the head on that trail."

"It's not that bad, is it?" Nick asked. "There can't be much crime at the beach."

"There have been twenty-three muggings this month, eight carjackings, three assaults and one rape," Detective Monahan said.

Chief Hawley squirmed a bit in his chair. "Uh, thank you, Detective."

Nick whistled. "All is not surf and sunshine at the beach. You've got something of a crime spree, I'd say. So what are you supposed to do about it?" Nick asked.

"Until you walked in the door, Nick, I didn't have much of a game plan, to be honest. But now I'm thinking that you and Detective Monahan will go undercover as joggers," Hawley said. "You could be our secret weapon, Nick. Several of the crimes have taken place within sight of witnesses. That's how blatant these perpetrators are. If you see someone being robbed, you arrest the robbers. Simple. Hell, you'll be working at the beach. It's like being on vacation. What do you say?"

Nick took a long look at his potential partner. He liked what he saw. Nothing was waiting for him back at the farm but a pile of wood to split. "Sure," he said. "Why not?"

• • •

Nick spent the rest of the afternoon asking Katie's roommates and co-workers when they'd last seen her—which turned out to have been at a party, in the company of a lifeguard. He had called that one, all right. He was planning on walking down to the beach and pestering the lifeguard on duty to find out where the lifeguards lived—he was fairly certain they would all room together, like members of a team—when one of Katie's friends tweeted the question.

"Crowd sourcing," she explained.

Less than a minute later he had the address of

the lifeguards' pad, located a couple of blocks from the boardwalk.

The place looked more like a frat house than a beach house, with a few empty beer cans tossed in the shrubs out front and some broken furniture on the lawn. Nick didn't bother to knock, but opened the door and went in.

A young man played a video game in the living room. The fact that he took his eyes off the screen just long enough to acknowledge Nick indicated it was indeed one of those beach houses where the party never really stopped, with people always coming and going. "Can I help you, dude?"

"I'm looking for my niece, Katie Thompson. I understand she hooked up with a lifeguard a couple of nights ago."

"I don't know anything about that."

"Then you won't mind if I look around," Nick said, already moving. "Are these bedrooms back here?"

He peeked inside one. Empty. Or at least, it appeared to be empty—it was a little hard to tell because it looked as if a bomb had gone off, scattering clothes and towels everywhere. He turned around to check the next room—and found the video-game lifeguard blocking his path.

"Dude, you can't just go searching our house."

"Can't I?" Nick started to push past him.

"Hey!" The lifeguard gave him a shove.

When Nick didn't so much as rock back on his heels, the lifeguard got a look of puzzlement on his face. Nick might have told him that splitting chunks of oak all day tended to build muscle better than pushing a button in front of a TV screen. The lifeguard shoved harder.

"Knock it off, kid, before you hurt yourself."

Just then there was an audible gasp from behind one of the closed doors. "Oh my God! That sounds like my Uncle Nick!"

Nick opened the door. The blinds were down, but he could see two bodies under a sheet, bare shoulders showing. The youthful profligates sat bolt upright when Nick leaned through the doorway.

"Katie," he said. "Call your mother."

CHAPTER 5

Rehoboth Beach was a morning town. The sun was just coming up, but already the beach was dotted with people out walking and running as the waves lapped gently at their feet. Dogs tugged eagerly at their leashes and they bounded along with their owners in tow. In the town itself, shops unlocked their doors and hung out their "open" flags. The town had begun as a camp meeting for the Methodist Church, and some of that wholesomeness still clung to the resort— never mind the fact that the population swelled from maybe 1,400 fulltime residents to 40,000 or more in the summer.

Nick had found a room at the Atlantic Sands on Rehoboth Avenue so he didn't have far to stumble to the nearest coffee shop. The staff at Browseabout Books had propped open the door and delicious smells of coffee and fresh-baked muffins drifted out. Customers came and went, stocking up on books and newspapers along with their morning caffeine. Off to one side, a local author was waiting to sign copies of a book called, "Delmarva Legends and Lore." Nick bought a copy, along with two coffees and a sack of muffins.

Nick felt like he had a handful of beach sand in each eye. Meeting Detective Monahan at police headquarters by six meant getting up by five-thirty, not his favorite time of day. She was already sitting behind the wheel of an unmarked car. Nick would have preferred to be behind the wheel, but he decided not to make an issue of it. She drove them out to the parking lot on Wolfe Neck Road at the midpoint of the Junction and Breakwater Trail.

He noticed that Detective Monahan looked wide awake as they sat in the unmarked vehicle, watching the runners and cyclists and dog walkers out for their morning workouts on the trail. He was suspicious of morning people, who tended to be healthy, trim and cheerful. None of them appeared to mind getting up early. This seemed like unnatural behavior to Nick. Of course, Karen had been a morning person, but he made an exception in her case.

"You look like hell, Logan," his new partner said, giving him a stare as if he was something unpleasant on the bottom of her Nikes. "Rough night?"

"Rough morning," Nick said. "I've always been more of a night owl, which was a good thing when I worked in Baltimore. I haven't gotten out of the habit. Even now, living out in the mountains, it takes a while for the sun to get over the peaks and down into the valleys. I get up with the chickens, but the chickens sleep late."

"You have chickens out there in the mountains?"

"Um. It's an expression."

"You were a homicide detective," she said. "I heard it from Bob Grabowski. He worked with you in Baltimore."

"Don't believe everything Grabowski tells you." Nick managed to avoid any detailed explanations by reaching for the bag of goodies from Browseabout Books. He didn't want to go into his past right now. "I brought us something to make morning a little easier," he said, taking out the two coffees. "There are muffins in the bag."

"I don't drink coffee," she said.

"What if I told you that it's decaf?"

"Doesn't make any difference," she said. "I don't touch the stuff."

"Then I'll drink it," Nick said, somewhat

irritated. "Have a muffin."

"No, thanks. I already had breakfast."

"So, you can still eat a muffin. Lighten up. Don't take this too seriously. Relax. We're supposed to be tourists."

"Don't remind me. I thought I'd be doing some real police work and here I am looking for muggers with a rent-a-cop who wants to shove muffins down my throat."

Nick was thinking his new partner might not be a morning person, after all. "Did someone piss in your cornflakes this morning, or what?" The rent-a-cop remark really rankled. "Detective Monahan, I haven't had nearly enough coffee yet, which means I'm kind of grumpy, so I'd advise you to shut up before I really do shove one of these muffins down your throat."

"I know Chief Hawley sent you along to babysit me, but let's get something straight. Don't think you can bully me," she snapped, her eyes sparking as she spun in the seat to face him. "What makes you think you can get away with saying that to me? You wouldn't physically threaten your partner if he were a man."

"Sure I would," Nick said, thinking, *yeah, but only if he was smaller than me and didn't know karate*. "You know what he'd say to me?"

"What?"

" 'Go to hell, Logan.' "

"Cute."

"Try it," Nick said. "That's all you have to do. If my partner was a man, that's what he'd say. So don't go nuts or anything. Just tell me to go to hell."

She wouldn't say it. "Let's get going. We're supposed to be patrolling the trail, remember?"

"I'm having breakfast," Nick said, biting into a muffin. He slurped noisily from his cup of coffee.

"You're a real charmer, Logan," his partner said. "Grabowski warned me about you."

"Yeah? What did he say?"

"He said you were trouble." She shrugged. "Look at how you're dressed," she said. "You don't even look like a tourist."

"What are you talking about?" He glanced down at his clothes, juggling a cup of coffee in one hand and a muffin in the other. They were supposed to be undercover, dressed as runners, so Nick had worn an old pair of gym shorts with rounded ends and white piping. He wore some cheap running shoes from a discount store. Tube socks with colored ends were pulled up to his knees. His T-shirt had yellow sweat stains under the armpits, something he hadn't noticed when he was pulling it on at five-thirty this morning.

"You're dating yourself," she said.

"That sounds kind of narcissistic."

"You know what I mean. It looks like you just came back from a run you took in 1985."

She had on pink and gray Lycra tights, and a

Lycra top covered by a loose T-shirt. Her running shoes were clean but they obviously had a few miles on them, like she actually used them for running.

"What?" Nick said through a mouthful of muffin. "I'm wearing workout clothes."

"Sure you are. You want me to play some Bee Gees so you can get psyched up to run?"

Nick gulped down the last of the coffee and swallowed another muffin. He thought he looked fine. If his partner had been a man, Nick knew he wouldn't be getting a fashion critique right now. His partner would be saying, *Let's go knock some heads.*

Nick shoved open the car door. "Let's go knock some heads," he said.

His new partner shook her head and began stretching. She put one leg on the car's bumper and leaned her head toward her foot. She was so flexible that her forehead touched her kneecap. Nick watched, fascinated.

"Aren't you going to stretch out and warm up?" she asked.

"I have to say, I think I'm plenty warmed up now."

Nick did try to touch his toes a few times, grunting with the effort. His fingertips fell well short of his running shoes. Then he swung his arms overhead, laced his fingers together and cracked his knuckles.

"Ready," he said.

They started out at a slow jog from the parking lot and picked up the trail that followed the Lewes-Rehoboth Canal. Ducks fed at the water's edge and a breeze moved through the trees. It was a pleasant morning, but Nick missed the mountains, his isolated farmhouse, the utter quiet apart from bird song and wind in the trees, his back porch that overlooked an old plow field yielding again to forest, his splitting maul and wood pile.

Splitting wood was a very different exercise from running. It was all about brute force, not cardio fitness. He was more of a sprinter than a distance runner. Nick tried to fall into some kind of rhythm, but his partner was running awfully fast for someone out for a jog, he thought.

"Hey, slow down," Nick said, already breathing heavily.

"I thought you were in good shape."

"Good enough shape."

"Then keep up."

Her legs moved easily and lightly, her feet barely making a sound on the mulched path. Another runner passed them coming the other way. He nodded hello.

"And happy whole wheat to you, too," Nick managed to gasp.

"C'mon Logan, step up the pace," she said. "We've got a lot of ground to cover." Her Lycra-covered legs pumped even faster.

Nick struggled to stay with her. His lungs felt like they were on fire. He hated to admit that maybe he wasn't in such great cardio shape and that he wasn't as young as he used to be. This woman was going to give him a heart attack.

"How far have we gone?" Nick panted.

"Maybe a mile."

His legs felt rubbery and sweat kept getting in his eyes, so he used the front of his shirt to swab his face. A mile had to be enough, he thought, but his partner kept going.

"We're supposed to be posing here," he said. "We only have to look the part."

"You're not looking like much of anything right now. Why in God's name did Hawley hire you for this assignment if you can hardly run a mile?"

The truth was that Nick knew very well why Hawley had hired him. It was pity. The sort of thing you did for an old buddy down on his luck.

While Nick could accept that, he just wasn't sure why he had agreed to take the job. He didn't need the money. Maybe he just needed to feel useful again. Maybe that part of him that had died with Karen was coming alive again.

Instead of answering his partner's question, Nick leaned over and vomited his breakfast against a tree.

Detective Monahan stood still and covered

her own mouth like she was going to be sick. "Oh my God."

Nick wiped his lips with the back of his hand. "What a great way to lose weight," he said. "I can eat all I want, then go run and puke it up."

"Ugh." Her face had turned a greenish color, but she was doing her best to keep from being sick.

"I'm going back to the car," Nick growled. "I'll do my surveillance from there. You keep running if you want to."

She hesitated, then said, "I'll head back with you."

"Music to my ears."

They returned along the path. At this slower pace, Nick was able to enjoy the scenery, which included his partner's shapely, tan legs. Hmmm. And just as quickly he pushed the thought away. It felt like cheating.

"You're awfully quiet all of a sudden," she said. "And you never answered my question."

"Yeah?"

"Why did Hawley put you on this?" she pressed. "We're supposed to be runners. You can hardly do a mile."

"My cover is that I'm some guy on vacation trying to shape up," Nick said. "I probably can't outrun a mugger or even chase him. I make the perfect target. What could be better?"

"I suppose," she said. "I know he put me on it

because I'll make a good decoy . . . a helpless woman. But he could have put just about anybody in your spot. There are plenty of young guys in the department who are in good shape. They would love a shot at working this. It's easy duty."

Nick sighed. Some strength was returning to his legs. They no longer felt like uncooked pizza dough. "They're not mean," he said.

"Excuse me?"

"I'm the meanest cop these assholes terrorizing people on this trail will ever meet," Nick said. "The chief knows that."

"Maybe you can scare them," she agreed. "You just won't be able to catch them."

"That's what you're for," he said. "You're the fleet-footed one."

They jogged along in silence, Nick taking deep breaths of the morning air. This slower pace was much better. He already felt rejuvenated. He was almost ready to believe the hype about the trail being one of the jewels in Rehoboth Beach's triple crown.

The mayor didn't want a few muggings taking the sparkle off one of those crown jewels. Normally, Rehoboth Beach had little violent crime—or crime of any kind, for that matter. There were a few drunken assaults and domestics. Homicides were almost unheard of. The retirees and vacationers who flocked to

Rehoboth from the D.C. suburbs and beyond didn't want to worry about crime of any sort during their sojourn at the beach.

If the beach resort was going to have a crown jewel, the Junction and Breakwater Trail was a good choice. The narrow, wooded band of park land roughly followed the Lewes-Rehoboth Canal. Paths mulched with wood chips followed the canal before curving into the trees, creating a path for runners, mountain bikers, bird watchers and dog walkers. The last thing any of them expected was to get roughed up and robbed.

"This isn't going to work," his partner announced. She stopped and looked him up and down as if seeing him for the first time.

"What?" Nick asked.

"Your outfit. It's awful. Nobody's going to mug you dressed like that. If anything, they'll run when they see you coming. We'll have to get you some real workout clothes. You'll need an expensive accessory, like a new iPod."

"I like what I'm wearing just fine."

"Men," she said, rolling her eyes. "Come on."

"Toss me the keys, will you?" Nick asked, once the car was in sight. "I've got to get something out of the trunk."

Monahan threw them over and Nick snatched them out of the air. He unlocked the driver's side door without going near the trunk.

"Hey," she said, crowding him at the door.

"What do you think you're doing?"

"I'm driving," he said.

"Give me the keys, you fricking chauvinist," she said. "I'm the one who signed the goddamn car out of the motor pool."

"You'll have to do better than that," Nick said, sliding in behind the wheel. "I mean, if the best you can do is *fricking* and *goddamn*, what kind of cop are you going to be? You've got to get creative with your vocabulary. Feel free to practice on me."

Monahan glared at him, but she walked around and sat in the passenger seat. She made a point of slamming the door.

Nick noticed that their spat had drawn the attention of a pair of nearby runners, who were looking their way and smiling. It amused Nick to know he and Monahan came off as a quarreling couple. That could make great cover sometime.

"Where to?" he asked.

"Head out to Route One," Monahan said, sulking. "We'll hit the outlets and see if we can find you something decent to wear."

The Rehoboth Beach area was known for its outlet stores. There were more than one hundred brand name stores for everything from shoes and handbags to kitchen ware. It seemed odd that the beach area had become a magnet for shopping, until you considered the number of rainy days, too-hot days, and the need for wives to get away from husbands and children for a few hours for a mini vacation of their own. Nick had to cruise the parking lot for several minutes in order to find a space.

"I don't know about this," Nick said.

"Come on."

Inside the sporting goods store, the young salesman was dressed in red nylon shorts, a white T-shirt with the store logo and athletic shoes so new they glowed. He wore a whistle around his neck. Nick thought that maybe the kid blew it at shoplifters.

The kid looked Nick over from head to toe, but if he saw anything funny about how Nick was dressed, he didn't let on. Good thing, Nick thought, because if this kid made a crack he might find that whistle stuck into some creative places.

Taking charge, Monahan spoke to the salesman. "We need everything. Running shoes, socks, shorts, T-shirts, sweats." She gave Nick an appraising look. "He probably needs underwear, too. I'm betting his briefs have holes and we don't want anything important popping out."

"I'm more of a boxers kind of guy."

Nick felt sheepish as he went around with the salesman and his partner, trying on pairs of running shoes, nodding yes to the clothes Monahan pointed out. Nobody had picked out clothes for him since he was thirteen, which was the last time his mother had taken him shopping for a school outfit. Monahan topped it all off with a package of Fruit of the Looms. "There's a color for every day of the week," she said.

"I usually just write the days of the week on the waistband."

He dumped the load of clothes on the counter next to the box with his new running shoes inside.

"Now your clothes will look the part," Monahan said. "It's the rest of you I'm not so sure about."

The clerk ringing them up said, "It's nice to see you take your dad shopping for clothes."

"Aw, Jesus. Did she pay you to say that?"

Monahan laughed and laughed. It was the first time she had really seemed to let her guard down. Looking at her, he thought: *Hmmm*.

CHAPTER 6

The surgeon was just heading *Windsong* into deep water when his phone began to play a Willie Dixon blues song. The song was familiar because it's what he often played in the OR. He immediately turned back to the marina because that particular ring tone meant one thing: he had just received a text from the hospital that there was an organ transplant waiting.

Two hours later, as he cut and probed, he listened to the rhythmic beeping of the perfusion machine that nourished the kidney. Other machinery made whirring and chirping noises. For the moment, he had forgotten all about his sailboat.

"Hemostat," the doctor ordered. He took the

instrument and squeezed off the blood supply to the iliac vein and artery. "All right. Nurse, please prepare the kidney, if you would."

The nurse detached the kidney from the perfusion machine, which was pumping a cooled mixture of plasma, saline solution, dextrose and other nutrients through the organ's vessels to simulate normal circulation. She wrapped the purplish-blue organ in a sterile towel and stood at the surgeon's side.

The doctor took the kidney in his hands and flushed it with saline solution. The organ was about the size of a small fist, and he noticed with satisfaction that the severed vessels and ureter were long enough for him to easily stitch into place. Whoever the surgeon had been on the other end, he knew his business, which was always reassuring.

He placed the organ in the pocket he had fashioned in the patient's abdomen. Before he began the anastomosis to weld the kidney's renal vessels to the iliac artery, he took a moment to study the organ. It looked good, although its color worried him because there was an unhealthy purple tinge, much like the color of a freshly thawed steak. He knew nothing about the organ's provenance, only that it had come from a regional hospital in Delaware. He could only hope it was healthy enough to be transplanted successfully.

The surgeon went to work. Connecting the vessels was a tedious process of making tiny stitches in the tough membranes and he stopped occasionally so that the nurse could sponge off his brow. Finally, he finished the minute stitching and released the hemostat. Blood rushed through the organ and it began to turn pink. He sighed behind his surgical mask. The kidney was healthy. The transplant appeared to be a success. The patient would have a new lease on life.

• • •

"I brought breakfast again," Nick said the next morning, producing another white paper bag from the cafe at Browseabout Books. He opened it with a flourish.

"More muffins?" Monahan said, peering into the bag.

"Yeah, but this time I got the bran ones."

"I hate to tell you this, Logan, but I don't think there's such a thing as a healthy muffin, great as that would be. Hey, what's that?" she asked, still looking into the bag.

"Well, you don't like coffee, so I got you chai tea."

Monahan smiled.

He felt pleased that this morning was getting off to a better start than yesterday. At the same time, he couldn't help wondering why he was going out of his way to make peace with her. He couldn't seem to stop himself. Getting soft, he supposed.

"That was nice of you," Monahan said, taking a sip of tea. "Maybe there's hope for you, after all. You know, considering that we've eaten muffins together and even gone clothes shopping, just like a couple of gal pals—"

Nick groaned. "Gal pals? Please don't use phrases like that in my presence."

"Anyhow, you can call me Sarah. I won't even sic the Sexual Harassment Task Force on you."

"Gee, thanks," Nick said as gruffly as he could. "You can call me Nick."

"Okay then. Nick it is. Let's hope everyone behaves today," Sarah said, watching through the windshield as a trio of teenagers came down the trail. They looked like local kids because they wore ratty sneakers and T-shirts—definitely not rich suburban kids on vacation.

"They're up to no good," Nick said.

"Eat your muffins," she said. "Then we'll take a run through the park and see what happens."

"I hope they are up to no good," Nick said. "Second day on the job, and I'm already starting to get bored."

"Sorry if I'm not entertaining enough for you," she said, sipping her tea. "I'll try to come up with some dirty jokes for tomorrow."

"Hey, I've got a lifetime supply of dirty jokes.

Knock, knock."

"Are you serious?"

"I believe you're supposed to say, 'Who's there?' "

"Who's there?"

"Ben."

"Ben who?"

"Ben Dover and I'll give you a big surprise."

"Spare me." Nick noticed she took a swig from her tea to hide a smile.

"Yep, definitely up to no good," Nick said, looking after the trio as they disappeared up the wooded trail. He took a big bite of the muffin, showering the front of his new T-shirt with crumbs. He chased the pastry with a gulp of black coffee from the oversize cup in his hands.

"You know what's a shame, Nick? We see three kids walking down a trail at the beach, and all we see is trouble."

"We're cops," he said. "It's our job to be suspicious."

Nick wolfed down the rest of his breakfast and banged open the car door. He felt like cracking heads. "Okay, let's go see what those poor, underprivileged children are up to," he said.

Sarah finished stretching and began to run, taking small steps for his benefit. After a hundred yards his legs began to loosen up. Thanks to the new Asics running shoes, his feet felt much lighter than they had yesterday.

"I think I could get into this jogging thing," Nick said. "It sure beats splitting firewood. Not as many splinters, for a start."

They ran up the trail, going deeper into the wooded section of the trail. It was another beautiful morning, and Nick found himself looking off into the trees as he pounded along. Sarah kept gaining on him, but he didn't give a damn.

She went around a curve in the trail and disappeared.

"Show off," he panted.

Nick rounded the curve half a minute later and what he saw stopped dead in his tracks.

Sarah stood in the trail, while the three kids they had seen earlier circled her like a pack of junkyard dogs. A middle-aged jogger stood off to one side, his nose bleeding, looking as if he couldn't decide whether to run like hell or help her fight.

Before Nick could cover the distance between them, one of the kids lunged at Sarah. She executed a perfect side kick, the heel of her foot smashing into the kid's face. His head snapped back and he went down.

The other two were on her in an instant. She gave the smaller one an elbow in the gut before whacking his nose with the heel of her open hand.

She wasn't quick enough for the last kid, a

chubby two-hundred pounder. He dropped his shoulder and hit Sarah with all his weight, sending her sprawling on the ground.

Nick ran up, relieved the kid didn't have a weapon, because Sarah would have been dead by now. At the small of his back under his T-shirt, Nick carried his Beretta in a nylon holster. He didn't reach for it. This screwy kid would probably lunge at him and Nick didn't want to shoot anyone today. It was too nice of a morning for that.

He walked up quietly behind the kid, who was waiting for Sarah to get to her feet. At least the kid fought fair, if you didn't consider the fact that he was a whole lot bigger. The jogger just stood there like a startled cow.

"Hey, asshole," Nick said.

The kid turned around. If he was surprised, he didn't show it. "You better run, yo."

"I hate to run. Besides, I'm a cop. So is she. You are in deep doo doo, my friend."

The kid shuffled toward him. He wore sneakers without any laces, and Nick wondered how he managed to keep them from falling off his feet every time he took a step. Maybe the kid just shuffled everywhere.

"What are you gonna do?" Nick asked. "Cool it, all right? Then everything will have a happy ending."

The kid rushed him, head down like a bull.

"Nick, look out!" Sarah shouted.

Like a matador, Nick simply stepped out of the way and let the kid go by, but he grabbed the kid's arm and twisted it behind his back. Nick dumped the mugger on his belly and put a knee between his shoulder blades.

"You move, dumb ass, and I'll break your back," Nick growled. He took out a pair of plastic wrist restraints and handcuffed the kid, then left him there like a beached whale. I warned you about this not having a happy ending. "You are under arrest for assaulting an officer. Make that two officers."

Sarah was busy putting restraints on the other two kids. The one she had kicked in the face had a bloody lip and the other mugger's nose was dripping blood and turning ugly colors. Nick sighed. Regrettably, there wasn't a mark on the kid he had arrested.

"You okay?" he asked Sarah.

"Yeah. Just knocked the wind out of me."

The jogger was still standing there, his eyes skipping from Nick, to the three kids on the ground, to Sarah. Nick could almost hear him thinking, *How the hell did I get mixed up in this?*

"Sir, we need you to come on down to the station and give a report," Nick said.

"I'd rather not get involved," he said. "I'm just here on vacation."

"At this point I'd say you are involved," Nick

said. His gaze settled on the man's bleeding lip. "What happened?"

"They came up and blocked my path as I was running," the man said. "It's narrow here and I couldn't get around them. I asked them what they wanted and the big one said, 'Give us your money, you.' "

"Yo," Nick corrected.

"I told them I didn't have any money," the man said. "Nobody takes their wallet with them when they go running. So the big one hit me."

"He punched you?"

"No, just kind of slapped me." He touched his face and grimaced. "It hurt like hell."

"Then what?"

"You and the other officer came up the trail."

"See, that's all you have to do, sir," Nick said. "Just come down to the station with me and explain what happened like you did just now. We'll have you in and out of there in no time."

The man touched his lip and his fingertips came away bloody. He stared at the blood a moment, apparently fascinated, then walked over to where the big kid was lying and kicked him in the ribs.

"Ow!" the kid hollered. "Jesus!"

"You dirty, thieving son-of-a-bitch!" The man kicked him again.

Sarah was jumping for the jogger, but Nick signaled her to wait. He watched the jogger kick the kid a third time.

"Okay, I think he got the message. That's enough."

The kid on the ground was swearing up a storm, trying to curl himself into a ball. Nick struggled to keep from laughing out loud.

"I'm sorry, officer," the man said. He was shaking. "I suppose you'll want to arrest me, now, too."

Nick shrugged. "Street justice," he said philosophically. "Or should I say trail justice. If you want, I've got some steel-toe boots in my trunk."

"I'll be happy to come down to the station and make a statement."

"Thank you, sir. Our car is in the parking lot if you want to meet us there. A tan Chevy."

"Okay," the jogger said.

The man started down the trail ahead of them, and Nick waited until he was out of sight before taking out his gun. "Everybody on their feet. Let's go. We're going to walk back to the parking lot now. If anybody tries to run away, I'll shoot him."

Sarah watched him anxiously. "Move it," she said, unable to take her eyes off the gun in Nick's hand. She helped one of the kids to his feet and shoved him in the right direction.

The second kid stood up, his eyes dancing down the trail into the woods. Nick pointed the gun at him. "Try it, yo."

The teen lowered his head and stood still.

It turned out that the biggest boy was the crybaby. "I ain't gettin' up," he said. "I'm hurt."

"Get up or I'll give you somethin' to cry about."

The other two kids looked nervously at each other and shifted their weight from foot to foot, their eyes on the gun in the big cop's hand. This guy looked like he meant business.

The big kid was still lying on his stomach. "Police brutality," he muttered. "Gonna get me a lawyer and sue your ass."

Nick had heard it all before. Where did they get this stuff? Far too many lawyers were advertising on late-night TV.

Tired of the kid's crap, Nick grabbed his bound wrists and pulled his arms backward, hauling the mugger to his feet.

"Aaahhhhh!" the kid screamed. "You're gonna rip my arms out."

"Shut up," Nick said once the kid was on his feet. He put a hand right between the kid's shoulder blades and shoved. "Get going."

"Come on," Sarah said, motioning them down the path with a nod of her chin.

It was only a short walk back to the parking lot, but the whole way they had to listen to the big kid whine about how he was going to sue.

"My lawyer is gonna pick your bones," the kid

said.

"How come you're such a goddamn crybaby?" Nick asked, losing his temper. "Some old middle-aged guy kicks you in your fat gut and you start whimpering like a puppy. They're gonna love your fat ass in the county jail, honey. You like that, *honey?* You think you're a big boy, but some skinny crazy old man in the county lockup is gonna make you and your lazy whimpering ass his girlfriend unless your mommy and daddy come quick to bail you out. *Yo.*"

Nobody spoke as they trudged out of the woods, the three kids hanging their heads and silently thinking over what Nick had just said.

Nick was wondering if he had been too crude, if his new partner would be offended by his little speech, when he spotted a woman with a fishing vest and a camera bag over her shoulder walking quickly toward them. Nick had seen enough reporters in his life to know one when he saw one.

"I'm with the Cape Gazette," she said.

"Get out of here," Nick snarled.

She ignored him, keeping her distance, snapping photos of their entourage as it wound down the path.

"What did they do?" she asked.

"I swear I'm gonna break that goddamn camera," he growled.

The photographer wouldn't give up. She

appealed to Sarah. "How about it?"

"They attempted to mug a jogger," Sarah explained. "See me in a minute and I'll try to get you some information."

Always the one with the answers, Nick thought, glancing back at his partner. Sarah appeared quite calm, and he wondered if maybe he should follow her example. That didn't stop him from reaching for the nearest kid and giving him a shove toward the parking lot.

"Time to go for a ride boys," Nick said, marshaling the teens into the back of the unmarked vehicle so that he could drive them to the county lockup. The thought of spending the next several hours filling out forms and writing narratives for charging documents made his stomach churn, but that was police work for you —a few minutes of action followed by endless paperwork.

The jogger who had been attacked was waiting patiently. "I just wanted to thank you," he said. "That was great work you and your partner did back there. I owe you one."

"All in the line of duty, sir," Nick said.

"I mean it," the guy said, after he had gotten their names. "I'll be in touch."

• • •

As the Rehoboth Beach Chief of Police, Hawley

made a point to know about every crime, big or small, in the resort town. If there was a domestic dispute at a motel on Route 1 or a shoplifting at the Outlets, he read the report.

His secret was that he also read the daily incident log and listened constantly to the scanner he kept in his office. He had one of the radio operators program in all the channels used by the local fire and police departments — even the unofficial channels where cops chattered away about everything from the incredible pair of hooters they had just seen to gossip about Hawley himself.

His ears pricked up when he heard the dispatcher say: *Patrol 19, respond to the parking lot of the Breakwater Trail on Wolfe Neck Road to assist an undercover unit there with an arrest.*

We're en route, said the cop in the radio car. *Station, can you elaborate?*

Detectives need assistance in transporting three subjects to the detention center.

Hawley jumped up from behind his desk and said, "Thank you, Logan." Then he began punching the speed dial buttons on his phone console, a feature his secretary had programmed for him—when it came to technology, the chief was a strong believer in delegating. The phone numbers put him right into the newsroom of every media outlet not only in the Rehoboth Beach area, but also to WDEL in Wilmington, the News Journal, and even the Washington Post, which occasionally ran news items from Rehoboth because so many people from D.C. vacationed there. Hawley hadn't made it to the position of police chief of the nation's summer capital without knowing how to pitch a positive story.

• • •

Nick groaned when he saw another reporter roll into the parking lot. This one jumped out armed with nothing more than a pen and a notepad, which was somehow reassuring. "What the hell are they doing here?" he demanded, looking at Sarah as if it was all her fault.

"How am I supposed to know?" she asked.

"We arrest three teenagers and suddenly we're surrounded by the media. What gives?"

"I don't know, but you better tuck in your shirt," Sarah said, nodding at the media people walking toward them.

The reporter introduced himself as Jorge Alvarez, and he seemed like a polite young guy, but he started firing off questions fast as a Gatling gun, aiming them at Nick.

"Jorge, why don't you speak with my partner, Detective Sarah Monahan."

"Actually, I go by George. The Hispanic byline thing is more about readership demographics."

"Yeah? Well, George, she can give you the details for benefit of your readership, whatever their demographics may be."

Sarah glanced at him, but she didn't hesitate. The young reporter took copious notes.

"Mayor Gates has assigned us here in an effort to sweep the Junction and Breakwater Trail clean of crime and make it a safer place for the citizens and visitors to Rehoboth Beach to enjoy," the detective said smoothy. "The three arrested today will be charged —"

Nick tuned out. All he knew was that where he would have fumbled in front of the camera, Sarah knew just what to say.

"Is there a crime problem here on the trail?" the reporter asked. Did he live under a rock?

"Nothing that the city police can't reverse," Detective Monahan said.

She was a natural-born public relations officer. Here was yet another hidden talent of Detective Sarah Monahan, although Nick thought it wasn't as impressive as a good karate kick.

The reporter moved off to interview the walkers, joggers and cyclists who had gathered to see what all the commotion was about. The guy they had rescued from the muggers was nowhere to be seen.

"You did great," Nick said to Sarah.

"Thanks," she said. "But don't let me grab all the glory."

"I've had my share of being in the spotlight," he said. "I'm not a big fan of the media."

"From the look on your face right now, I would say that's an understatement."

"Bad memories."

"You're supposed to be my partner," she said. "Is there something I should know about you?"

"You'll find out soon enough," he said. "But I won't be the one to tell you."

CHAPTER 7

"Hot damn!" Kreeger shouted as he merged onto Route 1. The highway was thick with summer traffic and Kreeger had to downshift and hit the gas to claim his place in the stream of cars. Other drivers gazed enviously at his silver sports car that looked like it was straight out of a James Bond movie.

Eat my dust. He punched the gas and slid into the fast lane. The speed limit was sixty-five, but he quickly edged past that.

There was some road construction going on, and as a result there was hardly any shoulder, just a narrow two-foot strip between the white line and the concrete jersey wall. The highway curved and Kreeger found his foot giving the car more gas, urging it even faster around the curve. The concrete flashed by on his left so close he could have reached out and touched it and on the right he saw the eyes of startled drivers in their side-view mirrors as he flew past.

Kreeger felt all the tension of the last few days drain away, replaced by raw adrenalin. He had a flashback of the long operations, huddled over the patients' warm and pulsing inner mechanisms, breathing through a sterile mask. The Aston Martin surged ahead and Kreeger laughed maniacally.

Out of nowhere a lumbering tractor trailer truck loomed on the curve ahead and Kreeger hit the brakes, feeling them grab, but not enough. For one sickening instant Kreeger thought he was going to crash. *Christ, my new car!* The back end of the tractor trailer was coming at him fast, big as a wall. One chance out of this —

He downshifted again, the engine shrieking in protest, and punched the gas to dart ahead of the line of traffic to his right. In the rearview mirror he saw the other drivers stare wide-eyed, too frightened to curse him.

Try that in a Honda! This was not a car. This was a driving phenomenon. He laughed again.

No sooner was he driving within the speed limit again than the realization of how close he had just come to being killed dawned on him. If there hadn't been a sudden hole in the line of cars to the right the brakes never would have stopped him in time, no matter how well the car handled. He and his brand new machine would have run right into the tractor trailer. Instant scrap.

And me without a donor card. Kreeger smiled to himself.

His pulse beating in a mix of euphoria and fear, Kreeger slowed down with everyone else as the highway gave way to the business district that was lined with stores and clogged with traffic. He exited toward Rehoboth Beach and then joined the stop and go traffic that plagued the resort from May to September, relishing the envious stares that the car earned him. *Eat your hearts out.* Kreeger figured he had a right to gloat, considering that the car had cost him almost as much as med school.

At one intersection, a jogger did a two-step dance waiting for the light to change, gazing enviously at the Aston Martin. In turn, Kreeger studied the jogger, noticing the man's muscular legs, the trim torso. The man bounced across the pavement on nimble feet as the light turned red.

Perfect donor, thought Kreeger.

Their organ donation operation depended on a good supply of kidneys. Keeping up the monthly payments on his new Aston Martin depended on a steady supply. But the ambulance routine had become dangerous. The man four days ago had been their fourth donor in a week.

That had been the plan, to take as many people as possible in a short time, before the police figured out what was going on. Another ambulance run would be too dangerous, and the police might arrest Grubb and Fat Boy that time. What those two knew would be disastrous for Kreeger and his partner.

There was also another problem relating to the quality of the supply. Relying on random accident victims meant that they were taking a chance that the organs were not damaged and that the victim was in good general health. It was a roll of the dice, a real crap shoot.

He drove home to his townhouse one block over from the beach. His neighbors all had expensive cars—a Lexus, BMW, Land Rover were parked shoulder to shoulder—and the parking area at the townhouse complex was ringed with security lights. His own townhouse had a garage, and he hit the remote to raise the door and then pulled inside. Kreeger walked once around the car, then patted the hood before heading upstairs. The living area was above the one hundred year flood plain, just in case the next hurricane decided to flood Rehoboth.

Once inside his townhouse, Kreeger switched on the TV. He disliked the silence of the empty rooms and left the television on whenever he was home, although he seldom paid attention to any of the programs. He just liked the noise it made.

Kreeger walked over to the large window in the living room that overlooked the street outside. If he looked carefully, he could just see a sliver of ocean in the distance. It was a view Kreeger liked to savor at night, sitting with the lights out and a glass of wine in hand.

He was too excited at the moment to enjoy the scenery. That Aston Martin could *move*.

He flipped open his MacBook to check the local news. Ever since they'd been snatching people with the ambulance, he had carefully monitored the news reports. There had been little or nothing about the disappearances, but Kreeger didn't want to push their luck.

Not much police news at all. He clicked on a video at the Cape Gazette website about an arrest on the Junction and Breakwater Trail.

"— part of the mayor's initiative to deter crime on the boardwalk as well as the Junction and Breakwater Trail," a female cop was telling the reporter, who was off camera. A rather attractive female cop, as a matter of fact. "The mayor and police chief wish to send a message that the trail, one of the jewels in the city's crown, is a safe place to exercise or simply enjoy this slice of nature here at the beach."

She was dressed like a jogger in provocative Lycra tights, Kreeger noticed. Behind her, just at the edge of the camera's eye, stood a burly man in running clothes. He looked more like a boxer than a jogger.

Kreeger recalled the runner he had seen waiting to cross the street downtown.

Joggers, he thought. *Joggers will be perfect.*

• • •

"Do me a favor and talk to this woman, will you, Logan?" asked the duty sergeant, catching Nick by the arm as he went by with a cup of coffee. Nick couldn't recall his name, but he was one of the temporary summer help cops. Not a bad guy —he had retired from a long career as a town cop somewhere up in Pennsylvania and he did a good job of dealing with the brush fires that popped up. "She wants to see someone higher up the food chain than me."

"Huh?"

"I want to speak with someone who's in charge," the woman said. Her voice was a bit shrill, and she had bloodshot eyes and a desperate look. To Nick, she appeared to be wavering between anger and tears.

"He's in charge, ma'am," the sergeant said. "He's a detective."

"You're in charge?" The woman rushed toward Nick, latching on to him. Behind her back, the sergeant was looking relieved that he had passed the buck.

"Yes, ma'am," Nick said, straining to be polite.

Inwardly, he groaned. This woman had "basket case" written all over her. All he wanted was to drink his coffee in peace and catch up on some paperwork left over from the arrest on the Junction and Breakwater Trail, not babysit this woman for the sergeant.

"What kind of detective are you?" she asked.

Good question. Nick wasn't so sure of the answer. Was he a detective or was he just keeping a few bad guys off a bicycle trail? "Right now, I'm the detective who can help you, ma'am. Why don't you tell me about why you came in here today."

"My husband went to work four days ago and I haven't seen him since. I reported it that night when he didn't come home but the police haven't found any sign of him."

The misery in the woman's face was plain to see. She stood before him, wringing a tissue so hard that it was shredding in her hands.

Nick cleared his throat awkwardly.

"Um . . . why don't you sit down over here, ma'am, right in this chair next to my desk," Nick said, holding it for her like a waiter as she seated herself. "Can I get you a soda or a cup of coffee or something?"

"I just want you to get my husband back." She sobbed into her open hands. Nick dug around on his desk and handed her a napkin that was still fairly clean. "What am I going to do? What do I tell my children? Why isn't anyone doing anything?"

Nick looked around the squad room. Nobody would meet his eyes.

"Do you know the name of the officer who took the report from you?"

"Yes, sir. Officer Jackson."

Nick sighed. The name didn't ring any bells, but Nick was new here, and he excused himself to ask the duty sergeant for help.

"Can you find me a missing person's report on Frank Wilson?" Nick asked. "It was filled out by Officer Jackson."

"Jackson will be back on duty in the morning. I looked for the report when she first came in and told me her problem," the sergeant said. "It's not here, which is weird, because Jackson is a stickler for details. The other funny thing is that Councilman Jenkins was in today inspecting files to make sure everything was in order. If we had a report, it would be on file."

"Guess I'll have to start over," Nick said. "Get me a blank form, will you?"

While the Rehoboth Beach Police Department was computerized, paperwork still began with actual paper. The information would be entered into the database later on. He sat back down across from Mrs. Wilson.

"What was your husband's name, ma'am?" he asked, pencil poised over the form.

"Frank Wilson."

"Height?"

"I went through all this with Officer Jackson —"

"Please, Mrs. Wilson, just bear with me for a few minutes while I get this down. Height?"

"Five-ten," she said. "And I know the rest of the questions from last time: One hundred and seventy pounds. Brown hair going thin on top. He was wearing khakis and a blue shirt."

Nick nodded as he filled out the form. "Your husband disappeared four days ago?" he asked.

"Yes. He was in an automobile accident on Rehoboth Avenue near the traffic circle," she explained. "That much I do know, because the police had an accident report."

Huh," Nick said.

"Officer Jackson called the officer who filled out the accident report when I was here last time and found out my husband was driving. The description matched." She paused and lowered her voice. "Frank had evidently been drinking. He was hurt, the other officer said, and they took him away in an ambulance."

"How do you know that, Mrs. Wilson?"

"The other officer, the one Officer Jackson spoke with, told him. Then Officer Jackson told me. They took Frank away in an ambulance."

"Did you call all the hospitals here?" he asked. Jackson, if he hadn't been lazy, had also done that.

"There's only one," she said. "I would have thought you'd know that. Southern Delaware General, and he's not there. So where is he, Detective? I think he could be wandering around somewhere with amnesia."

"Um." Nick nodded. "Could you please excuse me for a minute, Mrs. Wilson? I'm going to get another cup of coffee. Are you sure I can't get you anything?"

"No, thank you," she said.

Chief Hawley was out, so Nick left her and went into the chief's empty office to use the telephone, out of earshot of Mrs. Wilson. He called the state morgue.

"Yeah, this is Detective Logan with the Rehoboth City Police. I'm looking for a body."

The coroner's assistant sighed. "Ha, ha. That's original. We got all kinds of bodies here."

"Geez. Listen, do you have a Frank Wilson there?" Nick asked. "And if not, give me a run-down on your John Doe cases."

Nick heard the man tapping on a computer keyboard.

"No Frank Wilsons."

"You got a John Doe?"

"Three."

"Any middle-aged white guys?"

"Uh, checking." Nick heard him tapping a keyboard. "Well . . . a black guy, an old white wino, and some guy they fished out of the

Delaware Bay yesterday."

Nick had a growing sense of dread on behalf of Mrs. Frank Wilson. "The one they got out of the bay — was he a middle-aged white guy?"

"He was in the water for a while. They tend to look kind of bloated, but middle-aged seems about right."

"This guy, did he have brown hair, kind of balding?"

"It doesn't say here," the assistant coroner said.

"So go look," Nick said.

"I guess you want to make me do some work." The coroner's assistant sighed heavily and was away from the phone for a few minutes. "Yeah, looks like brown hair. And yeah, it could be a guy in his forties. Very white at this point. Fish belly white."

"Huh," Nick said. "What was the cause of death?"

"Well, uh, this one's kind of weird."

Oh boy. When the coroner's office thought something was weird, it tended to be *really* unusual. They saw a hundred typical ways people had died, everything from shootings to suicides to overdoses, so this must have been truly unique.

"So tell me. The suspense is killing me."

"Ha, ha." The clerk sighed. "You cops really are a load of laughs."

"Yeah, I hear you folks down at the morgue

really know how to have a good time."

The clerk snorted. "Officially, we're listing the cause of death as massive trauma."

"From the car accident?"

"Huh? Well, I don't think a car accident is what killed him. He was already dead when he went into the water. He didn't drown."

"So?" Nick asked, gripping the phone tight.

"Someone surgically removed his kidneys."

Now that *was* unusual. "I take it that's a step up from donating blood," Nick said.

"When was the last time you heard of a kidney drive?"

"You don't get many who die this way?"

"Nope," the coroner's assistant said. "This is a definite first."

"Thank you," Nick said. "I may have an officer bring the man's wife by to make a positive ID. That will clear one of your John Doe cases."

"My pleasure. Listen, I was hoping you could put in a good word for me with your chief. I would love to get a job with your department. Working at the beach all day! I mean, what do you do, arrest people for wearing sneakers with dress socks? I could run your lost and found or something."

"I'll see what I can do." Nick hung up.

Hawley had given up smoking some years ago, and Nick found a multi-pack of spearmint chewing gum on the chief's desk. He unwrapped a stick, chewed, thought about it.

There was never an easy way to tell someone that a loved one had died. And there was no way but hard for a wife to take the news that her husband's body was cooling in the state morgue.

In spite of the unpleasant task ahead of him, Nick couldn't help feeling curious and the least bit excited. A middle-aged man had been pulled out of the Delaware Bay with his kidneys missing. Such a mysterious death had homicide written all over it.

But Nick was not a homicide detective. He was working undercover as a jogger to catch teenaged muggers. Frank Wilson's death would be a matter for the Delaware State Police homicide squad.

Unfortunately, none of those homicide cops was handy, so Nick knew he had to be the one to give Mrs. Wilson the news about her husband.

He walked back out into the duty room, trying to keep his face neutral. A couple of cops who caught his expression read *uh, oh* in the air and found a reason to go elsewhere.

She was still sitting in the chair, her purse gripped tightly in her hands.

"Mrs. Wilson," Nick said gently.

Her head jerked up. "Yes?" The woman's eyes made it clear she understood his tone. *Bad news.*

"I think we may have found your husband."

CHAPTER 8

"Need some help with that?"

Grubb looked up into the leathery face above him. The man was thin, with a white beard and a cap pulled down over what was probably a bald head. Grubb tried to guess the man's age. Fifty-seven? Sixty? One of those aging health nuts.

"Sure," Grubb said. "This chain is always coming off."

"Let me take a look," the jogger said. He was deep into the trail but hardly sweating. Must have been in good shape.

"Thanks," Grubb said, trying his most normal smile. "I can't get the damn thing back on."

"You must be quite a cyclist," the man said, his gaze lingering on Grubb's bare calves. "You have very strong legs."

"Yeah, I'm a regular Lance Fuckin' Armstrong," Grubb said. He noticed the old dude was still checking him out. It look Grubb a moment to catch on, and then he almost cracked up. *Freakin' hilarious. This old pervert's hitting on me.*

As the jogger studied the bicycle's layered rear gears, Grubb studied *him*, then shook his head at a nearby clump of beach plum. Fat Boy's heavy face appeared from behind the branches. Grubb shook his head again and mouthed, "Din-o-saur."

"What's that?" the jogger asked.

"Nothing. I just said I'm kind of sore."

Over in the bushes, Fat Boy shrugged and disappeared behind some beach plums.

Something clicked in the gears, and the jogger spun the pedals. Grubb watched as the well-oiled chain slid back into place. The man's hands came away black and greasy.

"There," he said, smiling with satisfaction. "That should do it."

"I appreciate it," Grubb said. "Sorry you got all dirty."

The man wiped his hands on the grass, stealing another look at Grubb's legs. "No problem."

"Thanks again, man," Grubb said.

The white-bearded jogger nodded and gave Grubb a wistful smile, evidently disappointed this chance meeting was ending so abruptly. Grubb got on his bicycle and started to ride off.

The jogger disappeared down the trail and Grubb swung the bicycle around and returned.

Fat Boy shook himself free of the bushes and walked over.

"What was wrong with him?" he demanded.

"That old fart?" Grubb said. "Hell, he must have been seventy."

"Seventy is the new fifty. So?"

"So that ain't exactly prime rib, now is it, Fat Boy? Use your fat head. The Doc wants to cut out the organs and sell them, right? We are basically operating a chop shop like they have for stolen cars. That guy was like an '89 Chevy Cavalier. Who the hell wants a transmission from an old Chevy? Nobody. It's worth zip, nada, nothing. You want your stolen parts from a nice new car. It may help you to think in terms of snack foods, Fatso. That old man was like beef jerky, when what we want is Juicy Fruit."

"Okay, okay," Fat Boy said. "I get the point. It's just a lousy job hiding out in those bushes. There are bugs and shit, and it's so hot out here I'm sweating my balls off. I miss the ambulance. At least it had air conditioning."

Grubb had to agree about the ambulance. It was a much better gig, cruising the beach towns and checking out the sexy bitches in their teeny bikini bottoms. But the Doc hadn't steered them wrong yet, and he said the ambulance routine was going to get them caught. They needed a new strategy. So here they were.

"You got anything to eat?" Fat Boy asked.

"What happened to that box of Twinkies you bought at the WaWa on the way over?"

"Snarfed 'em, dude," Fat Boy said.

"You are a pig."

Fat Boy belched. "Just get back over there with the bike and see if you can't get somebody else to stop before I starve to death in the middle of goddamn nowhere."

"Seriously, there's enough blubber on you to last a month," Grubb said, but he jerked the pedals backward while yanking the gear levers back and forth. The chain popped loose.

Fat Boy took his place in the bushes and Grubb hunkered over the bicycle. Anyone coming along the path would have pegged him for a mountain biking enthusiast. His black hair was hidden under a bandana, although his hoop earring still winked in the sun. He wore a Go Brit T-shirt from the fish and chips place and a pair of spandex biking shorts that positively hugged his ass. It was a definite Mic Jagger outfit. No wonder the old dude had given him the eye.

"Think of it as silver mining," the Doc had said, explaining the idea to Grubb and Fat Boy in his shabby basement office at the hospital. "You follow a vein until the silver runs out, and then you go look for it somewhere else. The same goes for donors. That's our silver, boys."

The Doc had an annoying habit of confusing him and Fat Boy with a high school football team in need of a pep talk. Grubb doubted the Doc knew shit about mining, but so far he'd done all right with harvesting organs, so Grubb was willing to listen.

Kreeger had also warned them that some cops were patrolling the trail to scare off muggers, but Grubb wasn't worried about that. The Junction and Breakwater Trail was too long for the cops to be everywhere at once. Besides, ever since he was a kid shoplifting DVDs to sell on eBay, Grubb had possessed a sixth sense that allowed him to smell a cop a mile away. Even in running shoes and shorts, Grubb figured the police would be easy to spot. A pig is a a pig, right?

He heard footsteps on the trail and glanced up to see a young guy bounding along. He had so much gel in his hair it remained perfectly styled with each stride.

"You lost your chain," the jogger puffed, barely giving Grubb's broken bicycle a second look as he pounded by. Grubb was half-tempted to run after Captain Obvious and drag him back, but that was not part of the plan.

"Thanks for the help, asshole," Grubb called after him.

Fat Boy hissed from the bushes: "Nah, his name's probably Skippy."

"Sshhhh. You bushes aren't supposed to talk."

Fat Boy's head emerged from the brush. "This isn't working," he whined. "I've got so many mosquito bites it looks like I've got the measles."

"Shut up, you fat wimp."

Five minutes went by. Ten. Grubb was beginning to lose hope when he heard footsteps. He looked eagerly up the path, but it was only the white-bearded jogger coming back. He slowed, gave Grubb and little nod, but didn't stop. Evidently if Grubb wasn't interested, neither was he.

"There's a bike shop in the new Mermaid Zone in Rehoboth," the jogger called over his shoulder, still not winded after the four-mile loop. "They could take a look at it for you."

Grubb gritted his teeth. The Mermaid Zone. Just another goddamn tourist trap on the boardwalk. "Thanks," Grubb grunted.

The jogger disappeared and Grubb was left alone with his bicycle and the rustling clump of beach plum. After a few minutes Fat Boy's head popped up.

"This ain't working," he said.

"You got a better idea, Lardo?" Grubb asked.

"Yeah," Fat Boy said. He didn't like being called Lardo and was tempted to call Grubb something like Mr. Dye Job or at least *Gothmeister*. But he knew better. The guy was basically unstable. You didn't call Grubb anything but Grubb. No point in setting him off.

"So where?"

"Let's go over to the state park," Fat Boy said. "Out here we already missed most of the morning runners and bikers. It's getting too hot. There's gonna be a lot more people this time of day over at Cape Henlopen."

"We're going to grab someone out in the open like that?"

"Nobody's gonna notice."

Grubb shrugged, not convinced it was a good idea, but not wanting Fat Boy to think he was wimping out. He popped the bicycle chain back into place. It was risky, but he agreed they weren't going to catch anyone where they were now. "Sure, Fatso. You drive the van around and I'll meet you there by the bike rental place."

Fat Boy started down the trail to where he had left the van and Grubb rode the bike over to the rendezvous point. Cape Henlopen State Park consisted of 5,000 acres just outside the old seafaring town of Lewes, where the Delaware Bay and Atlantic Ocean came together. The area had once been a World War II Army base and it was dotted with towers where sharp-eyed soldier boys had been on the lookout for German U-boats. By some miracle the sand dunes and pine woods there had been saved from development so that it was now a sprawling oceanfront state park for campers, beach-goers and hikers. The more Grubb thought it over, maybe Fat Boy was right.

The state park was also the perfect place to snatch a victim.

Fat Boy had to drive the van all the way through town to get to the state park, which was no picnic in summertime traffic, but on the bike Grubb simply took the trails through the marshes and dunes. He waited for Grubb in the parking area of the bike rental shack. It operated on the honor system—the bikes weren't exactly new—so there was nobody working the shack. There were more people around, though none so close they could cause a problem or interfere once he and Fatso grabbed somebody. He sat in the shade and drank a bottle of water while he thought up song lyrics for his band, Dog Smell. They were due for some new material. The trick was coming up with edgy words that rhymed with things like *maim, anarchy* and *flay*.

The van finally drove up, and Fat Boy started bitching as soon as he got out. "Cost me six bucks to get in the park," he said. "Doc has got to reimburse me for that."

"I hope you got a receipt. You can declare it as a business expense."

"Huh?"

"Listen up, numb nuts, because here's the plan. You wait in the van. I'm going to do my broken bike thing right over there." He nodded at a shady path. "When I call you, you come running. We've got to be quick because there are a lot of people around."

Grubb liked to keep things simple. He rode the bike just a short distance down one of the paths leading away from the parking lot. The chain was hardly off again before Grubb saw a girl on the mountain bike slowing down to see if she could help. She looked to be in her twenties and judging by the way her sleek biking outfit showed off her curves, she appeared to be a healthy specimen in every way. *Perfect.*

• • •

Chief Hawley was positively beaming. He shook a newspaper at Nick. "You're famous! Have you seen the front page of the Cape Gazette? That's the best press we've had in years."

Nick slurped some coffee and reached for the newspaper Hawley was waving at him.

There he was with Sarah in a huge front-page color photo, gun at his side, guiding the trio of young muggers out of the park.

"Wow."

"And the clip of Sarah talking about the arrest is one of the most-viewed videos on their site."

Her performance in front of the news people who had shown up at the trail parking lot was impressive. She had known just what to say and how to say it. The News Journal also had a story.

By Jorge Alvarez
Staff reporter

REHOBOTH BEACH —Undercover detectives dressed as joggers arrested three muggers Tuesday who allegedly attacked a vacationing Washington, D.C., man who was running on the Junction and Breakwater Trail.

The victim was accosted by the trio as he ran on a path that connects Rehoboth with Lewes, police said. The men demanded money and when the victim refused, one of the alleged muggers struck him.

The man was saved from further injury by the arrival of the two detectives on the scene. According to police, Detectives Sarah Monahan and Nick Logan were on undercover patrol as part of the resort city's program to improve the safety of public areas.

A brief struggle followed, during which the three mugging suspects were subdued, police said.

"Subdued," he said. "I love it." Nick didn't need to read further. After the details of the arrest were given, the story quoted several city officials about how Rehoboth Beach was getting tough on crime and keeping it safe as a vacation destination.

He looked through the Gazette again, hoping for an article about the engineer whose body had been found in the Delaware Bay. Not a word.

"Hey, Logan!" someone called, interrupting his thoughts. He looked up to see an officer thumbtacking the newspaper photo to the bulletin board in the duty room. Beneath the photograph was a blank sheet of paper.

"Oh, no."

"Oh, yes. It's photo caption contest time," the cop said. "Do we have any contestants?"

Grabowski sauntered over and scratched his chin in mock thoughtfulness. "Hmm." He took out a pen and spoke the words out loud as he wrote: "So which one of you wants to get shot first?"

A few nervous laughs punctuated the room. Nick did his best to chuckle.

Another guy Nick didn't know very well took a pen and wrote, "You boys are so grounded."

The photo caption contest was a tradition that took place in many a squad room. The photo would stay up there for a few days, with cops adding captions to the sheet of paper. It was a way to blow off some steam.

The men in the room drifted back to what they were doing. Now and then a couple of guys would stop in front of the photo, add something to the sheet, and laugh. The longer the photo stayed up, Nick knew from experience, the raunchier the captions would get.

A civilian whom Nick didn't recognize walked

into the duty room. He was a tall, tanned guy wearing chinos and a shiny golf shirt. Chief Hawley came running out to greet him, but after a quick handshake with the chief and a back slap or two, the newcomer made a beeline for Nick.

"I see you're a real celebrity today," the man said, nodding at the newspaper on Nick's desk.

"Everyone has their fifteen minutes of fame."

"I'm Craig Jenkins, Rehoboth's police commissioner," he said, extending a hand. "I know from the photo here that you're Detective Logan. Very nice to meet you. I thought you and Detective Monahan would be back out at the trail again this morning."

"Not until this afternoon. She has a court appearance."

"Ahh," Jenkins said. "Well, keep up the good work, Detective, and welcome to the Rehoboth Beach Police Department. You're making us proud.

"Thank you, sir," Nick said, somewhat taken aback. His whole career in Baltimore, he had never seen an elected official.

He watched Councilman Jenkins walk back out of the room.

"You're a popular man this morning, Nick," Hawley said. He could see that his old friend was pleased. "It's good to have Jenkins on our side because he really goes to bat for us at budget time and in the town council meetings. He's a very hands-on police commissioner. Does ride-alongs and everything. We want to stay on his good side."

"Town politics."

"You got it, big guy. Got to play the game."

The chief went back to his office, and Nick finally got to finish his coffee. Sarah would be back from her court appearance that afternoon and then they'd return to the trail. Nick had decided to pass on patrolling by himself. He could only jog so much, after all.

Nick picked up the newspaper again, put it down. Time to get back to work. He grabbed for the phone.

All day he had been wondering about the fate of the engineer whose body had been pulled out of the Delaware Bay. It had been eating at him ever since the man's wife had walked into the squad room yesterday and told him about her husband's disappearance. Nick hadn't been able to get Frank Wilson off his mind.

It really wasn't any of his business and he didn't want to go meddling in anybody's case. Now that he was under the police commissioner's spotlight, he had enough to worry about. None of that stopped him from calling Grabowski, the Rehoboth Police Department's designated homicide detective.

In Baltimore, the gap between patrolman and homicide detective was wide as the Grand

Canyon. Nick had made that leap to detective during his career. Homicide detectives did not appreciate patrolmen offering their theories or showing interest in their work. Here at Rehoboth Beach he was back on the humble side of the canyon, but Grabowski knew him from their Baltimore days. He got Grabowski on his cell.

"That guy they found floating in Delaware Bay. Anything new on him?"

"No, that one's turning into a genuine whodunit," Grabowski said. "I mean, the man's organs were removed. His goddamn *kidneys*. That's a new one. I figure it's either devil worshippers—or somebody sold his kidneys."

"Sold them? C'mon, Grabowski, that's just an urban legend. Nobody steals kidneys."

"Maybe, maybe not. According to this doctor I asked, those kidneys were worth at least a couple hundred thousand. But I'm leaning toward the devil worshippers myself."

"I'm just curious, you know, because I'm the one who got his wife when she came in," Nick said. "I called the Delaware State Morgue, and *bammo*, there he was on a slab."

"Yeah," Grabowski said. "I saw your name on the report. You think maybe the wife cut out his kidneys and sold them somewhere? I'd think you need connections to do that. You can post your husband's golf clubs for sale on eBay, but not his kidneys."

"She said her husband was in an accident."

Grabowski cleared his throat. "Yeah, right in town on Rehoboth Avenue. I talked to the cop who investigated. He says an ambulance came and picked Wilson up. He was banged up, but nothing life threatening."

"He never checked into a hospital?"

"No record at any of the emergency rooms. But records aren't perfect. You know, things get busy, papers get shuffled out of order, things don't get entered in the computer. So it's possible it was overlooked. The thing that gets me is, after he got picked up by the ambulance, another ambulance stopped at the accident. This one was a county ambulance that had been dispatched out of fire headquarters. Nobody knows who the first ambulance belonged to."

"Huh. One of those private services."

"It gets weirder, my friend. It turns out there were two other accident victims picked up by ambulances last week. And you know what?"

"What?" Nick asked, feeling as if he was walking into a punch line.

"Those two people are missing, too. And in both cases, the county ambulance dispatched by fire headquarters got there behind this mysterious ambulance."

"So this mystery ambulance was listening to a scanner, and when they heard a 10-50 PI come across they ran on it," Nick said.

"And scooped up the accident victims and cut out their kidneys?"

"It does sound nuts," Nick agreed.

"Let me tell you something, Nick, which is that we rarely get so much as a single missing person report all summer, and now we've had three cases in a *week*. Just doesn't happen. This is Rehoboth Beach, not Baltimore. Do me a favor and keep it to yourself. Obviously, if this gets out . . "

"Don't worry," Nick said, disappointed that Grabowski had even mentioned the need to keep it quiet.

"So if you hear any rumors about devil worshippers or whatever, you let me know," Grabowski said.

"I doubt I'll hear much," he said. "I'm on trail patrol these days."

"Oh, shit, how could I forget that I saw your lovely face in this morning's Cape Gazette?" Grabowski asked. "Did they put the picture on the bulletin board?"

"Yeah. We've had some good ones already this morning."

"Ha, ha, I'll bet," Grabowski said. The line crackled with silence. "You know, Nick, that Hawley and I are hoping you stay a while. You were hot shit in homicide in your day and I know this isn't the same, but we could use somebody like you on a permanent basis. You'd make a better beach bum than a mountain man."

"Well, it's something to think about," Nick said. "It sounds like things are about to get interesting around here."

CHAPTER 9

Tara Conrad saw the guy up ahead with the broken-down bicycle and coasted to a stop.

"Trouble?" she asked, then slid off the seat and put her feet out to balance herself.

"The chain came off," Grubb said, looking up. He did a quick assessment: young, healthy-looking and alone. "It's been happening a lot lately. I should take it into the shop and see if they can fix it."

"There's a great bike shop in the Mermaid Zone at the boardwalk," Tara said. "Those are the new shops that are going in."

"Yeah, I've heard about it. I wonder if they make trail calls. If not, I've gone one long walk ahead of me," Grubb said, turning back to his bike. He took out a cheap phone and spoke one word into it: "Ready."

Tara gave him a puzzled look. *Ready for what?* While he fiddled with the bike, Tara took the opportunity to check him out. He looked kind of goth. Black hair. Earring. A stud under his lower lip. Guys with metal on their faces were not exactly her type, but she was on vacation. She was up for an adventure. There was no harm in having a fling at the beach. Live a little, right?

In her job as a medical home caregiver she got to know a lot of old people. They were nice people and all that, but it wasn't a job that did much for her love life. Tara dismounted from her mountain bike, flicked down the kickstand, and walked over. Her legs felt rubbery and wobbly from riding the bike so long. "Let me take a look," she said. "I don't know much about fixing bikes."

It was this crazy mountain biker she really wanted a closer look at. But when Tara knelt next to him, she immediately felt like getting back on her bike and riding away. This guy was spooky. His face was bony and ugly, a brutal fox-face. He was so thin that she could see his shoulder blades through the bike shirt. His eyes glittered with reflected pinpoints of light and he wore eye liner. That was taking the whole goth look a little too far, in her opinion, if you were older than, say, seventeen.

He fixed her with a strange, crooked smile. "I've got a problem, and you may just be the solution," he said. Then he cackled.

His laughter sent a cold chill through Tara. This guy looked nuts. Lock-up-and-throw-away-the-key crazy. She could see it in his eyes. "Just thought I'd try to, uh, help," she said lamely, wishing she hadn't stopped.

Time to ditch this weirdo. Tara was trying to get to her feet when out of the corner of her eye she saw a fat guy running toward them. She turned to watch him. What was he doing? He ran much more quickly than she thought such an overweight man could move. He was sprinting like the Pillsbury Doughboy on steroids. He was running right at them and he wasn't slowing down.

"Wha —" Tara started to say.

From behind her, the goth guy's bony but powerful hand clamped across her mouth, sealing in her screams. She struggled, trying to remember some moves from her self-defense class. She jammed an elbow into the guy's throat and she felt him loosen his grip.

Tara started to break away but thick arms pinned her own arms to her sides. Who — the fat man! She found herself being lifted. What was going on? Before she could scream, the bony hand was across her mouth again.

The two men half-carried, half-dragged Tara to

a van parked nearby. She tried to fight them, kicking her legs and attempting to scream, but they held on too tight. Tara's eyes darted wildly, looking for help, but the parking lot appeared to be deserted. They threw her inside the van and the fat one sprawled across her, holding her to the bare metal floor. She was being crushed by a mountain of lard. Tara screamed in his ear.

"Jesus, Grubb," the fat man whined. "Do something about that, huh?"

Tara was getting ready for another scream when the goth slapped some Duct tape over her mouth. More tape pressed her nose flat. She could hardly get any air. She gave up kicking and squirming and concentrated on breathing.

"That's it," the black-haired one said. "You've got the idea now. Come along quietly."

He moved quickly inside the van's dingy interior, his long hands deftly binding together her ankles and wrists with more tape. Soon all she could do was flop on the metal floor like a fish.

"Can she breathe?" the fat one asked, staring into her wide eyes. "We've got to keep her alive long enough to cut her up."

Tara tried to scream through the gag. She strained against the tape, trying to force a sound through the tape until her eyes felt ready to burst from their sockets. But it was no use. She jerked against her bonds and banged the sides of the van with her feet. Maybe someone outside would hear her.

"Hey, that's enough of that," the goth guy said. He grabbed her feet and secured them to the metal base of the van's passenger seat using a bungee cord. He wrapped it around her legs so tight that it really hurt.

"Man, all that exercise makes me hungry," the fat one said. "There's still a chocolate doughnut left in that bag up front, isn't there?"

"Is food all you ever think about?" Grubb shook his head in disgust. "Just watch her, will you? I'm gonna ditch the bikes."

Grubb slid open the side door of the van and looked around cautiously. The girl had made a lot of racket kicking the sides of the van. If anyone had seen him and Fat Boy grab the girl, that would have attracted attention. Grubb didn't need any curious onlookers or any police, either. A car rolled past on the main road through the park and Grubb tensed, ready to jump into the van and speed off. The car kept going.

Grubb hustled out and grabbed the woman's bike. He ran alongside it, heading for the pine woods. Once he was going good and fast he aimed the front tires for the trees and let the bike fly off into the woods. He ran back for his own bicycle and threw it into the trees. *Fingerprints. Evidence. Don't want that shit around.*

As Grubb trotted back to the van, he thought

with satisfaction of how well the broken chain stunt had worked. Fat Boy was already behind the wheel, licking chocolate icing from his fingers.

"There *was* a doughnut left, Grubb," Fat Boy said.

"Oh happy frickin' day," Grubb said. "Let's get the hell out of here."

Fat Boy hit the gas, and Grubb looked down at their prisoner. She lay immobile on the dirty floor of the van, flecks of oil and rust sticking to the bare flesh of her legs and arms. The tape held her tight, but the young woman continued to wriggle with some futile hope of working herself free.

Her big white eyes stared at him.

Grubb laughed. There were a lot of things he would like to do to that girl, but the Doc had warned him to leave her alone. He didn't want anything bruised, he said.

He put in a CD of his band's performance last weekend at the Cracked Saloon. His band, Dog Smell, had been getting gigs up and down the beach towns. Some geek from a college radio station had even been bugging them about making a demo so he could play some of Dog Smell's music on the university's station. Grubb, who was Dog Smell's lead singer, also made all the band's marketing decisions. He wasn't going to turn the music over to the radio station until he was positive that it wouldn't be too mainstream. Besides, he hated all those phony college kids, acting like they were cool while they studied to be chemical engineers.

Dog Smell was going to be famous one day, Grubb knew, but they weren't going to have a video on YouTube if he could help it. That was what everybody did now. Screw that. They would be famous in their own way.

Grubb listened to his recorded voice scream out the lyrics:

My mom she is an old gray yuppie
She never heard of Skinny Puppy!
Every day she drives off to work
In my dad's foreign car — that jerk!

"You know what, Grubb?" Fat Boy said
"What?"

"You can't sing," Fat Boy said. "In fact, you kind of suck."

"That's the idea, Lardo," Grubb said. "I'm not trying to be the next Frank Sinatra. We're Dog Smell. Our motto is eat shit and die."

"More like *listen* to shit and die."

Grubb gave him a hard look, and Fat Boy hunkered down behind the steering wheel and shut up. Grubb turned around in his seat and looked at their prisoner.

"Good music, huh?"

"She's probably a Taylor Swift fan," Fat Boy said.

Grubb cackled and thumped the dashboard with his hand. He laughed until he was gasping for breath. "Are you trying to make me laugh until I puke or what, Lardo?" He turned back to the girl. "Who do you like, huh?"

Fat Boy made his voice sound high and girlish, "I have all of Justin Bieber's albums."

Grubb hooted with glee. "That's a good one!" he shouted. "A Bieber Believer!"

The young woman just stared at them with eyes like saucers.

• • •

"We'll have another shipment going out today if everything goes according to plan," Doctor Kreeger said into the phone.

"Excellent," said Roger Cramer, the hospital administrator. "We've got just the place for Grubb and Fat Boy to do their collecting."

While it had been Kreeger's idea to use joggers as donors, Smith had suggested the Junction and Breakwater Trail as a hunting ground. They had been wildly successful. "You're sure they won't have any trouble?"

Smith gave a short laugh. "If you've seen something in the news, it's all just hype, Kreeger. My source tells me there are only two officers on that patrol. This is the Rehoboth Beach police we're talking about, not the FBI. They'll catch a couple more kids shaking down joggers, get a couple more mentions in the newspaper, and that'll be it. The mayor wanted the police to crack down. I don't think we have anything to worry about as long as our timing is right."

"You should know," Kreeger said.

"I'll be in touch later to find out how it turned out," Smith said. "For God's sake, be careful, huh? Those organs are worth a lot of money."

"Don't worry," Kreeger said.

"Okay." Smith hung up, and Kreeger left his office and headed for the operating room in the basement.

He went down the hall, whistling as he walked. He knew the nurses he passed were smirking at him behind his back because of the Aston Martin. He had overheard some of them gossiping about how silly he looked driving the sports car. Overcompensating, they said. They never said what he was overcompensating *for*. Kreeger would have liked to hear their theories. He didn't care much about what the nurses were saying. The silly bitches were just jealous they couldn't afford one of the finest driving machines ever made.

The elevator was broken again, so Kreeger had to use the stairs. Good thing there were only three floors — four, if you counted the basement. The whole damn hospital was falling apart and the administration didn't seem to be doing anything about it. It wasn't any secret that Southern Delaware General Hospital had financial problems. But if they couldn't even keep the elevators running, maybe the hospital was in worse straits than Kreeger had imagined.

Kreeger changed into his green smock, scrubbed up, and donned his cap and surgical mask. *Another donor*, he thought gleefully. If this kept up he could buy a Ferrari to go with his Aston Martin. He shouldered open the door to the basement operating room and Fat Boy helped him slip surgical gloves over his sterile hands. Neither Grubb nor Fat Boy wore surgical gowns, but they weren't going to be sticking around for the actual operation.

"What have we here?" Kreeger said through his mask.

The young woman didn't answer. She was strapped to the operating table, her eyes darting from Kreeger, to Grubb, to the door, as if she expected help to arrive at any moment. Kreeger could tell she was fighting the shot Grubb had already given her. The anesthesia hadn't yet taken hold.

"Where . . . where am I?" she asked. She sounded surprisingly calm, Kreeger thought.

"You're here for the plastic surgery, right?" Kreeger asked. He turned to Grubb. "Funny, her nose looks all right to me."

The woman was shaking her head. "I was

kidnapped . . . " her voiced trailed off. Sounding sleepy, drugged. The anesthesia starting to cloud her mind.

"What should we do with her, then?" Kreeger asked, looking at Grubb. "I mean, I put all this stuff on, we've booked the operating room for the next hour . . ."

"Let's cut out her kidneys," Grubb suggested.

"What an excellent idea," Kreeger said. "You wouldn't mind, would you?"

"What . . . " She shook her head. "No . . . "

"I can't believe you guys brought me the wrong patient again," Kreeger said. He sighed. "Well, it's too late now." He began to mark her exposed belly with betadine solution. She cringed at the touch of the cold swab.

"No . . . no . . . "

"Put her under," Kreeger ordered.

Fat Boy lowered the mask over her face.

Grubb cackled again. To Kreeger it sounded like a mule braying while someone in the background dragged their fingernails across a blackboard. He wished Grubb would shut the hell up.

"You're hilarious, Doc," Grubb said. He choked out one last cackle, like the dying gasp of a crow. "You've got a real good bedside manner."

"Thanks, Grubb. That's means a lot coming from someone like you. Now pass me a scalpel, will you?"

• • •

Just a few miles away, Nick was getting used to his new beach house. It turned out that the jogger they had rescued from the park had connections. When he heard Nick needed a place to live, he found him a great deal, house sitting a place for a couple spending the summer in Europe. It was a definite step up from the motel room—and a whole lot cheaper, considering that he got to live in a million dollar beach house for free. The owners loved the idea of a police officer keeping an eye on their place.

Though the house was nice and the view of the beach and sea was great, he was still feeling lonely. He wished he could talk to Karen. She had always been able to help him through the blues.

He found himself roaming the beach house, walking from the kitchen, through the living room, into the bedroom, then back again. He wandered into corners and stared at the empty white walls. The place was decorated in a beach theme with the requisite whitewashed wicker furniture and pastel colors, but by night it felt cold and sterile. He could hear the surf outside.

He slid open the door and went to stand on the deck. In the darkness, he could see the glow of the waves breaking on the beach. The water must have contained something phosphorescent.

The wind off the sea felt fresh and helped to clear his mind. The ocean at night seemed cold and lonely, dark as death itself, and was small comfort. He felt the blues coming on sure as the tide was rising.

Tough guys weren't supposed to get lonely, but even out in the mountains, he'd had his share of nights like this. The good thing was that splitting wood usually left him too tired to think much.

Before Karen, Nick never had bad nights. It was only after. Before Karen he had never been home. Early in his career he'd always been in the squad car, working extra shifts, or pulling double duty at one of the nightclubs or theaters as a privately paid cop in city uniform. Then he got on the homicide squad. Crazy hours when it was busy, nine to five when it was slow.

Then Karen.

Don't think about her, he warned himself. Just forget her. He left the deck, pulled the door shut, and was back in the kitchen, his last beer already somehow gone. He opened the fridge and grabbed another.

She had been a part of his life for three years. She should have been his wife, but Nick always had been afraid of marriage. It seemed like too much of a commitment, even though they already lived together. Marriage was what Karen had wanted, and Nick would always regret not making her happy. He should have married her.

Don't do this to yourself, he thought. Not tonight. But it was too late.

He had crammed his memories of her, had crammed those three years of his life, into the farthest corner of his mind. It was the same as shoving everything into a closet. One day you cracked open the door to take a peek, and everything came tumbling out.

He grabbed his phone and flipped through the pictures of her. Nick felt guilty about the fact that he sometimes had trouble remembering her face, but he had never forgotten how beautiful she was. Long chestnut hair, green eyes, a playful smile on her lips. They'd had three years together. He wished it could have been a lifetime.

Why tonight? It had been a long time since he let himself think about Karen.

He thought it might be because of Sarah Monahan. She reminded him of Karen in many ways, especially their senses of humor, although the two women were very different people. Nick had to wonder if he was falling for his partner, even though he knew better. It wasn't professional. More importantly, women like Sarah did not go for the Nick Logans of the world, he knew. She was on the fast track toward the upper echelons of the police department. A woman, especially one with her capabilities, was a feather in the cap of a police administration. Put her in front of a microphone, let the reporters quote her. The Rehoboth Beach Police Department would look very progressive.

Well, to hell with Sarah Monahan. Nick didn't need another woman cluttering up the closet space of his mind. He would keep things on a strictly business level between them for the rest of the assignment.

Nick headed for the refrigerator and grabbed another beer, hoping it would help him sleep. He drank it on the deck, looking at the dark sea, then pitched the bottle toward the waves. He thought about another beer, reminded himself that he had to get up in a few hours, and went around turning off lights instead. He crawled into bed, thinking that he wouldn't be able to sleep, but the sound of the surf was like a lullaby. In a minute, he was out.

CHAPTER 10

Grubb grabbed the microphone and wrenched it in his hands like he was wringing a chicken neck.

They call this world a place to be somebody
What about me? A dedicated loser, a nobody.
I think I'll burn this goddamn town,
Spread the ashes, make it sacred ground.

The crowd howled and gnashed its teeth for more. Dog Smell's lead guitarist, a young man with a shaved head and a tattoo of a gargoyle over his left ear, launched into a solo. The kids in the mosh pit in front of the stage bumped and mashed each other, screaming along until flecks of spittle flew from their lips. Grubb danced a crazy, lone dance on the stage, moving as if all his bones had been removed and he was a rubber puppet dangling on the end of a string.

The chords came around and Grubb snatched up the mic.

I saw a Boy Scout help an old lady cross the street.
My motorcycle roared as I screamed "Dead Meat!"
They had these sweet, tender smiles on their faces.
I put them on the road to a better place, yeah!

Set this world on fire! Pour the gasoline, yeah!
This place must burn. Burn it down, yeah!
It's the only way the drones will ever learn.
Set it on fire! Yeah! Make it burn, make it burn!

Grubb flicked his head and sweat whipped from the tips of his black hair. He danced again, this time with the mic. The guitarist was giving it to them. The kids grated and ground. Mostly college pukes, working jobs at the beach for the summer. They didn't know what it was all about. Grubb stood on the edge of the stage, hating them all. So fake, so phony. The kids held out their hands for him. They wanted him to jump, wanted to catch him and pass him overhead from hand to hand, supported like a Hindu on a bed of nails.

Laughing, Grubb leaped.

Arms and hands caught him, held him aloft,

and soon he was crowd surfing. He flew over the heads in the mosh pit, dipping and rising like a plane in turbulent weather. Grubb cackled insanely as the hands kept him in the air, kept him moving. Then they carried him back toward the stage, pushing him along in a human wave. He crawled onto the rough wood and jumped up in time to grab the mic and scream:

Set this town on fire! Pour the gasoline, yeah!
This place must burn. Burn it down, yeah!
It's the only way those drones will ever learn.
Set it on fire! Yeah! Make it burn, make it burn!

Grubb screamed the last words and the guitarist played his final lick. Then they were finished. The kids shouted, going absolutely wild, begging for more Dog Smell, for more music. They were like a pack of jackals.

"More!" they screamed. "One more song!"

"Screw you!" Grubb screamed back over the mic. "Screw you all!" He flicked them the finger.

The crowd howled, loving it.

"You suck!" he yelled at them. "You're all a bunch of phony assholes!"

"More," they shouted. "More Dog Smell!"

But Grubb was done. To hell with all those college pukes. Then the guitarist dug into one last song and Grubb found himself caught up in the angry, throbbing beat. His head bobbed, keeping time.

He stepped forward and sang. The kids mashed even harder down on the floor, getting the last of their energy out.

Grubb sang, screeching out the words with such force that the stage lights backlit droplets of spit. Then the guitarist hit the last chord, slashing down on the strings, and the lights flicked on and off in the club.

He finished singing, panted for a moment under the eye-stinging house lights, then started running.

"Hey, Grubb, man — " the guitarist called, but Grubb was already across the stage, headed for the back door. He slammed out the door and into the alley behind the bar as if demons were chasing him.

His bike was chained up out there. A lime green Kawasaki Ninja ZX-6R that went from zero to 60 in less than five seconds. A real crotch rocket. Grubb paid cash for it, thanks to the organ business.

The alley was dark and damp, stacked high with cardboard boxes full of empty beer bottles and plastic trash bags. Grubb reached behind a tower of trash and pulled out a cheap nylon rucksack, the same kind those college dweebs in the club carried on their way to political science class.

He hefted it and felt the weight inside. Good.

Everything was there. From inside the club, he heard the sounds of the crowd and the electric squealing of amplifiers as Dog Smell packed up. They wouldn't be too happy with him for running out and leaving them with all the work, but he was Grubb. The center of the band. He called the shots. He could do what he wanted. Just being inside that place had been making him sick. And he had something special planned for tonight.

Grubb unlocked the motorcycle, slipped his arms through the straps of the rucksack. He climbed on the Ninja and it kicked right over. He kept it in neutral and rolled the accelerator forward a couple of times, making the machine snarl like a rabid hyena on steroids. The engine noise was deafening in the narrow alley. He slipped into gear then darted out of the alley and into the street without bothering to look for oncoming cars.

He rolled the accelerator forward again, putting all 636 CCs to work, and surged effortlessly up to fifty, then sixty, flying through the mostly vacant streets. The engine noise echoed off the houses and shops he passed, making a spooky mechanized howl that could be heard far across the beach town, like some beast on the prowl.

• • •

Grubb headed for the boardwalk. Straight ahead he could make out the dark expanse of the sea, dappled here and there with moonlight. It was after 1 a.m., but there were still a few people out on the boardwalk or walking the beach, maybe looking for a quiet place to make love under the summer sky. Some couples held hands, forming picture-perfect romantic silhouettes against the pools of light along the boardwalk.

Grubb hated them, hated the boardwalk, hated all the fake tourist bullshit. The question might be why Grubb hung around, but the answer was that he would have hated just about anywhere. This was as good a place to hate as any, and he had a good job to boot.

He still had Dog Smell's lyrics screeching in his head and his ears rang from the gnashing guitars. He preferred burned-out warehouses, waterfronts stinking of dead fish and mud, streets littered with wine bottles. Reality. The down-and-out versus the rich. He swung the bike right onto the boardwalk and raced down its length.

Finally, he braked to a stop in front of the entrance to the new Mermaid Zone shops, his back wheel slewing around on the sandy surface so that Grubb had to throw out a foot to keep from dumping the bike. The Ninja weighed a bit over 400 pounds—dead weight if he laid it down. Then he was off the bike, kicking down the stand, tugging the heavy rucksack from his back.

Grubb took out a Molotov cocktail. He had mixed it up inside an empty vodka bottle. The bottle was filled with high octane gasoline, the same kind Grubb used for his motorcycle. He had screwed the top back on the bottle. Now, he uncapped it and took a long strip of what had once been an American flag from his rucksack. Working quickly, he spilled a little of the gasoline onto the cloth, then jammed the strip into the bottle to stopper it. The remnants of the flag wicked into the gasoline inside.

He had never made a Molotov cocktail before, much less used one. *Thank you, YouTube*. Now, hefting the gasoline-filled bottle, he thought *whoa*. He was about to cross some kind of line here between someone who just talked about doing something, and someone who actually did it. Somewhere in the back of his mind he thought this was crazy; this was nuts. He shook the bottle in his hand. It was also pretty awesome. He wasn't just singing about anarchy. He was about to become an anarchist.

Grubb studied the plate glass window of the shop facing the boardwalk. He had imagined himself simply hurling the bottle at the store and then watching everything go up in flames. But the window looked thick, and if the bottle shattered against the glass, the burning gasoline would cascade uselessly to the concrete surface of the boardwalk.

Break it., he thought. Grubb had brought along a one-inch wrench in his rucksack. He could never use it to fix his bike, which was metric. But the heavy tool was good to have if you needed to fine tune any assholes who gave you trouble. Moving like a cat, Grubb hustled up to the window and smacked it with the wrench.

The tool bounced harmlessly off the glass.

"Shit!" Grubb shouted. The echo clattered down the boardwalk like an old hubcap. He used two hands on the wrench the second time, swinging it like a baseball bat. He shut his eyes and flinched his head away as the steel connected.

The window gave way. Not all at once, but Grubb had punched a hole big enough to throw the Molotov cocktail inside. A burglar alarm trilled. Grubb hadn't imagined that part, either.

He was starting to get nervous. He already had been here a few minutes. Somebody could have called the cops about him riding on the boardwalk. The Ninja was hard to ignore. Cops might be on their way right now.

He looked around for the bomb. "Where . . "

It was still back by the bike. He ran to the street, grabbed the vodka bottle, and held it carefully away from him as he flicked the lighter he pulled from his pocket. The gas-covered cloth ignited in a burst of flame. *Holy shit, look at that!* He hurled the bomb through the hole in the window. Then he dove for the sidewalk.

Whump.

The fireball blew out what was left of the window. Shards of glass like icicles showered down and shattered up and down the boardwalk. The interior of the store was ablaze. Grubb scrambled to his feet, and he could feel the air being sucked through the open window to feed the fire.

Grubb stood there a moment admiring the fire. The ocean breeze fanned the flames. He beat his chest and howled. "Oooo! Ooo! Ooo! Oooooo!"

Then he jumped on the bike and took off. He turned down the first street he came to. He was working through the gears, only half a block down, when he saw the car.

It was a beautiful gray Mercedes. Four doors, sleek as a groomed thoroughbred. Grubb braked and was off the bike and into his rucksack in a flash. He had one more Molotov cocktail.

Already he could hear sirens in the distance, so Grubb worked as quickly as he could, willing his fingers not to fumble. He hammered at the driver's side window until the safety glass dissolved into tiny beads. The car alarm started going. He poured gas on another strip of flag, spilling a lot on the pavement. The rag slipped into the bottle.

Red and blue lights flashed toward him down the street. It was just his luck that one of

Rehoboth's finest had been nearby.

Grubb had the lighter out. He flicked it at the gasoline-soaked rag. The flame guttered out. *Flick.* He touched the lighter to the cloth, which caught this time, then tossed the cocktail into the Mercedes.

The cop car was almost on him, framing him in the headlights. He jumped on the bike and twisted the accelerator. *Outta here.* The Ninja surged ahead so quickly that Grubb felt the G forces tug at the skin on his face like he was a freakin' astronaut headed for the moon.

In the next instant the Mercedes blew up and filled the street with fiery light.

What looked like a rear view mirror whipped past Grubb's head, even though he was doing seventy. He chanced a quick glance over his shoulder. What he saw made him brake.

The police car had been passing the Mercedes just as it exploded. Shock waves—or maybe the cop's reaction—forced the patrol car onto the sidewalk on the opposite side of the street. The front end of the police car was now wrapped around a tree.

The luxury car was a flaming hulk. A second explosion wracked the street as the gas tank went up.

Grubb threw back his head and screeched with delight. Then he was gone into the night, leaving behind only the echo of his machine.

CHAPTER 11

"How did I do this morning?" Nick asked, digging into the white paper bag. "Orange juice. Bananas. Plums. And, voila, bran muffins."

He put each item on the stakeout car's dashboard, creating a makeshift breakfast buffet. He also pulled out a copy of the News Journal, which had a story by Jorge Alvarez about the firebombing on the boardwalk.

"You've got something else in the bag," Sarah said.

"Well, uh, it's a cup of coffee and a cup of chai tea."

She laughed, and Nick felt a stab of emotion that he hadn't felt in a while. It took him a moment to realize that it was happiness. Then he remembered his vow of the night before. He wasn't getting involved with his partner, even if she did by some chance become interested in him.

"All right, you did good this morning," she said. "Keep it up and I you might make a decent partner."

"Gee, thanks."

She blew steam off the cup of chai tea and looked at him over the rim. "Don't take this the wrong way, Nick, but you smell a little like a brewery right now."

"Let's just say I had one too many last night."

"So, is that a habit with you? Having one too many?"

"Every now and then the blues come on, if you know what I mean."

"I think I do. Listen, next time you're having one of those nights, just give me a call. I'll tell you a knock-knock joke to cheer you up."

Sarah reached for a banana and began peeling it. Logan watched her.

"That's incredibly erotic, you know," he said.

She paused with her mouth wide open, ready to take a big bite of the banana. "Let your imagination run wild, Logan," she said, then chomped. "Mmmm."

Watching Sarah eat the banana was making him kind of aroused. He attempted not to stare as she took another bite. He tried to think about something else. "That was one hell of a fire last night on the boardwalk," he said, sipping his coffee.

"What I want to know is, why would some nut throw a firebomb into a surf shop?"

"Who knows? Revenge, maybe? A fired employee or something. Surfers can be intense."

"What do you know about surfers? This is Delaware."

"There are surfers in Delaware." Nick had seen them down at Indian River Inlet, a popular surfing spot. His niece had invited him down there to watch her surf. Her new boyfriend—the lifeguard—was teaching her. Both of those kids were still embarrassed about Nick finding them in the bedroom. As it turned out, the lifeguard seemed like an okay kid.

"A firebombing is a little unusual," Sarah said as she stripped away more banana peel. Was she doing that on purpose, or what? "If he's a disgruntled employee, at least he didn't walk in and start shooting. That seems to be the modus operandi these days."

"One of our guys got hurt, though. He spotted the firebug and tried to run him down. Only a second firebomb went off in a car parked on the street just as he passed it. They had to fly him to the burn center outside Philly."

"When we catch the son of a bitch, we ought to burn his ass, see how he likes it," Sarah said.

Nick grinned. Maybe he was beginning to rub off on his partner. She hadn't acted this tough before. "Grabowski is the lead investigator on that. I'll tell him to give you a call," he said. "Maybe he'll let you strike the match."

Nick took a tentative bite of his bran muffin, which tasted like it was made out of sawdust or straw. He washed the dry mouthful down with a gulp of coffee, made a face. A chocolate doughnut would have been so much better.

He took another gulp of coffee, willing the caffeine to hurry up and kick in. Too early for him.

Sarah finished her banana, took a sip of chai tea. "I'm going to start stretching," she said.

"Just a banana?" Nick asked, looking at the food spread on the dashboard. "Don't you want something else?"

"Maybe later," she said. "I don't want a full stomach, just enough to settle it. Besides, I don't want to eat another banana in front of you. You might get over-excited or something." She slipped out of the car.

Nick smirked at her through the windshield. He was liking this woman more all the time. She gave the appearance of being completely professional, but deep down she was tough and flinty. She was a woman who has going places in her career. *She's not for you, Logan.*

He gulped down the rest of his coffee, hoping

the caffeine wouldn't give him a heart attack when he began exercising, and slid out from behind the steering wheel. Ever since the day Nick had claimed the keys, Sarah hadn't argued about letting him drive. She knew a pig-headed man when she saw one.

Nick put his leg up on the hood of the car and tried to bend his upper body toward it. He managed only a few inches, like the way an oak might bend in a windstorm. Reluctantly. Nonetheless, he felt his hamstring stretch.

"You do this every day, you'll get more flexible," Sarah said, watching him struggle. She was doing the same stretch, and her ear was touching the laces of her running shoe.

"Maybe I like being inflexible," Nick said. With a grunt, he pulled his leg down and kicked up the other one.

They finished stretching and started out running. Nick's legs no longer felt as sore as they had. He was in fairly good shape from the farm work, but running definitely used a different set of muscles. While he was hardly ready for the Boston Marathon, at least he was keeping up with his partner.

"This is getting easy," Nick said as he chugged along beside Sarah.

"We're just warming up, Nick," she warned. "Think of this as first gear. I think we should run all the way into the state park this morning.

Think you're ready?"

Nick felt good. "Let's do it."

They ran the Junction and Breakwater Trail all the way into Lewes and then cut over toward Cape Henlopen State Park. For some distance, they ran along the Lewes and Rehoboth Canal, keeping pace with the occasional kayaker and the ducks. There was the usual mix of runners and bicyclists on the trail this morning. Once in the park, they followed the trail through shady black pines that grew on the sand dunes. There was sand beneath the pines, along with patches of prickly pear and beach plum. Nick's eye was caught by the sight of two boys struggling to pull something free out of the underbrush.

The boys, who couldn't have been more than eleven or twelve, were trying to drag two bicycles out of the woods. The bikes were for adults, the seats and tires all out of proportion compared to the size of the young salvagers. Something didn't look right.

"Hold up a minute," Nick said.

"It's just a couple of kids with bikes."

Ignoring her, Nick trotted over. The two boys were working to get the bicycles free of the brush, which had developed into a tug of war between them and some stubborn briers. They looked up, startled, as Nick approached.

"That's a strange place to leave your bikes," he said to the kids.

"Somebody left them here," one boy said. "We saw them back in the trees and thought we'd get them out."

"Let me get this straight," Nick said. "Somebody left these two perfectly good bikes here in the bushes?"

"Yep."

"Look, I'm a police officer. You boys go wait with the lady over there," he said. The boys started to leave, but he called them back. "Did you two, uh, borrow these bikes?"

"No." Both kids shook their heads emphatically. "Uh, uh."

Nick sighed. "Okay. Go wait over there."

The boys walked slowly away, kicking at the ground. Then they started running like hell.

"Kids." Nick shook his head. He didn't even think about going after them. They were quick as rabbits, gone in a flash.

"What was that all about?" Sarah asked.

"Those boys said they found these bikes." Nick shrugged, then looked down at the bicycles. "What were those bikes doing back in the woods?"

"Somebody probably stole them, got tired of riding them around, and ditched them."

"They're nice bikes," Nick said. "It looked to me like they were trying to get them out of the brush, not the other way around."

"Let's report them as recovered stolen

property," Sarah said. "What's that yellow one? A Trek? It's worth a few hundred bucks. Nobody ever bothers to see if we have their missing bicycles, though. So we can ride them ourselves on trail patrol." Sarah grinned and punched Nick playfully in the thick meat of his arm. "It would sure beat running, huh?"

• • •

Nick was still figuring out what to do with the abandoned bikes, dreading more paperwork, when his phone rang. Grabowski.

"I thought you'd like to be the first to know," the detective said. "We got a missing person report. Another one, can you believe it? A woman disappeared. Last seen yesterday. She was on vacation and decided to ride her bike in the state park. I figured you and Detective Monahan would be out there this morning."

"Uh oh," Nick said.

"Exactly," Grabowski said.

"Is there a description of the bike? Is it a yellow Trek?"

"Uh ... yeah."

"Then I think I'm looking at it right now."

"Nick, you may be the luckiest cop in Rehoboth Beach. We ought to put you on finding Blackbeard's treasure, which is supposedly buried somewhere in the sand dunes around here."

"I'd be a whole lot luckier if I knew why we have two bikes here, when there's only one missing person."

"At the rate you're going, you'll have it figured out by lunchtime."

As it turned out, it would take Nick a little longer.

• • •

"The flames were everywhere," the man said to the TV reporter. "It was just terrible."

"You lost your surf shop?" the reporter asked, jerking the microphone to his own lips, then aiming it at the shop owner once again.

"Everything."

Kreeger watched as they cut to video of the early morning fire. Firefighters scrambled everywhere, dragging hoses and shouting. The TV lights glowed in the reflective strips on the firefighters' turnout coats. Flames fed by the ocean breeze licked at the nighttime sky.

Cut back to the reporter, live at the scene. That in itself was unusual, because Rehoboth was a newspaper town. TV reporters generally only showed up at the beach when there was a hurricane coming so that they could film the businesses boarding up their windows and the surf coming onto the boardwalk. But a firebombing at the famous Rehoboth Beach boardwalk was almost as newsworthy as a tropical storm.

"Officials are telling us they still don't know who set the fire early this morning. The first police officer on the scene, Patrolman Bill Donovan — who is in stable condition now at Chester-Crozier Burn Center — radioed that he was in pursuit of a man on a motorcycle just moments before he was injured in a second firebomb explosion in which a Mercedes Benz was destroyed. Rehoboth Beach Police will not release any details about this mysterious motorcyclist and say they have no suspects at this time. I'm Tom Hunter, live from the boardwalk at Rehoboth Beach."

Kreeger thumbed off the remote and poured himself a cup of coffee. Crazies throwing firebombs, blowing up stores and luxury cars — thank God it hadn't been his new Aston Martin. Relieved, Kreeger went back to munching on a bagel.

His mobile rang as he was pouring his second cup of coffee. He saw it was the hospital's number.

"Dr. Kreeger." He immediately recognized the voice of Roger Cramer, the hospital administrator. "Can you get down here right away?"

"Another donor?"

"Yes."

"Is he just dying to meet me?" Kreeger asked.

Cramer missed the joke for a moment. "Yeah." He laughed half-heartedly. "Just get here quick as you can, will you?"

Kreeger hurried to get ready. Behind the wheel of the Aston Martin, he would get there in record time.

CHAPTER 12

"We haven't found any sign yet of our missing woman," Chief Hawley said. "The state police are going to put some K-9 patrols into the dunes and woods and see what they come up with. But we have to keep it low key. We don't want the Cape Gazette or the News Journal over there shooting photos of us looking for a body."

"Bad public relations," Nick said. He didn't necessarily agree with keeping a lid on the missing person case, but he was beginning to understand that tourism—and tourism alone—was what fueled the local economy. Abducted vacationers was not the kind of story that the chamber of commerce wanted to promote.

"The mayor will not be happy," Sarah agreed.

"Tourism is very important to him," said Craig Jenkins, the city councilman whose role it was to oversee the police department. Hawley wasn't always thrilled about a "civilian" sticking his nose into police business, but to be fair, Jenkins seemed content to be kept in the loop and rarely meddled. It didn't hurt that he always made sure the department's budgetary bread had plenty of butter. "He's not going to let some bad publicity destroy Rehoboth's reputation as a safe haven, especially not during the summer season."

Nick nodded, took a sip from his mug, grimaced at the taste of cold, sour coffee. Since early that morning, he and Sarah had been looking for leads out at Cape Henlopen State Park. They talked with joggers and bicyclists, fishermen at the pier, dog walkers and bird watchers. No one had seen a thing.

Nick was convinced the two bicycles he had pulled from the woods were the key. The missing young woman was part of a group of friends who had rented a beach house in the Pilot Point community. A roommate verified that one of the bikes belonged to the missing woman. The second bicycle had been reported stolen from a family staying at the state park campground. Prints had been found, but some were Nick's, others belonged to the two boys, and there were a couple more unidentified partials. It turned out that bicycles did not provide the best surfaces for fingerprints.

Chief Hawley sighed. "You know, I have to say that I'm a little disappointed in the two of you. The idea was that you'd be patrolling the park so things like this wouldn't happen."

"We've been out there every day, Mike," Nick said. "But it's a big park and it's just our luck that the abduction happened when we weren't around."

"You'd almost think somebody knew we wouldn't be there," Sarah said. "Like they planned it that way."

Hawley leaned back in his chair, shook his head. "Hey, forget I said anything. I know you two have done good with the trail patrols. I'm just getting frustrated. I mean, what the hell is going on? This is the beach, right? The hardest part of our job should be handing out parking tickets and fining underage drinkers. I don't even know—"

Chief Hawley never finished the thought, because at that moment the door swung open and the mayor walked in. Everyone in the room shuffled to their feet. The Honorable Edward Gates, Mayor of the City of Rehoboth Beach, was a man who liked everyone to stand when he walked into a room. He was tall, white-haired, tanned and lean—like he played a lot of tennis. Though past sixty, he looked to be in good shape. At the moment, he also looked unhappy.

"What the hell is going on in Cape Henlopen?" he demanded.

"Well, sir, it looks like we've had an abduction," Hawley said. "A young lady was out riding her bicycle and she disappeared."

"I know that," the mayor said, sounding irritated. "How did it happen? I thought there were supposed to be extra patrols on the Junction and Breakwater Trail to prevent just such occurrences. This is not a good sit —"

"Ed, come on now," Jenkins said. "We're doing the best we can. Have you met detectives Logan and Monahan? They're the ones who caught those muggers on the trail. I'm sure you remember it was on the front page of the Gazette?"

Mayor Gates nodded coolly at Nick and Sarah. Nick had never met the well-known mayor, and despite the fact that the man was not happy, Nick was impressed. Mayor Gates looked like the mayor of a beach town straight from central casting—he could have been the model who stepped out of a magazine advertisement for a beachfront retirement community. Gates found a chair, dragged it into a corner, and sat with his arms folded across his chest.

"Pretend I'm not here," the mayor said. "I just want to hear your plan of action."

"Well, uh . . ." Hawley stumbled.

"Here's the situation, Ed," said Commissioner

Jenkins, who rushed to the rescue. "The young lady went off to ride her bicycle in Cape Henlopen State Park and the Junction and Breakwater Trail, and she hasn't been seen since. Her bicycle, along with another bike, was found abandoned in the dunes by Detectives Monahan and Nick, which was a good bit of police work in itself. The detectives have been out at the park all day asking people if they saw anything. There are some rather isolated areas along the trail and in the park itself. No houses nearby. I don't want to speak for the chief here" —Jenkins nodded deferentially to Hawley—"but this afternoon I believe the state police are sending some K-9 patrols out to see if they can find a body, or any clothing."

Mayor Gates rocketed to his feet. "That's just what we don't need, TV footage of the police searching for a dead girl in the park! She was supposed to be on vacation. First the boardwalk nearly burns down, and now this incident at the state park. What the hell in going on? I'd say our beautiful beach resort is beginning to have an image problem. When people come down to the beach, the worst they expect is a sunburn or an overpriced margarita. Being murdered is not on anyone's list of things to do at the beach."

Jenkins shrugged. "If we keep it quiet, the media won't be there. And if they do show up, we'll make the point that we've pulled out all the stops to find this woman. If a crime took place, we'll vow to catch the perpetrators. We need to look like we're on top of things. We need to reassure people that spending time at the beach is perfectly safe. We need to show that we are going to catch whoever did this and nail his ass to the barn door."

"Hawley, is that right?" the mayor asked. "You have to search with dogs?"

"Yes, sir."

Mayor Gates clapped his hands together and got to his feet. "Jenkins, you are goddamn brilliant. We need a show of force. What's everybody sitting around for? Get out there and find out what happened to that poor young woman!"

CHAPTER 13

Doug Keller couldn't believe he was watching a man have a heart attack. Doug wasn't a doctor, but he knew what he was seeing as the fat man clutched at his chest, gurgling noises escaping from the thick lips. He looked too young to be having a major coronary, but the man's eyes bugged out of his head and he was trying to mouth some message for help as he staggered down the jogging trail.

Keller slowed his pace, trying not to panic. *CPR.* He had learned it five years ago when he was a Boy Scout camp counselor his first summer out of college. How the hell was he supposed to remember what to do? *Five compressions, two breaths.* Or was it four compressions, one breath?

"Help me," the man wheezed. "My heart —"
The next thing Keller knew, the fat man was slumped on the ground.

Keller sprinted over, his own heart pounding wildly. He had only done CPR on practice dummies. This was it. The real deal.

"What's wrong?" He crouched at the man's side. "Are you having a heart attack?"

"Help me," the fat man said. He groaned.

I ought to call 911, Keller was thinking. But he hadn't brought his phone on the trail and nobody was in sight. He was vacationing at the beach to get away from his phone, for God's sake. He had to stay and help the guy. If another jogger came along Keller could ask him to get help.

He went over the steps for CPR in his head, trying to think straight. Find the end of the sternum and measure two finger-widths up . . . but how the hell was he supposed to find anything on a guy this fat? Might as well try to find the sternum on a walrus. He had learned CPR on a skinny practice mannequin called "Resusci-Annie." This guy was more like Resusci-Whale. The instructor had wiped down the mannequin each time with alcohol wipes. Nice and clean. This guy smelled like an Italian sub and Mountain Dew. He wasn't in any hurry to put his lips on that.

Doug was still waiting for the man to quit breathing so he could administer CPR when he

felt the arms encircle him from behind. *What the*
—

"Hey!" He tried to break free, but whoever had grabbed him was crazy strong. Doug was over on his belly in a second, pinned to the ground. Someone's knees pressed painfully into his back between his shoulder blades.

"Listen, I was only trying to help," he struggled to say. "I think this man here is having a heart attack."

"Not me," the fat guy said, getting to his feet. "You looked like the one who was going to have a heart attack. White as a sheet."

"What's going on?"

He felt his wrists being taped together. Doug was so surprised he didn't even try to struggle. "Look, I don't have any money," he said. "Take my car keys. They're in a little pocket on my running shoes. It's an Optima."

"We don't want your car," hissed his attacker, who was still unseen behind him, taping up his wrists. The voice sent a chill through him.

"Then what *do* you want?"

The fat man stood nearby. A candy bar had appeared out of nowhere and he was patiently unwrapping it. "We want your heart, buddy. Maybe your corneas, too. But most definitely we want your kidneys. Do you have any medical defects we should know about? Any social diseases?"

"Let me go, you assholes!" His voice was shrill. Doug felt himself giving in to terror and he struggled against it. There had to be a way out of whatever was happening here.

His unseen assailant slapped the side of his head, making his ear ring.

"You're not HIV positive or anything, right?" Fat Boy asked. "Hepatitis? High cholesterol?"

"Even if he is, we still got to kill him," the other man said. "He knows too much. He's seen you."

"But I haven't see you," Doug said to the voice. "You could let me go now. I have herpes! I've got AIDS!"

"Nice try, buddy, but I think you're just fine."

Keller felt himself being rolled onto his back. In a moment he was staring up into the face of the man who had tackled him. He flinched. The man looked bone thin and ugly, with the face of an emaciated rat. His black hair hung in clumps and a tattoo of a spider crawled along his neck.

"Now you've seen me," Grubb hissed, his face just a foot away from Doug's. "Guess we've got to kill you."

• • •

Kreeger hadn't counted on joggers being so ... fit.

One minute the patient was being wheeled into the operating room on the gurney. The next minute he had somehow broken free of the straps and was running for the door.

"Grab him!" Kreeger shouted.

"You're all crazy," the man screamed. "Let me out of here!"

Grubb darted to intercept him. Quick as a snake, he leaped to block the man's path. Grubb was fast because he didn't have an ounce of spare flesh on his skeletal body. The man was much bigger and heavier, and he slammed Grubb with his shoulder, sending him into a tray of surgical instruments that scattered on the floor, ringing like gunshots as they hit the tile. Grubb landed on top of the implements and swore as something sharp dug into him.

"Hold on there," Kreeger said, trying to stay calm but already worrying about what would happen if this one got away. He wished Fat Boy had picked some other time to visit the snack machine down the hall. "You shouldn't be so hasty to leave."

The man stopped, momentarily obeying the authority in the doctor's voice. People listened to doctors. Kreeger noticed that the young man looked mad as hell. Good thing his hands were still secured behind his back.

"What the hell is going on?" he demanded.

Kreeger advanced toward him with his scrubbed hands out just as he had held them to accept the surgical gloves.

• • •

All that Doug Keller saw headed toward him was a shapeless figure in a green surgical smock. The head and face were covered and the eyes appeared unnaturally huge behind the thick lenses of the surgeon's magnifying glasses. His hands were bound, so he lashed out with one muscular leg as the doctor approached and kicked him squarely in the chest.

Kreeger crashed back against the operating table, lost his balance, and hit the floor, too stunned to even use his hands to break his fall. His face banged against the floor and the frames of his glasses cracked.

Then their next donor was out the door and running down the hallway.

Pipes and wires hung overhead in the open basement ceiling. The hallway was lit by flickering florescent tubes. He might have been running through the corridors of an old space ship. Doug felt as if he were in some nightmare aboard *Battlestar Galactica*. Where the hell was the door to get out of this place? He chanced a look over his shoulder. Nobody was following.

He was going to get away.

Just then he rounded a corner and ran headlong into Fat Boy, who was unwrapping a Snickers bar from the vending machine.

The collision knocked Keller flat. The jogger got to his feet, eyes wild and desperate. The man feinted left then ducked his head and tried to get around Fat Boy on the right. All Fat Boy had to do was grab him, then lock his arm around the man's neck in a chokehold.

"Sorry, but Doc will be wondering where you are," Fat Boy said.

The jogger kicked and tried to knee Fat Boy in the nuts, but Fat Boy just tightened his hold until the jogger began to gag. Then Fat Boy lurched down the hallway toward the operating room, dragging the patient along by his neck. He used his free hand to lift the candy bar to his fat lips and take another bite.

Grubb came running out and met them in the hallway. Fat Boy caught the crazed, dangerous look in his eye and subtly maneuvered his own body between Grubb and the patient. It didn't stop Grubb from getting in several rabbit punches with his bony fists.

"Hey, don't damage the goods," Fat Boy warned.

"I sat on a scalpel thanks to this asshole," Grubb growled. "I might need stitches in my ass."

"Let's just get him back to Doc in one piece."

They dragged the patient into the operating room. Kreeger was putting his broken glasses back together with white medical tape.

He barely looked up. "Strap him down properly this time," he said calmly.

Kreeger's surgical instruments were scattered in disarray across the tiled floor. Kreeger reached down and picked up a scalpel. It was really the only implement he needed. There was no time to put it back in the autoclave, so he merely squirted it with Betadine solution.

"Hurry up and shut the door," Kreeger said. "With all that racket we'll have half the staff down here to see what the hell's been going on."

"Where's the needle?" Fat Boy asked. The syringe with the anesthesia had gone missing in the scuffle.

"Do it without," Grubb hissed. "Do it without!"

Why not? Kreeger thought. The bastard had broken his glasses, after all. "Tape his mouth."

Fat Boy had to take his hand away from the patient's mouth long enough to put on the tape. "You sons of bitches!" he managed to scream before Fat Boy covered his lips with tape.

Someone was knocking at the door, then trying the locked doorknob. "It's security, Dr. Kreeger," came the voice through the door. "Everything okay in there?"

"Fine, fine," Kreeger shouted back. "One of the surgical trays got knocked over, that's all."

"Should I come in?" the guard asked.

"No!" Kreeger shouted, then caught himself.

He added more calmly, "I mean, no, please don't. You'll violate the sterile conditions."

"Okay, Doc. Whatever you say."

Footsteps receded down the hall.

"Showtime," Kreeger said. His repaired glasses slipped down his nose. He pushed them back up. Then he lowered the scalpel.

The patient's eyes lit up like his finger had just been stuck into a light socket. He strained against the straps on the operating table.

"I'll bet that smarts," Kreeger agreed, bending to his work. He soon stopped, however, and turned to Grubb. "You'd better anesthetize him, after all, Grubb, or we're never going to get those kidneys out in one piece."

CHAPTER 14

"The disappearance of Tara Conrad is now officially a homicide investigation," Hawley said. "Since the discovery of her bicycle in the park, we have sufficient reason to suspect that foul play was involved."

"A homicide without a body is not the easiest to solve," Nick said. "We have no witnesses, no clues other than the bikes. Nothing, nada, zilch. This is not good, people."

"Any kind of homicide at the beach is not good, particularly when the mayor takes an interest," Hawley said. "I was hoping to retire from this job someday, not be fired from it."

"Don't worry, Chief," Grabowski said. He clapped Hawley on the back. "We'll figure it out."

Chief Hawley's office fell silent and all five of them — Hawley, Jenkins, Grabowski, Logan and Monahan — stared at the carpet. All of them knew that some cases didn't get solved, never mind what Grabowski said. The more time that passed, the colder the trail became.

And yet, Nick felt far from subdued. He was strangely elated. While it seemed wrong to feel that way, considering a young woman was missing and probably dead, he was finally working a real case again, not chasing down muggers.

He was the first to break the silence. "So far, the scenario we have is that she was fooled into stopping to help a bicyclist," he said, going over what they already knew. "After the perp abducted the victim, he threw the bicycles into the woods. We know one bike was the woman's. The other was taken from campers at the state park."

"Was there any kind of struggle?" Hawley asked.

"We don't know for sure," Nick said. "But the evidence doesn't point to it. What I think happened is that this guy — I think we're talking about a man here, even though no one saw him — popped the chain off his bike and waited for someone to stop and help him. And someone would—this is the beach, not the big city."

"But how did he subdue the victim?" Grabowski asked. "And what was his motive?"

"I'm sure he simply surprised her and then

overpowered her," Sarah said. "It happens all the time. As for a motive, who knows? Just another sick son-of-a-bitch."

Hawley raised an eyebrow at her language. She had never talked that way before. *Nick Logan must be rubbing off on her,* he thought. "Okay," he said. "There's still a lot of work to be done on this case to try and nail something down. Meanwhile, how the hell do we keep it from happening again?"

"We don't," Grabowski said.

"That's not what the mayor wants to hear," Councilman Jenkins said. "The body found in the bay is already attracting a lot of attention. We don't need any more bad publicity. Not unless we want an off beach season."

Grabowski grunted. "Is that what you call it, bad publicity? We got people on vacation disappearing and it's bad publicity."

"We don't know what the hell to call it," Hawley said. "This is uncharted territory in this part of the world. People are here to get a tan, not get murdered. All I know is that we have to take some action."

"We'll step up patrols in the state park and on the trail," Nick said. "Saturate the place. If someone makes a move, we'll see them."

"If this guy tries it again, we'll only be forcing him to operate somewhere else," Sarah warned.

"Unless we catch him," Nick said.

"What about the media?" Sarah asked.

"Screw the media," Grabowski said.

"No, Sarah is right. We should get on top of this. I'll hold a press conference," Hawley said. "The mayor may want to say a few words. Detective Monahan, I'd like you to make a brief statement to the press concerning the progress of the investigation."

"We haven't got anything!" she blurted out.

"Never mind that," the chief said. "I know you'll make it sound good."

• • •

Even in the era of indie bands it didn't hurt to have a record label behind you. There might be some bands that could leverage social media, a grueling live show schedule and digital downloads to something like success, but Dog Smell wasn't one of them. Grubb knew that a recording contract was his band's best shot at fame, and he had taken the train into New York to meet with a record producer. He'd heard somewhere that Ron Rodale had a summer place at Rehoboth Beach and so he had played up that angle in contacting him.

For his own part, Rodale had agreed to meet with Grubb mainly on the basis of Grubb being from Rehoboth Beach. The truth was that Rodale had no real intention of signing Dog Smell to his label, but he figured there was no harm in giving a little encouragement to a beach band. He certainly hadn't made any promises to Grubb.

Rodale kept Grubb waiting in his office for over an hour. The receptionist, who had seen more than her share of strange-looking musicians, kept glancing anxiously his way. All Grubb did was stare back at her.

Rodale Records was a mid-size label that had managed to thrive even in the rapidly changing music scene, mainly by focusing on regional acts. Ron Rodale's talent was recognizing bands that filled a niche — for instance, if a band was playing a lot of bars in a university town, Rodale would release a CD that sold well in music stores and coffee shops frequented by the university students. When a retro heavy metal band had exploded on a local scene, Rodale had signed them to a recording deal and thousands of high school headbangers bought the resulting CD. Even in the digital age, there were still enough CD sales for Rodale to have some skin in the game and make some money.

Hardly any of the bands ever made it big. Every four years the population of any university town underwent a complete overhaul, filling with kids who had different tastes in music from the students of four years ago. Rodale simply picked up the latest popular band. One of Rodale's success stories was a heavy metal group that had gone on to produce videos that aired on MTV, although with their soaring sales they had been snapped up by a major label.

You didn't have to be big, but you had to be big enough. And you also couldn't suck. Rodale was thinking Dog Smell had already struck out on both counts.

Grubb hoped Rodale Records would be interested in Dog Smell. The band sounded better than ever, partly because with the money Grubb made working with Doc Kreeger he had been able to ditch their second-hand equipment for state-of-the-art electronics that made them sound louder than before.

"Are you sure you wouldn't like to come back some other time, Mr. Grubb?" the receptionist finally asked. "I'm sure Mr. Rodale must be very busy if he hasn't seen you yet."

"I can wait," Grubb growled. "I got nothin' better to do."

"I could schedule another appointment for you."

"I said I'll wait," Grubb snapped. "It's very important."

"It always is. You know how many bands have been in here to see Mr. Rodale this week?"

"I dunno."

"Guess, Mr. Grubb. Just take a wild, crazy guess." The receptionist was losing patience. Musicians all thought they were great artists.

They thought they didn't have to be polite. She thought they were a pain in the ass. At home she made a point of listening to bluegrass music, which was about as different from the bands they represented as she could get.

"Ten thousand," Grubb said, staring at the floor like a sulky teenager. She thought he was a little old to act that way. So many of the musicians she met seemed to be locked in a state of permanent adolescence.

"Thirty bands. Thirty, Mr. Grubb. In fact, you're number thirty-one. And the week isn't over yet."

"Hey, lady, are your kidneys in good shape?"

She stared. "I beg your pardon?"

"If you want to keep them, then shut the hell up."

She was just thinking about calling security to remove Grubb when Ron Rodale walked in.

"Dog Smell?" he asked.

"That's me," Grubb said. "I mean, I'm one of them."

"Sorry to keep you waiting." He grinned at his receptionist. "Just imagine, I've kept the lead singer of Dog Smell waiting! What was I thinking! Come in, uh, what was your name again?"

"Grubb."

Ron Rodale may have been a music producer, but he looked nothing like a musician. He wore dark blue dress pants, a white shirt and a red tie covered with tiny white treble clefs. His suit jacket was hung on the back of his chair. The only thing that distinguished him from a lawyer or an accountant was his long ponytail of graying hair, which made him look kind of like a tall Willie Nelson. Every inch of wall space in his office was covered with photographs and posters of bands. The wall behind his desk was taken up with shelves full of CDs and vintage albums, even a few cassettes.

He sank into a leather-upholstered chair. "Mr. Grubb." He smiled. "I listened to the demo songs you sent me. Dog Smell. Very angry music. Very outraged."

"Yeah," Grubb said. "That's us. I mean, that's me. I'm the one who writes all the lyrics and I'm also the lead singer."

"Uh huh. I couldn't help noticing you seem to have an obsession with fire. The words 'burn, scorch, flames, char and blacken' kept popping up, to name a few. Maybe you should change the name of the band to Burned Dog. Or Hot Dog!"

Rodale laughed. Grubb didn't. He was too busy staring at a point on Ron Rodale's forehead, thinking how much he'd like to place a nail there and drive it in with a hammer. This asshole was making fun of the band, which was a cardinal sin in Grubb's book. The band and everything it stood for was *holy*.

"Listen, Mr. Grubb, I'll be frank with you. Punk is out. I can't sell it —"

"The Cracked Saloon is always jammed —"

"Yes, but the Cracked Saloon is one club out of many. One little club at the beach, as a matter of fact. It's the only place in the area that offers raw bands like Dog Smell. How many people are in there on a Friday night? A couple hundred? It's the same people every week. And there you have it. I can't put out an album that's going to sell two hundred copies. It won't even pay for itself."

"But if we had a CD —"

"Nobody ever heard of Dog Smell outside of the Cracked Saloon, Mr. Grubb. You're playing music which simply doesn't have a wide appeal. Here's my advice. Update your sound. Get current. Maybe package yourself as an emo band. You're the new Billy Joe Armstrong! Get it! Then send your demo CD around and get some air play on the college radio stations. Try to book some new clubs. Philadelphia and Baltimore have several worth trying. Put some videos on YouTube. Get around, get heard, and then come back."

"But —"

"You can also produce your own album, Mr. Grubb. That works well for a band like Dog Smut —"

"Dog Smell —"

"— with a small following. Rent some studio

time. Philly has a couple of good places. Mrs. Loudon out front can give you the information. Make a good quality CD, get it professionally mastered, and sell it at the Cracked Saloon between sets. You can even turn a nice little profit on it if you keep the costs down. It's a way to give yourselves a raise."

"Hey —"

Ron Rodale stood and offered his hand, indicating that the meeting on which Grubb had pinned so many of his hopes was over. "Do that and come back, Mr. Grubb. Don't think of this as a door being slammed. I prefer to keep the door open to talents like yours."

Grubb ignored the extended hand. He was staring again at the point on Ron Rodale's forehead, imagining how if a fire started there it would burn outward toward the edges. As Grubb watched, he pictured the eyes melting, the long white hair curling up and turning into black ash. Grubb's nostrils flared as he thought he smelled the singed flesh.

"Mr. Grubb, Mr. Grubb, are you okay?" Rodale came around from behind the desk, looking concerned. "I certainly didn't mean to upset you. I'm just offering a reality check. Can I get you a glass of water or something?"

Grubb backed out of the office, still staring. He imagined the man in front of him as nothing more than a puddle of bubbling skin and bones.

Then Grubb turned and rushed out.

Rodale stood for a moment in his office and loosened his tie. His forehead was sweating and for some reason he suddenly felt very warm.

CHAPTER 15

Nick locked his truck and started down the boardwalk. He had splashed on a bit of cologne and he caught a whiff of it now. He had paid a second visit to the Outlet shops and was wearing a new polo shirt and khakis, along with new Sperry Top-Siders without socks. Everything about him screamed *hot date*. In reality, he and Sarah were meeting for dinner to talk about the case. Strictly business. Or so he told himself.

A woman he passed on the boardwalk caught his eye and smiled at him. *Hmm. Must be the cologne.*

Something about the soft light of an evening at the beach took the hard edges off the world. Even after the sun set, twilight seemed to stretch on and on. The breeze fell away and the miles of sand, streets and sidewalk warmed the dusky air by radiating the sunshine absorbed all day long. On a summer evening like this, he could almost forget that there was a murderer on the loose at the beach.

He saw her on the sidewalk in front of the restaurant, wearing a pale blue sundress patterned with a white floral design. Apparently, he wasn't the only one who had gone to the trouble of dressing up. Sarah's bare arms stood out in contrast to the fabric because the long days patrolling the trail were turning her skin bronze. The last of the day's sunlight seemed caught in her hair. A middle-aged couple passed her on their way into the restaurant, the man's eyes lingering on the younger woman as he held the door for his wife. *You old dog*, Nick thought. Then again, who could blame him?

Nick realized he was admiring Sarah without thinking about Karen at all. Sometimes whole days went by now when he didn't even think of her, and then the memories would come out of nowhere and nearly overwhelm him. *Karen*. Guilt hit him like a fist in the gut. He was forgetting Karen. Damn Sarah Monahan in that dress! With a pang, he realized that he and Karen had never visited the beach together. She would have loved it here, tonight, in this soft summer twilight. Until his sister's phone call had summoned him, he hadn't been to the beach since he was a kid. Maybe that was why he associated all things beach-related with children; it was hard for him to get used to the idea that grownups went there all on their own.

"There you are," Sarah said, breaking into a smile when she spotted Nick walking up from the corner. No matter how old a guy was, there was no better feeling than a woman smiling at you, happy to see you. "I thought I might have to eat alone."

"You wouldn't be alone for long, looking like that."

"Like what?

"Like dessert."

His partner gave him her offended-feminist look and Nick groaned. Here comes the lecture. "You just can't get around thinking of me as a sex object, can you?"

"Save the speech for later, Monahan," he said. "Then we can have a little *whine* with dinner."

"Ha, ha," Sarah said. "Very funny. I guess you're just working as a cop until you get your big break on the stand-up circuit."

"Look, Monahan, before you get your panties — " Nick stumbled as he saw her eyebrows arch dangerously "— I mean, before you get your *undergarments* in an uproar, the answer is *no*, I don't always think of you, in all your female-hood, as a sex object. The truth is, when I saw you standing out here by yourself a minute ago, I just thought you looked very nice."

"Oh, shove it, Logan —"

"No, I mean it, Sarah. You . . . look . . . uh, very attractive."

She blinked, somewhat stunned. "Thank you — I think."

They stood awkwardly a moment, both of them wondering what to say next. Nick felt like an idiot. He had said more than he should have, opened a door that should have remained closed. This woman was his partner, goddamnit. He had to work with her. He couldn't be telling her she was — *attractive*. Sweet Jesus, had he really said that?

"Did you get us a table?" he asked, hurrying to change the subject.

"Oh? Um, yes. We're on the waiting list."

"There's a wait to get a table on a weeknight?"

"This is the beach, Nick. It's summertime. Of course we have to wait."

"How long? I'm kind of hungry."

"Walk in and the smell the gnocchi, Nick. One whiff of the great smells coming out of that kitchen and you'll wait forever. Besides, I'll buy you a drink."

The hostess took Nick's name, but then the owner, a real Italian grandma, came over. "I've seen you on TV, trying to catch that killer," she said to Sarah. "For you, we make room." She led them to the only vacant table in the cramped restaurant.

They ordered a carafe of the house chianti when the waitress came with the menus. Nick decided to try the special, stuffed peppers. Sarah ordered mussels marinara.

"I know we're not here to talk shop, but I was listening to the radio on the drive into town and they mentioned the body found in the Delaware Bay," Nick said. "The DJ made a couple cracks about how the sharks and jellyfish weren't bad at the beach this year, but the murderers and muggers were getting kind of thick."

"Oh boy," Sarah said as they sipped wine and nibbled the bread. "The TV stations are having a field day with this. Both the Philadelphia news shows also had segments on the murders. News Eight is claiming a link with satanic rituals because some of the organs were cut out."

"Where the hell do they come up with this stuff?"

"I'll bet Grabowski leaked it to them, just to yank their chain," Sarah said.

"Sounds like him," Nick agreed.

"It would even be kind of funny, if it weren't our investigation," she said.

"One thing I'm learning is that News Eight never worries much about being right as long as it sounds good. They come down here from Philly whenever some kids die of alcohol poisoning or there's an unusual killing. Sources? Hell, some uniformed cop in a doughnut shop says, 'I'll bet it's devil worshippers' and that's good enough for them. I can just hear that blond bimbo reporter now: 'Sources close to the investigation say devil worshippers may be carving people apart for their vital organs.' "

" 'Blond Bimbo?' " Sarah said. "Sounds to me like you have it in for her, and for everybody else in the media. What's that all about?"

Nick shrugged. Took a long sip of the red wine.

"You're not going to tell me, huh?" Sarah smiled. "Some deep, dark secret from your past?"

The look that crossed Nick's face made her wish she hadn't said it. "It's been my experience that TV reporters are only interested is what sounds good," he growled.

She nodded, deciding to back off. She had really touched a nerve in Nick. He looked like he was about to punch somebody. She would have to ask around and find out what past case had gotten under Nick Logan's tough hide. "The people who see it on TV don't know what is and what isn't true. The whole town will be freaking out," she said.

"It's going to get hot for us in the department," Nick said. "If there's one thing Mayor Gates can't stand, it's bad publicity. Hawley could be in trouble."

"Would Gates go that far?"

"You never know."

The waitress came with the antipasto Nick had ordered as an appetizer. He started heaping some on Sarah's salad plate.

"Just a little for me, thanks," she said.

"What do you mean? It's salad. It's healthy."

"Are you kidding?" Sarah said, picking daintily with her fork. Nick noticed she avoided the prosciutto and the olives. "This stuff is loaded with oil. It's very fattening. So are all these olives."

"I love olives," he said. "Stick those over here on my plate."

Sarah continued picking at her antipasto. Nick finished what was left on the platter and ate Sarah's olives as well.

He was just setting his fork down when the waitress came with the food. The stuffed peppers were swimming in a sea of thick, meaty sauce with a serving of linguini on the side. Nick's mouth was watering as he dug in.

He noticed his partner was only picking at her plate of ravioli.

"Not hungry?" he asked.

"It's not that," she said. She sighed. "What are we going to do, Nick?"

"I don't know," he said. "We'll finish this, Maybe get some coffee and tortoni for dessert—"

"The case, Nick. I'm talking about the abduction from the park. Once the media gets wind of that, they're going go be all over us." She rolled her eyes in exasperation. "Can't you ever be serious?"

"What are we supposed to do, huh?" he snapped. He couldn't believe she didn't think he was taking the case seriously. "The plan was to make a few arrests of muggers and it would make the TV news and the newspapers and both the police department and the mayor get some good press. That was the plan, Detective. But then the woman disappeared. There is no longer a plan. This was not supposed to happen."

"But it did," she said. "So what do we do?"

"Catch the bastard who grabbed her."

"Okay. But how?"

"We start by asking *why*, then *who*. A girl is down here on vacation and she disappears from the park. No clues." Nick sliced open his second stuffed pepper. Steaming, delicious smells rolled out. "Now, why?"

"To rape her," Sarah said stonily. "I don't know what else. Torture her. Kill her."

Suddenly the smell of the thick, red meat sauce and ground beef in the stuffed peppers sickened Nick.

"You okay?" she asked, watching him push his plate away.

"We have to catch whoever is doing this."

Sarah nodded. Her eyes were studying his face. Nick let her gaze slide over him, taking the opportunity to study her in return. The long blond hair framed her features, made even more lovely by the restaurant's candlelight. His stare dropped lower, following the neckline to the collarbone and stopping just at the border of her sundress. He had a sudden, dizzying desire to see her naked.

He broke off his stare and took a sip of chianti. *Focus on business, Nick,* he told himself. When he looked back at her she was blushing. Had she guessed his thoughts?

Nick had to wonder if she left the York police department simply to advance her career. Had there been someone else in her life, a broken relationship that demanded distance to heal?

"What would you do if you weren't helping me catch bad guys, Nick?" she asked.

He looked up, locking onto her hazel eyes. "Splitting firewood."

"I can tell you really love being a cop," she said. "You could always stay on after the summer and make this a second career."

"Being a cop has its moments," he said. Nick shrugged. "We'll see. It's going to be a short second career if we don't put an end to these disappearances. Listen, what do you want to do after dinner? We could have a drink somewhere."

Sarah looked sideways at him. "And after the

drink? What's your motive here, Detective Logan?"

"Nothing, I mean, it's just a drink, right?" He had a sudden, nightmarish image of himself up before some committee on sexual harassment charges.

"Right," she said. "But I think I'll take a raincheck, Nick. I'm kind of tired. Besides, I want to get an early start again tomorrow." She shrugged it off, not making a big deal out of his suggestion.

Sarah insisted on splitting the check with him.

"I'll walk you to your car," he said once they were outside.

The evening air had the tang of salt and waves murmured on the beach.

"Thanks for the nice dinner, Nick," Sarah said. She drove a new Honda Accord in a metallic green color. Nick was glad he had parked his old pickup truck a few blocks away.

"Rest up," he said. "Tomorrow we've got some serious work to do."

He watched until she had pulled away from the curb and was driving down the street.

On the walk back to his truck, he could have kicked himself for asking if she wanted to get a drink. It was a rather transparent way of saying he wanted the evening to last a little longer. Sarah had let it slide, thank God. He didn't want that kind of awkwardness being like a barbed wire fence between them for the rest of the time they spent working this case.

That was the last thing they needed, if they were going to catch a killer.

CHAPTER 16

"Gimme one of them chocolate-iced doughnuts," Patrolman Dunleavy said.

"Better get two," said the waitress behind the counter. Her chewing gum snapped and popped in her mouth as she spoke. "This has got to last you until morning. We close at two."

"Since when?" Dunleavy asked. He was so fat his belly flopped over his utility belt. Riding in a radio car all night eating chocolate-iced doughnuts could do that to a man.

"Since last week. Mr. Stepowicz — you know him, he owns this place and that new gourmet cupcake shop in the Mermaid Zone on the boardwalk — he says we don't take in enough money between two and six."

"Businessmen," sniffed Dunleavy. "They're all a bunch of cheapskates." This was one of the few doughnut shops open all night in the area. The next closest one he could think of was way the hell up in Dover near the Air Force base.

"Whaddya mean cheap, honey?" said the waitress. She snapped her gum at him. "With all the free coffee you guzzle, I'm surprised Mr. Stepowicz ain't bankrupt."

The cop sighed and plucked a couple of napkins from the steel dispenser on the counter. It was true that the doughnut shop was on the list of late-night places that encouraged cops to stop by with the lure of free coffee. They had to pay for the doughnuts, but an eye-opening dose of caffeine at three in the morning was free. It was cheap insurance against robberies and drunken teen-agers to have police officers popping in from time to time.

The cop noticed the waitress looking past him out the plate glass window, staring at something in the parking lot.

"What is that kid doin' to your car?" she asked, squinting and leaning forward to get a better look.

Dunleavy turned, and so did the assortment of night owls sitting at the counter, mostly old men and insomniacs.

"What the hell?" Dunleavy said.

"Who's he?" asked the waitress.

"Damn freak is what he is," commented one shrunken old man. "They ought to bring back the draft in this country. The Marine Corps would straighten his ass right out, yessirree."

Freak was a good word for the young man in the doughnut shop parking lot. He had hair so dark it was like a black hole in the summer night, earrings and tattoos, and a skeletal build. He was holding something in his bony hands and Patrolman Dunleavy strained to make out what it was.

"It's a bottle of booze," Dunleavy announced incredulously, getting ready to bite into his doughnut. "Damn drunk kid. I'll go out in a minute and shoo him away."

It was a warm night and Dunleavy had left the windows of the radio car down. Rehoboth had its share of crime, but it wasn't like L.A. or Detroit, where the bad guys sometimes stole police cars. In the entire history of the state of Delaware, nobody had ever stolen a police car.

"What's he doing now?" the old man asked.

Out in the parking lot, the goth kid was staring into the open window of the police car.

Patrolman Dunleavy sighed. "Honey, better get me a cup of coffee to go. I might have to run him down to the station. Teach him a lesson."

As they watched, the kid calmly took out a lighter and flicked it. He held the flame to the end of the bottle, which everyone now realized was stoppered with a rag.

"I seen them do that in Vietnam," the old man said. "He's going to blow up your car, son."

Dunleavy butted his way through the heavy glass doors of the doughnut shop, unsnapping the holster of his service weapon as he went. His hand was shaking, and not just because he was mad. In his entire history as a police officer, Dunleavy had never drawn a weapon on anybody. The local police did an excellent job without the need for weapons.

The goth spotted him and tossed the bottle through the open window of the patrol car. Then he took off like an Olympic springer. Dunleavy could hear him laughing as he ran. It was a weird, high-pitched laugh.

Patrolman Dunleavy trotted toward the car. He noticed the dim, guttering light of the burning rag-fuse on the driver's seat and reconsidered the wisdom of approaching the car. He ran like hell back toward the doughnut shop. He just had time to duck inside the foyer of the doughnut shop before the Molotov cocktail went off.

Whoomp.

It was less like a bomb exploding and more like what happened when you threw too much lighter fluid on a stubborn charcoal grill. But fire was fire, and Dunleavy's radio car was a bright orange fireball.

"Woo-wee," said the old man at the counter. "Just like Napalm."

Dunleavy was back outside as fast as his overweight body could move. He was already thinking about how much trouble this was going to get him in. He had to catch that kid.

He heard the high whine of a motorcycle.

Dunleavy yanked his weapon free of the holster again. If he was going to be suspended, he thought he might as well make it worthwhile by shooting somebody.

The black-haired goth roared out of the darkness on a motorcycle. He was screaming something, and as he entered the light cast by the burning car Dunleavy saw that kid's face going past, twisted with crazy.

At that instant Dunleavy fired four rounds at the rider, jerking the trigger of the semi-automatic with each shot. The goth wobbled, ducked his head, and kept going until the machine was only an echo in the night.

"I don't think you got him," said the old man, who had come out of the doughnut shop just in time to see Dunleavy blast away at the goth.

"Winged him, maybe," Dunleavy said.

"Nah. You can't shoot worth a damn. I'll bet you weren't even in the Army. The Coast Guard, maybe."

"Somebody call the fire department," Dunleavy shouted.

"Ha!" the old man snorted. "I'd say it's a little too late for them to save your car."

"Will you go stand over there, please," Dunleavy said, as patiently as he could, pointing to the sidewalk under the eaves of the doughnut shop. If the old guy made one more wisecrack, Dunleavy was afraid he might lose his temper and bust the old man's head for him. "This is a crime scene."

The waitress came out and joined Dunleavy in watching what was left of his patrol car burn. It looked like the flaming, blackened skeleton of some giant insect. "Not a good situation, is it?" she asked.

"No, it's not," Dunleavy said. "The word 'suspended' comes to mind."

"In that case, I think you might be needing this," she said, handing him a takeout box. Inside were a dozen chocolate-iced doughnuts.

● ● ●

Nick fumbled the phone as he reached for it in the dark. He glanced at the number, saw it was headquarters.

"Sorry to wake you, detective," said the dispatcher. "I know it's early —"

"What's up?" He was completely awake now, sitting up in bed. He had shoved the alarm clock aside in grabbing for the telephone and he reached to turn the digital face toward him. Three a.m.

"Chief Hawley wanted me to call you," she said. "He said you should get in here as soon as possible."

"Jesus Christ," he growled into the phone. "What is it?"

"Something about another vacationer being abducted. Or maybe the fire bombing tonight. Who knows?"

"Okay." Nick jabbed at the phone. Thought a minute. Picked it back up and called Sarah.

"This is Nick. Do you know what's going on? Hawley wants to see us." He hung up.

Waking up in the middle of the night was something Nick never quite got used to, even as a cop. Back when he worked homicide, they used to call Nick when they had a body late at night because there wasn't a 24-hour squad. In those days he had told the dispatchers to call him first, and became a hero to the other detectives. They had families. Nick just had the job. Although later, he had Karen. He took the phone off the hook a lot of nights then.

The beach house was dark and empty. He looked out at the dark expanse of Delaware Bay. Waves tumbled on the beach. He grabbed his jeans off a chair where he had thrown them. He was sure someone had either found the abducted woman's body or made an arrest. He tugged on a

T-shirt and thrust his feet into scuffed Nikes. The night was cool, so he snagged a sweatshirt off the hook by the door.

He hoped it wasn't a body. There had been enough of those lately. Please let it be an arrest, he prayed silently, combing his hair back with his fingers as he went down the steps.

Nick gunned his truck down the empty streets, slowing at the red lights but not stopping. Beach towns never really slept—even in the middle of the night the streets were lit up, although there were only a few stragglers and insomniacs out. He dumped the truck in the "police vehicles only" area in front of the headquarters building on Rehoboth Avenue. Headlights pulled in behind him. He recognized Sarah's sporty new Mazda.

"What's going on?" she asked, meeting him on the sidewalk.

"I dunno, they got something for us," he said, adding, "I'm impressed. You almost beat me here."

"Nick, don't jerk me around. It's the middle of the night. What the hell are we doing here?"

He shrugged. "Beats me. Hawley called us in."

She hadn't asked yet why the dispatcher had called him at home, not her. Nick didn't know why himself; he just figured Hawley hadn't even thought of it. A mental block because she was a woman. Hawley's old-school mind had passed right over her. Chauvinism died hard in the police department.

They punched a code to unlock the door.

"I just want to duck in here a minute," Nick said, slipping away to see if anything was up in the squad room. The duty sergeant was drowsing over a cup of coffee and a young, disheveled woman sat in a chair nearby. Their eyes met briefly and Nick nodded to her.

He knew then Hawley hadn't called them in because of a body or an arrest.

He hustled out again and walked down to Hawley's office, passing dark offices as they went. Somewhere, someone was running a copy machine. Like the town, the police station never really slept, either. It just waited in suspense for morning.

"Who was she?" Sarah asked, meaning the woman who'd been waiting in the squad room.

"She's the reason we're here."

It was the middle of the night, so when they walked into the chief's office only Hawley and Bob Grabowski were there. Nick caught Chief Hawley's sheepish expression as Sarah entered and smiled to himself. Just as he'd suspected, Hawley had forgotten to have the dispatcher call her. Nick had saved his butt on this one.

Hawley and Grabowski nodded hello. It was too early in the morning for casual greetings.

"Sit down," Hawley said. Bags of dark, loose

flesh hung under his eyes and gray stubble covered his face. Nick had never seen his old friend looking so rough. He was wearing the same clothes he'd had on earlier in the day.

"Have you been home tonight, Chief?" Nick asked.

Hawley shrugged. "What do you think? The mayor is giving me a shit storm. All hell is breaking loose this week. Not only do we have an abduction, but we found a body with the organs carved out. It doesn't help that there's some jerk running around firebombing the city. The same asshole torched a radio car tonight, by the way, while the patrolman was inside eating doughnuts. Doesn't get any better, does it?"

"That's going to do wonders for our public image," Detective Monahan agreed.

"Mayor Gates said the same thing. He thinks we need to get our asses in gear. He wants whoever was driving that phony ambulance around caught yesterday. He wants whoever took the girl from the park behind bars. He wants this nutty arsonist locked up, too. What does he know about police work, right? He has unreasonable expectations, but believe me, heads are gonna roll if something doesn't break soon."

Nobody spoke. Nick realized they were seeing the Hawley who had scratched his way up from Baltimore beat cop to Rehoboth chief. He could be a son-of-a-bitch when the need arose.

"Now there's a new wrinkle," Hawley continued. "Which is why we're all here in the middle of the goddamn night. We have another missing person. Bob?"

Grabowski jumped in. "A man named Doug Keller went out for a run yesterday morning on the Junction and Breakwater Trail and never came back. His wife is downstairs."

"We saw her," Nick said.

"Why a man?" Sarah wondered out loud. "This must not have anything to do with Tara Conrad."

Nobody answered. Nobody knew.

"Grabowski, you're in charge of finding the bodies. Because by now I'd say there are most certainly bodies. It's your investigation. Do whatever it takes. Also, I'm putting Logan on your team.

"Monahan, you're still new here, but you're smart," Hawley continued. "If you stick around, you'll probably be the police chief one day. We need someone to work the press on this, someone they can focus on. As of tomorrow morning, we are going to get a shit storm of press attention, thanks to the latest development. That's what you did in Pennsylvania, right? You handled the two dailies, a couple of radio stations, a TV station. You know how to play the game. You're going to be our cop in the field and our public image person. But watch yourself, because we'll be sure to get some attention from the Washington Post and maybe even the New York Times, both of which are the man-eating jaws of journalism compared to our local paper. This is the big time."

"Yes, sir," she said.

"Finding some bodies would help," the chief said. "At this point we've got two missing people."

"Give it time," Grabowski said. "We'll find them."

CHAPTER 17

"Downshift, you idiot, downshift!" Kreeger yelled at the TV.

Kreeger watched the driver in the video finally do the only thing possible to keep his car from spinning off the track.

The driver downshifted as the instructor's voice emerged on the soundtrack over the scream of a revving engine: "The driver has just made an error. Always avoid downshifting in a curve, which can cause you to lose traction, and, in turn, your ability to stay on the road. Instead, try to anticipate the curves so you can shift to a lower gear just before entering —"

Kreeger snapped off the remote. The video on high-speed driving techniques would have to wait now that Grubb and Fat Boy had secured another set of kidneys that needed tissue typing.

The jogger that Grubb and Fat Boy brought in had a rather unusual set of antigens that made him hard to match with potential organ recipients. It was a difficulty Kreeger could have done without, but with Fat Boy and Grubb picking the donors at random, an occasional rare blood type had to be expected.

Kreeger finally found matches in Minneapolis and Boston. He had sent Grubb on his way to the airport early this morning. Because of the distance and the fact that a regularly scheduled flight was not leaving the Philadelphia airport for several hours, the Minneapolis hospital had opted to charter a plane to deliver the organ. Kreeger knew time was all important once the organ was out of the body, but he still marveled at the expense and effort that went into securing organs for transplant patients.

With what he was going to make off the man's organs once the insurance money came in, Kreeger could buy another Aston Martin if he wrecked his because he hadn't gotten around to watching the driving techniques video. Besides, he had a busy day ahead of him at the hospital. A mountain of paperwork was waiting, thanks to the organs they had been sending out. All those kidneys were bringing in reimbursements from insurance companies to cover the cost of the harvest operation and other expenses.

Insurance companies didn't simply hand over the money. Forms had to be filled out. Stacks upon stacks of forms. And to keep any insurers from becoming suspicious about the number of donors originating from one particular hospital, it was up to Kreeger to be creative in coming up with causes of death and phony names and addresses for the donors.

Definitely no time for watching high performance driving videos this morning, Kreeger told himself. There was work to be done and money to be made. And if he didn't hurry, he was going to be late.

While his coffee brewed, Kreeger left his condo and went down to get that morning's News Journal. He stepped off the front porch of the condo complex and took a quick walk to check on his Aston Martin. The car was just as he had left it, gleaming red and frosted with dew in the early morning sun, waiting for him. Kreeger smiled and blew it a kiss, then retraced his steps.

Back in his kitchen, he popped a whole wheat bagel into the toaster to go with his low-fat yogurt. Kreeger would have preferred bacon and eggs for breakfast, but he had seen enough of what cholesterol could do to a man's arteries and heart. If he was going to live dangerously, he'd do it in his sports car, not at the breakfast table.

The bagel popped out. Kreeger spread the

orange marmalade and settled at the dining room table with a cup of coffee and unfolded that morning's paper.

The headline wasn't the top story, but it was on the front page: "Woman abducted from park."

That was the trouble with newspapers, he thought. They became outdated so quickly. The headline should have read: "Two abducted from park. More missing joggers likely."

Kreeger took a sip of coffee and began to read.

By Jorge Alvarez
Staff Writer

REHOBOTH BEACH — Foul play is suspected in the disappearance of a woman who went for a bicycle ride on the popular Junction and Breakwater Trail and never came home, Rehoboth Beach police officials said Thursday.

Tara Conrad, 25, was last seen by her roommates at a beach house in Lewes last Friday as she headed for the trail and Cape Henlopen State Park. Her roommates said the Trolley Square woman had been taking daily afternoon rides while on vacation. Her route included the trail, recently dubbed one of the jewels in the beach resort's "Triple Crown" of attractions.

When Conrad did not return home by nightfall, friends drove the short distance to the park to look for her. After finding no trace of Conrad, her friends called police.

"We're looking into several leads right now," said Detective Sarah Monahan, police spokesperson and a member of the investigative team delving into Conrad's disappearance. "At this point we don't know what happened. Unfortunately, foul play has not been ruled out."

Sources close to the investigation say the police department is baffled by the vacationing woman's disappearance. Until now, they have been reluctant to release any information about the case, which was classified as a homicide only Thursday.

Police patrols at the trail and state park have been stepped up considerably recently in the wake of several muggings. Officers have been posing as runners and bicyclists. Just last week, Monahan and Detective Nick Logan arrested three north Rehoboth youths who allegedly attempted to mug a jogger.

Conrad, a University of Delaware graduate, worked at Chase Bank as a junior loan officer . . ."

Kreeger put down the paper and chomped his bagel. He didn't want to read on and learn anything personal about Tara Conrad. Her name was more than enough. In his mind, Kreeger simply wanted her to remain Victim X, a young white female with a certain set of antigens, whose particularly fine kidneys had been sent to transplant centers in Atlanta and Chicago. He wanted her to remain as anonymous as the cadavers he had worked on in medical school. He preferred his victims to be as anonymous as the steak on his plate. He knew thinking of them as people would only get in the way of his work.

The newspaper story was to be expected, he thought. He'd been checking the paper every day and was surprised the story had taken so long to come out. It had only been a matter of time before their organ-harvesting operation attracted attention. He had hoped they would be able to harvest organs from more than one donor before they generated headline news. This was only going to make things harder.

The donors who had been picked up by Grubb and Fat Boy's pseudo ambulance hadn't gotten much attention. The discovery of the first victim's body had only been worth a brief in the News Journal. At that point, the police hadn't quite been sure what they had. Tara Conrad's disappearance had turned up the heat.

"Time, Kreeger, time!" he warned himself, glancing at his watch. He had paperwork to do if they were to be paid for the organs, and if Grubb and Fat Boy had luck today there would be more organs to harvest, more antigens to type.

He clapped his hands together, eager to get to the hospital so he could start work. Besides, the Aston Martin was waiting.

• • •

Bob Grabowski fed his change into the soda machine and punched a pad marked "Coca Cola." He waited a moment, expecting the internal rumbling and final thunk of the soda can in the bin. Nothing happened. He punched the button again. Silence.

He threw his shoulder into the machine, sending it rocking backwards. The lights blinked as it slammed upright again. Still nothing came out. "Piece of junk," he growled.

"Let me try," said a voice at his side.

Grabowski turned to find Sarah Monahan standing next to him. She smiled.

"It's all yours," he grumbled, stepping aside. "Damn thing doesn't work right."

Sarah pulled down the coin return switch. Change tumbled out. "You're short a quarter," she said.

"Huh," Grabowski said.

He fed in the money. This time, his soda came out.

"Looks like I owe you one," he said. "What will you have?"

"Something that's caffeine free, sugar free."

Grabowski punched the pad for a Diet Sprite.

"You're just like Logan," she said. "You were ready to start punching that machine, weren't you."

"Depending on what mood Logan was in, I'll bet he might have tossed this thing out a window."

"I wouldn't take that bet," she said, taking the cold can from him. "Men are all alike."

"Women are so logical," Grabowski said. He lightened his voice an octave. " 'Gee, the machine doesn't work. Let me make sure I used the right amount of change.' It's far more satisfying to beat it."

"Your words, not mine," she said.

It took Grabowski a moment to catch his accidental double entendre. And then he smiled. "Logan is beginning to rub off on you."

"Oh yeah? I would have thought I was rubbing off on him."

"Maybe you are." Grabowski smiled noncommittally. "You like it here so far? I like to say the beach would be a great place to work, if it wasn't for all the damn tourists. Despite what's going on lately, there's usually not much crime."

"I suppose my next step would have been a bigger city, but I was kind of done with all that. Rehoboth seemed like it would be a good place to work. I didn't want the insanity of a D.C. or New York or Baltimore. They average more than a murder a day in Baltimore."

"It's all that heat and humidity down on the Chesapeake Bay, plus the Natty Bo beer," Grabowski said. "It's a bad combination."

"The crack and meth don't help, either."

Grabowski smirked, studying her with a sly sideways look. Sarah could understand now why this unimposing, roly poly man made such a good homicide detective. He looked like a bag of dirty laundry. People felt at ease with him. Meanwhile, mentally he was picking your bones apart.

"I've seen you around the department," he said. "We've never really had a chance to talk, except for this morning."

"Three o'clock in Chief Hawley's office hardly counts," she said.

They stood awkwardly for a moment, holding their soft drinks.

"Um," she said.

"What is it?" Grabowski asked amiably, taking a sip of his soda. Pure sugar and caffeine, Sarah noticed. It was what most cops lived off, whether they got theirs from sodas or coffee and doughnuts.

"I want to ask you something about Logan," she said.

Grabowski raised an eyebrow. "Like what? Please tell me he's our suspect. You think he's doing a little devil worship on the side? Carving people up? I mean, what the hell was he doing out there in the mountains, right?"

"With Logan, nothing would surprise me," she said. "What's his deal? It seems like something bad happened to him and he hasn't gotten over it."

"A good cop can read people, so you must be a good cop." The lines of Grabowski's furrowed brow deepened. "I don't know if I'm the one who should be telling you. It's really up to Logan."

"He hasn't brought it up," she said. "I've got the feeling he wants me to find out on my own."

"I don't know."

"Why not?"

Grabowski stood a moment, working it over in his mind.

"If you want to hear this, we better find a room where we can shut the door behind us." He hesitated, then jerked his head toward the hallway. "C'mon. Let me tell you a ghost story."

• • •

"What the hell is going on in that park?" the caller barked in Nick's ear without making any introductions. Nick smiled. It was George Alvarez, the police reporter from the News Journal.

"I don't know," Nick said, playing dumb. He had a copy of the morning paper on his desk with Alvarez's story about Tara Conrad's abduction. "Is there something going on?"

"Logan, don't give me that," Alvarez said. "A second guy disappeared from there. A jogger this time, not a bicyclist."

"Huh. Where did you hear that?"

"From a good source," the reporter said. "I'm just looking for confirmation, maybe some details. A name, for instance."

"I'll get back to you," Nick said lazily, hanging up. He glanced at the clock on the squad room wall. It was barely ten a.m. Give Alvarez an hour and Nick knew he'd be calling back, pestering him for information. Nick would let him sweat a little. Eventually he'd give the reporter a name, if he didn't already have one by then. Doug Keller. Maybe some details. Tossing him a bone like that could pay dividends later if Nick needed something.

"Hey, Logan," the duty sergeant shouted from across the room. He looked up, blinking and reaching for his coffee cup. He had already been awake for seven hours.

"Yeah?" he said, getting up and crossing the squad room. A blue-haired old lady stood in front of the sergeant's desk. She clutched a small white purse nervously in her bird-like hands.

"This lady here has something to tell you about that girl that got grabbed from the park."

Nick wondered where the hell Grabowski was. The homicide detective was now officially in charge of the investigation, and it should be his responsibility to interview any potential witnesses. Nonetheless, Nick felt his sluggish blood begin to flow a bit faster. So far, the investigation into Tara Conrad's abduction was at a dead end. A living, breathing witness might have just volunteered herself by showing up at the police station. A citizen doing her duty. It was too good to be true.

"Where's Grabowski?" he asked the duty sergeant.

"Dunno." The man shrugged.

Nick turned to the woman. "Right this way, ma'am. My name is Detective Nick Logan."

"Eloise Pritchard," she said, extending her hand. Her handshake was firm, her eyes like two clear blue marbles as they met his. No signs of senility that he could see. Nick's hopes rose yet higher.

"Please have a seat," he said upon reaching his desk. He cleared a space in the clutter of coffee cups and fast food wrappings so he could write on a notepad.

"I don't know what I saw," she said. "Or if I even saw anything out of the ordinary. But after I read the newspaper article this morning I just had to come in."

"Well, it's about the young lady abducted from Cape Henlopoen State Park, right, ma'am? Even the smallest item may be helpful in this case. What did you see?"

"Well, this happened on the day that the newspaper said the poor girl disappeared. I know the day, because our birdwatching club was meeting. We were going to check on the plovers, just to make certain the surf fishermen were avoiding the nesting areas."

Nick nodded. He was impatient to hear what she had to say, but old ladies didn't come with a fast forward button.

"The plovers were fine."

"I'm glad to hear that." Nick nodded encouragingly.

"Afterwards, Mary Kowalski, who was driving, asked if we'd mind if she drove past the big field on the main entrance road so we could see the deer. They're often grazing in the big open field there. Well, as we drove through the park, I noticed a van. It was pulled off to the side of the road. I've driven through there since then and I've realized it's an unusual place to pull off, because there is no shoulder, only grass."

"Yes," Nick said. He was leaning toward her now so that he wouldn't miss anything.

"There was a man standing beside the van. A young man." She twittered. "Of course, when you get to be my age, any man seems younger."

Nick smiled encouragement at her. "Go on."

"He was, as I said, a young man. He had black hair. Coal black, like one of those bunk rockers —"

"Punk," Nick corrected.

"— and an earring. Oh, and he was so thin he looked like a skeleton, like the skin was stretched right over the bones. He was just standing there."

Nick felt his excitement rushing in like the tide. "Is that all you saw?"

"Yes," she said. "I know it's not very much. I asked my granddaughter why someone would have hair like that and look that way, and she said maybe he was gothic. It's a word I would use to describe a cathedral, not the young man I saw, but I haven't kept up with the times."

"Let's go back through it, if you don't mind," Nick said. "I just want to get some of the times straight, maybe get the names of the women who were in the car with you."

"I don't believe any of them noticed anything. I already asked. We were chatting away about the plovers, you know."

"Well, still, this helps, Mrs. Pritchard. I mean, you've told us there was a van in the area when the girl disappeared, and that this goth character was standing next to it. That's exactly the sort of clue that may help our investigation."

"Oh, and there's one more thing," she hurried to say. "He looked so unusual that I just had to wonder what he was doing there. I mean, just standing along the road? And so when we stopped, I looked back. I watched him throw two bicycles into the woods. I thought it rather odd."

All Nick could do was stare at her.

Bicycles.

Nick had pulled two bikes from the brush just

at the spot where this woman had seen someone throw them in.

Nick grabbed for the phone and punched Grabowski's extension. Where the hell was he? It was a bad time for him to disappear, considering they now had a description of a person of interest in Tara Conrad's abduction.

CHAPTER 18

"I can't believe you never heard any of this stuff about Nick Logan," Grabowski said. He and Sarah were sitting in the lieutenant's office, which was empty and lit only by a gray light filtering between the slats of the window blinds. He took a swig of Coke. Sarah sipped her Diet Sprite.

"I've only known him a few days," Sarah said. "I didn't know he went around killing people."

"He doesn't make a habit of it." Grabowski looked hard at her. "We have to be clear on one thing, now. Whatever I say can't leave this room. You tell anybody else and I'll deny it."

Sarah slowly nodded her head. "Agreed," she said.

• • •

It was every cop's nightmare, becoming the victim. The call came in on a Friday evening. Guys in the department were thinking about the weekend, about putting up drywall in the laundry room or whether or not they should put twenty bucks on the Ravens for Sunday's game. A neighbor dialed 911 to report seeing a suspicious man leaving a townhouse. The dispatcher sent a radio car by to make sure the residence was secure.

It was on the same street where Nick lived with his girlfriend, Karen Richardson. That registered with a couple of people listening to the scanner in the squad room, but they didn't give it a second thought.

The patrolman could be heard on the scanner a few minutes later. "Requesting backup at number one-oh-two Fourteenth Street." He sounded nervous. "We have an apparent homicide."

They found out later the thief had hit several houses on the street. It was a residential neighborhood and most people were away at work. Maybe the thief got greedy, pushing his luck as the afternoon ran on and the risk increased of someone coming home while he ransacked a place. Maybe he didn't really care because he had a gun. Maybe he was too high to care.

It was easy to piece together what happened.

Karen came home from work a little early that Friday, unlocked the front door, went in. The burglar heard her and was waiting in an inside room.

"Sweet mother of Jesus," said the first cop on the scene. "This is bad."

He touched the radio on his shoulder and called it in as a homicide.

Karen worked as a loan officer at a bank downtown. She enjoyed dressing up and going to work in the stately bank offices. She liked going out to lunch with the other women who worked there. Some might consider a job like hers to be so much number crunching, but Karen didn't see it that way. People came in and she helped them get the money they needed to buy a house, start a business, pay for their children's college tuition. She believed she was a positive force in their lives.

She had dark hair and green eyes, pale skin, and a pretty, fine-boned face. Men noticed her. Some of the customers even flirted with her when they came in to discuss a loan.

She and Nick had been living together for three years. Karen wanted to get married, but Nick kept putting her off. "Soon," he promise her. "Maybe in a couple of months."

Karen didn't like Nick being a cop. She disliked seeing the gun he kept strapped in a holster under his arm. But she knew that was all Nick ever wanted to be. She saw how he turned silent and brooding whenever she tried discussing what else he might enjoy doing for a living. She might even be able to get him a job in security at the bank. She quit bringing it up, accepted his career and the oddball hours. After all, he was doing good, making a difference in people's lives. Karen thought this mattered.

The cop who had been first on the scene trudged back out to the street. The small crowd that was gathering made way for him as he went down to his radio car.

"What's going on?" a neighbor asked.

"We don't know yet," he said, ducking his head away. He was sure his face would give him away.

"You know, a cop lives here," someone else said.

"What?"

"Yeah. Do you know him? Nick Logan. I think he's a plainclothes or whatever you call them."

"Sweet mother of Jesus," the officer groaned again.

Karen never had much of a chance against an armed thief who surprised her in her own home. Out on the sidewalk, the cop saw Detective Logan coming up the steps of his townhouse and hurried to block his path.

"Detective, you shouldn't —"

The cop had been reaching for Nick's arm, but the look in Logan's eyes stopped him cold. The patrolman didn't know him that well, but Logan always had looked like a mean son of a bitch.

Logan went in.

"Did they catch the guy?" Sarah asked. She thought about Nick walking in on that, and shivered.

"The idiot left fingerprints. He'd been arrested six times previously and he left prints. It was as good as a business card. Also, there was a witness, the neighbor who had seen him leaving. She picked him out of a photo array, and we knew immediately who we were looking for."

Wallace Green was a skinny little thug who had been in and out of jail most of his life. He was like a poster child for small-time cons right down to his weasel's face and bad teeth.

Why he had turned vicious enough to murder a woman in her own home was anybody's guess. Maybe it was the drugs. Maybe he just didn't give a damn anymore.

Nobody knew why. But there was no doubt Wallace Green was the perpetrator. Law enforcement officials across the state put out an APB.

Logan found him first.

"I was the first one at the scene," Grabowski said, staring off into the shadowy corners of the shaded room. "Nick was just standing there in a daze. That guy Green lived like a pig. Jesus, I still remember how dirty the sheets were on his bed. They were actually brown. The things you remember."

"Nick killed him?"

"Officially, Wallace Green fell out a sixth-floor window. It certainly fit with the fact that just about every bone in his body was broken."

"Nick got away with it?" Sarah asked.

Grabowski shrugged. "Got away with what? The suspect jumped out a window. It was a clear case of suicide."

• • •

"So now you know the deep, dark past of Detective Nick Logan," Grabowski said. "I'm telling you all this not because I like to gossip like a schoolgirl, but because if he acts like a jerk at times, there might be a reason."

"I had no idea he went through all that," Sarah said.

"Have you changed your mind about him?" Grabowski asked. "Do you still want to get, uh, involved?"

"What do you mean by that?"

"Oh, I think it's obvious." Grabowski winked. "I'm a detective, remember?"

CHAPTER 19

"Where the hell have you been?" Nick asked, finally catching Grabowski in a hallway. "I've been looking all over for you. We've got a witness. She saw our abductor."

"You're kidding me."

"We've got a goddamn description of the guy." Nick knew he was acting like an overexcited rookie, but he couldn't help it.

Nick told Grabowski all about what Eloise Pritchard's had seen on her birdwatching expedition in the state park.

"It's a step in the right direction," Grabowski said.

"What do you mean, a step? It's a frickin' leap. We've got nothing else."

"Exactly," Grabowski said.

• • •

Nick stared into the tangled scrub pines and tried to see what their witness had: a man with black hair throwing bicycles into the brush. Had this man abducted both Brandon Keller and Tara Conrad? What about Frank Wilson?

Nothing but questions, and precious few answers. He started running, passing the spot where the elderly witness said the van had been pulled off the road. It couldn't have been there long, he thought, noting the narrow grassy shoulder. Patrols visited the park regularly and would have noticed the van or questioned the black-haired man. Just in case, he would ask the state park officials for all the tickets written since last week to determine if any had been issued to vans. It was a long shot, but you never knew.

It would have helped if he and Sarah had seen something on the day Tara Conrad had gone missing. But neither of them had been in the park. The abductor had been lucky enough to catch them at a time when they were out doing something else.

They were looking for a young man with black hair. Was he the killer? To Nick, it seemed unlikely. If you were out to abduct people, you'd want to appear as inconspicuous and harmless as possible. The goth look would scare off most people, not put them at ease. But that was expecting the killer to think rationally, and Nick knew from experience that was expecting a lot.

Woods closed in around him and the dappled shadows created a twilight effect. The thick pines overhead muffled the rumble of the surf. Nick began to hear birds, the sound of his running shoes on the wood chips, some small animal rustling in the underbrush. His breathing was deep and easy.

Nick kept running. With each stride some worry fell away, leaving him feeling lighter. Soon he was alone with his pumping heart, his lungs filling and emptying of air, his legs eating up the distance. He burst into a clearing and felt the warmth of the sun on his bare arms and legs. Then he was back in the shadows, running, forgetting.

He ran for nearly an hour. Still panting, he got down and did 100 pushups, then rolled over and did 100 sit ups. He'd been doing that every day now since coming to the beach, and with that and the running he hadn't lost any of his wood-splitting muscle.

Winded, his arms and legs quivering, Nick walked it off, coming back to the spot where the bicycles had been found. It all came back to the black-haired young man, Nick thought. If they could find him, they would be one step closer to getting to the bottom of the disappearances.

Nick leaned back and took a deep breath. He arched his back and flexed his burning muscles. Someone watching would have noticed it was the same lazy way that a big predatory animal stretched—maybe a lion or a wolf.

The goth was the key. *Gotta find him.*

• • •

As Dog Smell's leader, Grubb had called an impromptu band meeting backstage at The Cracked Saloon. A fifth of vodka was going around, getting the band primed for that night's performance.

"Tonight after the show we're going to party," Grubb said, passing the vodka.

"Like what else is new," said Twiggy, the bass guitarist. "We party after every show."

"Tonight we *really* party," Grubb said. "I guarantee you it's going to be like nothing we've done before."

The drummer and the sound board man looked around nervously. Grubb was crazy. His idea of partying, whatever it might be, was sure to be dangerous and highly illegal.

"What you got in mind, Grubb?" Twiggy asked. He dragged on his cigarette and laughed nasally. "An orgy? Or do you just wanna go down to the landfill and shoot rats?"

"Even better," Grubb said, and opened the top of a rucksack next to his chair. Inside were several empty vodka bottles filled with a pale liquid. Also visible were several shredded rags and some cigarette lighters.

Puzzled, Twiggy leaned close to the bottles and sniffed. What was Grubb trying to get them to drink, peyote extract? Psychedelic tequila?

"Whoa, dude," Twiggy said, jumping back as soon as he smelled gasoline. "You want to blow us all up? That's *gasoline*."

"I know that, asshole. So put out your cigarette."

Twiggy stubbed out his cigarette. The drummer and soundboard man kept looking toward the door as if they wanted to run out of the room. But they didn't want Grubb to think they were spooked.

"So those are, like, Molotov cocktails?" Twiggy asked, trying to sound cool with the idea.

"Yeah. We're going to make this city hot tonight after the show."

"Grubb, you're one crazy mo fo," the drummer said. "I'm not helping you burn anything."

"If we get caught . . . " the soundboard man said.

"Nobody's gonna get caught," Grubb said. "Believe me, the cops in this city aren't capable of catching criminals. Besides, we'll get high first."

"Huh?"

"If you commit a crime while you're high, you can't be held responsible," Grubb said.

"Oh," the drummer said. He nodded. Anything that involved getting high sounded good to him. "This is all beginning to make sense now."

"I knew it would," Grubb said. "Besides, it's good for marketing. Gets our name out there. You know what they say—there's no such thing as bad publicity."

The other members of Dog Smell nodded as if they were savvy advertising executives. Then Twiggy said: "What the hell are you talking about, man?"

"If we get caught for firebombing Rehoboth Beach, big deal. It gets us noticed. We'll be all over TV and they'll play our songs on the air. Think of the headlines, Twig man. 'Punk band terrorizes city.' 'Dog Smell makes beach resort howl in terror.' "

"All I can think about is prison," Twiggy said.

"Nah, we'd be high," the drummer said. "So it wouldn't be our fault."

"Then there's the CD."

The three band members leaned toward Grubb. "What CD?" So far, all the band had been able to afford were some recordings of shows right here at The Cracked Saloon. They were all right, but half the time you could hardly hear the band because of the clinking beer bottles and the shouting.

"We're gonna be doing a compact disc," Grubb announced. "I've already reserved some studio time for us starting next month at this great studio in Philly. We make the recordings, they'll make the CDs. Just for demos to send around to radio stations and to sell here. We'll have to work late though, between one a.m. and seven, because that's when it's cheapest to use the place."

"How about Dog Smell T-shirts?" the drummer asked.

"Why not?" Grubb said.

"Uh, Grubb, man, this sounds great," Twiggy said carefully, choosing his words. Grubb was getting that glazed look in his eye that meant trouble. Twiggy didn't want to push him or Grubb might decide to set off one of those Molotov cocktails right here. "But where are we supposed to get the money for all this?"

Grubb grinned. "Don't you worry about that," he said. "I have a little something going that will finance Dog Smell's ride to fame."

A little something going? Twiggy tried to remember if there had been an unusual number of liquor store holdups in the newspaper lately. Or was Grubb dealing? The truth was, Twiggy didn't really give a damn what Grubb did if it meant Dog Smell might get to play someplace besides The Cracked Saloon for a change. It was

Grubb's ass, not his.

On the other side of the wall, the music playing over the club's sound system began to get louder. That was their cue. Dog Smell began to stir itself. Grubb refastened the rucksack and stuffed it into a corner. The drummer drained the bottle of vodka. The soundboard man slipped out to take his post.

Grubb burst out onto the stage, barking like a dog at the audience. They screamed profanities at him. Grubb howled and grabbed the microphone:

I'd like to invite you all to my barbecue
We'll have ribs, chicken, and a cop or two.
Vegetarians can eat salad or some green thing
Won't be as good as the pig I'll be roasting.

My pig recipe is really quite easy
Cook him quick till he's sort of greasy.
Salt, pepper, season him real well
Light a fuse and blow him straight to hell.

CHAPTER 20

Sarah was just sitting down when her cell phone rang. Damn. She thought about letting it go to voice mail, then glanced at the number. *Logan.* Late as it was, it could only be something to do with the case. With a sigh, she took the call.

"Logan?"

"Are you hungry?"

"God, Logan, it's almost ten o'clock. You haven't had dinner yet?"

"Nah," he said. "I went for a run at the park, and that took the edge off my appetite until now. Listen, though. I want to talk the case over with you. You could at least use a drink."

"Okay," she said.

"See you in twenty." They agreed to meet at a

watering hole on Rehoboth Avenue. Nick hung up.

Sarah looked at her phone and shook her head. Nick was a hard man to figure out. One minute he was playful, the next he was rough and tough. And he could be moody. According to Bob Grabowski, Nick Logan was also a killer. Was it any wonder that he was a little hard to figure out?

She still had a hard time imagining Nick as a cold-blooded killer. Nick may have been acting out of revenge when he killed that man, but he had broken the rules all the same. In the same situation, what would she have done? She hoped to God she never found out.

Pushing those troubling thoughts from her mind, she focused on getting dressed. She had put on sweatpants and a sweatshirt as soon as she came home from work. She considered changing but then thought, why bother? It was just Nick she was going to meet. He wouldn't notice if she wore a gunnysack. She strapped her gun under her sweatshirt and hurried out.

The bar was in an old brick building that crowded up against the street like an Irishman brooding over his drink. It was about the closest thing to an Irish pub you could find at the beach, and the proximity to the ocean gave it a seafaring air. She hoped Nick was already there. It was late and she was in no mood to deal with sloppy pickup attempts. Whenever she went to a bar alone, she felt more hit on than a punching bag.

She ducked inside and stood a moment to let her eyes adjust to the dim lighting.

"What are you drinking, honey?"

She blinked up at a tall man standing to her right. His eyelids drooped at half mast and his tie was a haphazard afterthought around his flabby neck.

"I'm here to meet someone," she said and spun away.

"Then you came to the right place, honey!" he called after her.

Silently, she cursed Nick for not being there to meet her at the door.

She came out into a long room filled with round tables. At the far end was a small bar crowded with drinkers. A man with a guitar and another with a banjo were singing Irish songs on a modest stage. She scanned the scattered tables. Where the hell was Nick? The whole place seemed filled with vacationers who had shown up for happy hour five hours ago and never gotten around to leaving.

A man was waving at her. Nick. She hurried to join him.

"You could have met me at the door," she said reproachfully.

Nick shrugged. "I was hungry. I wanted to get my order in before the kitchen closed. You want anything? I told them not to put everything away just yet because you were coming."

"No thanks," Sarah said. What had dinner been? A frozen slab of vegetarian lasagna heated in the microwave. She gazed enviously at Nick's roast beef sandwich as the waitress arrived. Her mouth was watering. "I'll have one of those, too, please," she surprised herself by saying. "Lots of horseradish." The waitress hurried off.

Nick tore into his sandwich. "You'll have to forgive me if I don't wait for you to be served," he said through a mouthful of food. "I don't like my food to get cold."

"It's already cold, Nick. It's a sandwich."

"Whatever," he said. He took another huge bite.

"Notice anything at the park today?" Sarah asked.

"Yes and no," Nick said. Between mouthfuls of roast beef sandwich, he told her about the witness who had come forward to report seeing a black-haired man hurling the bicycles into the scrub pines at Cape Henlopen.

Sarah felt a flush of excitement. "My God, Nick, we have a description of a suspect. That's incredible."

"Yep. Or at least someone we should definitely try to find."

"A skinny, black-haired goth. He shouldn't be hard to track down."

"Sure. There's probably only fifty or sixty

college kids working at the beach who look like that," Nick said. "The description really narrows it down."

Sarah's sandwich arrived, along with a pint of Harp ale. She tore into it. She couldn't remember the last time she had eaten red meat. It tasted wonderful. Ever since she had been partnered with Nick, she had been breaking all sorts of rules.

"At least we have something now," Nick said. "I think he'll come back to the park or the trail. And if he does, we'll nail him. But we may have to help things along . . ."

"What's your plan?"

"We should split up. A lone jogger makes a much better target. Still, we stay close, keep in contact. Hawley gave me the okay to bring in more joggers so that the park and trail are constantly patrolled."

That made sense to Sarah. If nothing else, the police patrols could force the abductor to move someplace that generated less publicity. Wilmington would be good. Or better yet, Philly. "I'm also asking Grabowski to assign a radio car to sit in the lot at the trail head all night. You never know."

"You're right," she said, taking a long drink of ale. She was amazing herself. Food hadn't tasted this good in a long time. She sipped more ale. At the moment, the idea of running the beach trails alone while a crazy man with black hair stalked her seemed to be only a hypothetical scenario, not something she'd be doing first thing tomorrow morning. "If we split up we have a much better chance of catching this psycho, although I have a feeling I'm the one who's going to make a good target. In fact, the word 'decoy' comes to mind."

"Like I said, we'll stay close," Nick said. "Be sure to pack."

"I'll put my .357 in a speed holster," Sarah said. "I know it's big and clunky, but it'll stop a fucking elephant."

Nick blinked in mock astonishment. "Detective Monahan. Such language."

"That's Detective Monahan to you, buster," she said. "And since when would anyone in this tavern be offended by the f-word?"

"In that case, I hope you'll excuse me." Nick drained his Guinness Stout down to the creamy froth. "I've got to see a man about a horse."

Sarah watched him go, thinking *hmm*. She realized she was beginning to have a weird fondness for him. Nick Logan did have a kind of charm if you were the sort of girl who also liked Sherman tanks.

"Excuse me." A voice just beside her. She turned in her seat, expecting the worst. She got just about what she was expecting.

The man looked harmless, but drunk. His face

was contorted in an alcoholic grin he evidently thought was seductive. His Hawaaiin shirt shouted tourist. Loudly.

"Go away," she said, turning back to her pint of Harp.

"I was just wondering if your legs were tired," he insisted.

"Huh?" She glanced back up.

"I thought your legs might be tired because you've been running through my mind all night."

Sarah looked at him deadpan. "You can't be serious," she said. She noticed a couple of his buddies at the bar, elbowing each other in the ribs. "You are serious, aren't you? That's got to be the worst pickup line I've ever heard. Get lost, huh?"

"Hey, c'mon, it's a great line," he said. "I got it from a book." He put his hand on her shoulder.

"Don't touch me," she said.

"C'mon now, Beautiful. Don't get upset. Did anyone ever tell you that you've got amazing eyes?"

Sarah started to get up. He was crowding her to one side and the chair wouldn't slide back easily on the wood floor. Somehow her feet got tangled in the confusion of chair legs. She started to stand without any footing under her. So much for looking tough and cop-like. She stumbled and went down to her hands and knees on the floor. Real smooth.

"You've got her right where you want her!" one of the pickup artist's buddies shouted. Another hooted. The man grinned down at her stupidly, started to say something —

— and was slammed against the wall as Nick came out of nowhere. The man sputtered and grabbed Nick's wrists, trying to free himself. His hands tugged powerlessly on Nick's forearms, which danced with cords of muscle. He looked toward his friends, who had taken a step forward, then stopped. They were middle-aged, flabby men out for a couple of beers and definitely not looking for real trouble. One wore wire-rim glasses and a pink polo shirt. Nick could have beaten them silly with a bar napkin.

"I tripped," she said, trying to stay calm for Nick's sake. "It's not his fault." Nick was frightening her more than a little right now because he looked mean and mad as hell. A drunken banker she could handle. She didn't know about her angry partner. What was it Grabowski had said about Wallace Green? *Just about every bone in his body was broken*. She had to defuse this, and fast.

"That's enough!" Sarah shouted.

Nick let him go.

The bouncer arrived. He was a college kid, a preppy weightlifter type with styling gel in his hair. The kid got a worried look when he saw Nick, and glanced around for help. Nick turned to face him, his fists bunched like two rocks at his side.

Sarah scrambled to her feet, getting between the bouncer and Nick. She was imagining the headlines: *Cops arrested in barroom brawl.*

"We're leaving," she told the bouncer. He got out of the way. "This was all a misunderstanding. I tripped over a chair. No harm, no foul." She dug in her purse for a couple of twenties, threw them on the table.

She motioned for Nick to come along and he backed toward the door, then spun and followed her out.

On the sidewalk, she heard sirens. Sarah had a momentary twinge of worry that they were screeching toward the tavern, but then two fire engines roared past in the street. They were so close she could feel the rush of air as they went by.

A police car zipped past, lights flashing. Then another. In the distance she could hear sirens in other parts of the city.

"What the hell is going on?"

"It's probably just the boardwalk burning down," Nick joked. "Let's walk around the block, huh? I need to cool off."

"I'll say," Sarah said reproachfully.

"Look, I'm sorry. I really lost it in there. I thought that asshole shoved you or something —"

"Logan, for God's sake. I started to stand up to tell him off and I tripped. I was clumsy. That's not to say he wasn't an ass."

"Yeah, but all I saw was you on the floor, that dumb bastard grinning —"

"I *am* a cop. I can handle myself."

"You didn't look like one down there on your hands and knees," Nick said. "You looked, well — "

"Like a helpless woman?" she demanded. Sarah felt herself getting steamed. It was all she could do to keep from slugging him. She could understand now how he had almost lost it in the bar. Anger. It was almost a pleasure to give it to it. A release.

"Look, I didn't mean —"

"Forget it, Nick. I appreciate your help." She gave him a wan smile. "I just thought I'd be the one who had to explain to Hawley why you had been charged with assault."

"Oh, c'mon. I wasn't that bad."

"Says you." She giggled. Caught herself. *God, what is it that this guy does to me?* There was never a dull moment when he was around, that was for sure. "You looked positively homicidal."

Nick shrugged. They walked side by side. The tavern was a few blocks back from the beach and most of the places they passed were closed up for the night. Doors locked, lights burning in the windows. People came to Rehoboth Beach to relax, not party all night.

"It's this damn case," Nick said. "I forgot how frustrating homicide cases can be when there's no clues, no witnesses to the crime, no body. Christ. Fortunately, in most situations the suspects are so stupid the only part they don't do is drive themselves to jail."

"We have what our witness saw," Sarah reminded him. "We can build off that."

"Tomorrow we'll start patrolling singly," Nick said. "That should bring the bastard out."

They had walked around the entire block and found themselves back in front of the tavern. Even from the sidewalk they could hear the raucous Friday night sounds inside. Laughter, odd snatches of guitar and banjo from the Irish ballads, clanking mugs. Sarah regretted that they couldn't go back in.

Another radio car whipped past, lights blazing. Definitely one of the summer cops having some fun. What the hell was going on? She thought about calling in, but decided not to. She'd hear about it soon enough if it was anything big.

She began digging in her purse for her car keys. "I guess I'd better be going," she said. "Let's plan on being on the trail early."

"Sure you wouldn't like to come over to my place for a nightcap or a cup of coffee or something?" Nick asked.

In the dusky light cast by the street lamps,

Sarah tried to read his face. Was Nick making a pass at her? This was the second time he had invited her for a nightcap. But who was counting? In the semi-darkness she could only make out shadows — his angular nose, a dark swipe of mouth, the hollows of his eyes. All she had to do was say yes, and part of her wanted to.

"I'll take a raincheck, Nick," she said breezily, trying not to show she had read anything into his offer of a cup of coffee. "It's almost midnight. We'll be running a lot of miles come tomorrow morning."

"You're right," he said. She heard grit crunch beneath his shoes as he shifted his weight uneasily from foot to foot. It wasn't too late for her to change her mind. The moment hung there in front of them both like an open-ended question, then just as suddenly evaporated.

"Walk me to my car, will you?" she asked.

She had pulled her Honda right behind Nick's pickup truck. She unlocked the door, slid behind the wheel, rolled down the window. "Good night, Nick," she said.

"See you bright and early."

She pulled away from the curb and headed home, glancing once in the rearview mirror to see Nick looking after her car, big-knuckled hands shoved into his jeans, shoulders hunched, his face in shadow.

● ● ●

Idiot.. Nick wasn't sure what made him feel more like a fool: losing his temper in the bar or the not-so-subtle attempt he'd made at getting Sarah to come home with him. *Definitely an idiot.* What was even more infuriating was that he knew *she* had done the right thing by turning him down, while he himself had taken the typically male course of action and made a pass at her. Maybe Sarah was right about him being just another chauvinistic pig.

He dug in the fridge for a beer, then grabbed a hard pretzel to munch. A "no fat" snack, according to the package. No more greasy potato chips.

What was happening to him? In the back of his mind he knew it all came down to Sarah Monahan. Not since Karen had a woman had such an effect on him. He was watching what he ate and drank because of Sarah. He was even honing himself with workouts because of her. Splitting all that firewood had gotten him into good shape, but now he was moving in new directions. Four miles on the trail today along with a hundred pushups and sit ups! No way he would have done that a few weeks ago.

With a twinge of guilt, he remembered that Karen had also changed his life. He had lived recklessly until meeting her, then had three years of what Nick liked to believe was a normal life. That crackhead burglar had destroyed what they had and taken Karen away. He had killed Wallace Green in the hopes that revenge would make him feel better, but in the end it was no different from exterminating any sort of vermin. Karen left a hole that revenge couldn't fill.

When Nick saw Sarah on the floor with that drunken asshole hovering over her, the rational part of his mind shut down. Instinct took over. He didn't think so much as react. His muscles themselves took over until he snapped out of it and realized that he was choking some drunk guy in a shirt and tie. Nick had made a scene, embarrassing the very woman he was trying to protect.

He had already let Karen down by failing to protect her. He wasn't going to let Sarah down as well.

Too many thoughts began eating at him. He opened the fridge to get another beer, then changed his mind. He'd been down that road more than a few times, and it always came to a dead end and a hangover.

He went out on the deck for a few minutes, listening to the surf. It was a soothing, ageless sound. The vastness of the dark sea also put things in perspective. Hell, some Dutch explorer had probably been standing in this spot four hundred years ago, looking out at the sea, pondering his own version of woe is me. A lot of good it did anybody. Nick walked around the beach house snapping off lights. Got into bed. Some nights, when he'd had trouble sleeping, Karen had told him to focus instead on someplace that made him happy. Nick imagined he was back in the mountains splitting firewood. That calmed him down. He started to drift off.

There would be plenty of action in the next few days, and he welcomed it. Nick knew it was what he did best.

· · ·

Sarah put on some Adele and poured a glass of wine. She was coming unglued. All because of Nick Logan.

She really didn't want to become involved with anyone. Not at this time, at least. Becoming involved with another cop was definitely not part of the plan, especially when it was someone like Nick. She had a feeling he might even hurt her chances of climbing the career ladder at the Rehoboth Beach Police Department.

She picked up her wine and wandered through the apartment. It was a small place, but she had decorated it as best she could on her salary and in the limited amount of time she had. Most of the furnishings had come from Ikea and Pier One Imports, but she'd added some items from the shops in town. The result was trendy as something in a magazine, with a little beach kitsch thrown in.

She flipped through her CDs: Cheryl Crow, Amy Winehouse, Bonnie Raitt. Her musical tastes ran toward women who stood alone against the world.

Sarah paused to top off her glass. She needed it. The scene with Nick in the bar had jangled her nerves. The man was a ticking time bomb. What had gotten into him? He nearly throttled that drunk guy. And yet, when was the last time someone had had her back like that? It felt kind of good, just knowing Nick would do that for her. She tried to think of a word for it. *Unconditional.* She shook her head, as much to clear it of wine haze as thoughts of Nick Logan.

Sarah poured the rest of her wine in the sink without finishing it, rinsed out the glass, then looked around at the framed prints on the walls, the trendy furniture, the houseplants. Her cat slept under a chair—yes, it was a sure sign of where her life was headed that she had a cat, an indifferent one named Cagney, to boot.

She felt lonely, goddamnit. She needed something—someone —to fill the void. Not new furniture. And definitely not a cat.

But Nick Logan?

Better look before you leap, she warned herself. The trouble was, she'd already fallen.

CHAPTER 21

Kreeger hoped to find a recipient soon for their latest kidney. He looked over to where the perfusion machine beeped insistently as the blue organ pulsed and glistened. The machine pumped a nourishing solution through the organ, keeping it healthy. It had already been hooked to the assortment of tubing for nearly twenty-four hours and time was running out. Sell it or smell it, baby. Better get back on the UNOS database and see what he could come up with.

Just as he settled at the computer terminal, there was a knock at the door.

Kreeger froze. This area was strictly off limits and it was so early that the hospital should have been deserted except for the nightshift nurses and a resident or two. All the basement entrances were kept locked to keep curious staff members out. Couldn't have some nurse wondering what all those organs were doing down in the basement. Kreeger disliked the idea of prison.

He tried to remember if he had forgotten to lock any of the doors behind him. Didn't think he had.

"Who's there?" he called nervously.

"It's me."

Kreeger scurried across the makeshift lab to unlock the door for the hospital administrator, Roger Smith.

"Hard at work again, huh, Dr. Kreeger? You never stop."

"We had another couple of donors come in yesterday afternoon," Kreeger said. "Their organs had to be harvested, then all the groundwork had to be done. I didn't get on the network until nearly three this morning."

"I guess you missed all the excitement," Smith said.

"What excitement?" Kreeger asked. He had been in the lab all night, busy typing tissues and babysitting the organs. He didn't think he had missed anything exciting at all. Quite the contrary. There was no use trying to explain this to someone who wasn't a doctor.

"I guess you couldn't hear the sirens down here," Smith said. "It's all over the news. Some gang was running around the city setting fires. I'm just glad they stayed the hell away from the hospital. I came in just to be sure."

"Something like this happened before," Kreeger remarked. He was thinking back to the burned bicycle shop on the boardwalk and the firebombed Mercedes.

"That's what they were saying on the news," Smith said. "But it's a lot worse this time, believe me. I swung by the boardwalk just to see. I swear, it looks like a bomb hit."

"Maybe these bombings will draw some of the attention away from us," Kreeger said. "The press will have something else to report."

"I guess you're right," the administrator said. He glanced toward the beeping perfusion machine, and raised an eyebrow. "How are things going?"

"You'll be glad to hear I'm sending Grubb to the airport with three kidneys."

"Excellent," Smith said. "Send Grubb and that fat buddy of his over to the beach trail as soon as they get back to see if they can find anyone else for us. Our source at police headquarters says the extra patrols at the park won't be part of the work schedule until Monday morning so there shouldn't be any problems there for us today."

"I'll give Grubb a call."

Smith nodded toward the perfusion machine. "What about that one over there?"

"I'm having a little trouble placing this fourth kidney," Kreeger admitted. "It's rather an unusual blood type. This is the second time this has happened. The luck of the draw was evidently against us."

"Luck or no luck, that piece of meat over there is worth at least a couple hundred thousand to us in insurance money," Smith pointed out. "Find a home for it. Sell it at a discount if you have to."

Kreeger suppressed a laugh. Here was yet another hospital administrator who knew about balance sheets but nothing about medicine. "You want me to hold a two-for-one sale?"

Smith glared. "You know what I mean, Kreeger. Just get rid of it. Ship it to somebody. That thing only has forty-eight hours, right? How long has it been around already?"

"Getting close to twenty-four."

"Off-load it," Smith insisted. "Lie about the antigen matches if you have to."

"They'll check it on the other end," Kreeger said. "Even if they don't, the recipient will reject the organ. Some of these people barely have the strength to survive the transplant operation. The emotional strain alone of a rejection episode could kill them."

"Kreeger, you're being silly," Smith said. "Don't tell me you're worried about some kidney patient on the other end. Don't forget that you're the one who cut up these so-called donors on *our* end."

Kreeger tried to think of the "donors" Grubb and Fat Boy brought in the same way he had thought of his cadaver in medical school. Just a body, a piece of flesh. He didn't appreciate Smith reminding him otherwise. "If you don't mind, I have work to do," he snapped.

"Just make sure you ship that kidney out today," Smith said before pulling the door shut behind him.

Dr. Kreeger picked up his cell phone. He'd tell Grubb to get out to the park with Fat Boy. Then he'd start cold calling hospitals like a goddamn telemarketer.

Funny how things worked out. Back in medical school Kreeger never thought he'd be selling body parts.

• • •

Not long after dawn, Nick and Sarah were in the parking lot off Wolfe Neck Road, ready to head out on the Junction and Breakwater Trail.

"Be careful," Nick said, looking into Sarah's face to see if she was okay with what they were about to do. Both of them knew going it alone was risky. She gave him a crooked smile and nodded toward the woods.

"Don't worry, I'll shoot first and ask questions

later," Sarah said.

He wondered if maybe splitting up was a tactic that relied too much on good luck and underestimating this creep who was abducting people. Nick tried to reassure himself. He had been running alone in the park only yesterday, but chances were this wacko with the black hair was going to leave someone like Nick alone. He had a bad feeling about letting Sarah serve as a target, but there was no talking her out of it now.

As if he didn't have enough to worry about, he still felt like a perfect ass for making a pass at her the night before. He was glad there hadn't been time to dwell on embarrassment this morning. He was grateful to Sarah, too, for concentrating on the details of their trail patrol. She hadn't brought up the subject of last night.

"You feeling okay?" Nick asked.

"Fine," she said. "It's just hard to wake up. It's damn early, in case you haven't noticed. My internal clock is thrown off."

"I thought you were a morning person."

"I am when I'm not out late the night before."

He couldn't argue with that, and he didn't particularly want to talk about last night. "If something starts, don't let it go too far," Nick added. He began stretching to limber his muscles. "Shoot the bastard if you have to. Don't take any chances."

"You're going to give yourself an ulcer, Nick,"

she snapped. Her head had started pounding in anticipation of running four miles. That damn wine. "I can take care of myself."

"I know you can," Nick said. "So get going."

Sarah set off down the trail. Nick waited until she was out of sight, then started after her. If there was trouble, he be just behind her.

It was not a pleasant morning. Anyone hoping for a good beach day was going to be disappointed. Ocean fog clung to the woods, making the tree trunks stand out black and wet amid the blanket of gray. So far his pumping arms and legs hadn't been enough to warm him and goosebumps formed on his flesh even beneath his sweats. His movements felt sluggish as if the misty morning air was weighing him down.

Nick felt uneasy, and he couldn't blame it all on the horror movie quality of the scenery. Splitting up to cover more ground seemed like a good idea in theory. Now, he wasn't so sure. He just prayed Sarah kept an eye out. This was not a morning to let your guard down.

He began to see other people moving in the fog. A couple of joggers and a mountain biker passed him coming the other way on the trail, their forms emerging from the gloom like wraiths. He nodded good morning, watching for black hair. After what had been going around in the news about Cape Henlopen and the beach trail, he couldn't believe these health nuts were still running the paths.

He wished the department had some small two-way radios he and Sarah could use. Something inconspicuous, like the FBI or Secret Service had. But high-tech gear was expensive and not all that in demand in Rehoboth Beach.

Nick pounded up the trail, feeling his legs begin to loosen and his breathing deepen. Damn, but he felt good. Up ahead he saw a fat man, a younger guy, coming his way. Not much of a jogger because the guy was clearly laboring to move it along, roly poly and panting, but you had to give him credit for getting out there. His T-shirt was dark and sweat-stained where it was clenched in a roll of fat around his waist.

As Nick watched, the fat man tripped over his own two feet and fell.

It was all Nick could do not to laugh. He ran up and stopped beside the man, who was huffing badly as he tried to regain his feet.

"You okay?" he asked.

"Yeah." The man groaned and struggled to sit up. "I hate this jogging crap. My wife is making me do it. Some vacation, huh? She says I'm overweight and I've got to lose thirty pounds if I ever want to have sex with her again. Can you believe that shit?"

Nick fought back a smile. Overweight? This guy's poor wife must have gotten tired of getting humped by a walrus. "Maybe she's just worried about you. All that health stuff on TV is scaring her."

"That's just the trouble," the fat man said. "My wife expects me to look like one of those TV hunks."

"Yeah," Nick said, thinking it was going to take more than losing some weight to turn this guy's wife on. "You know, maybe you should start out walking instead. It's less of a strain on your body."

"You think so?" The fat man grinned. "Maybe. But it takes so long to lose any weight just walking. I figure that if I go running, I'll either get skinny in a hurry or die of a heart attack."

"You better —"

There. Something was moving in the trees. Nick's peripheral vision detected a shifting in the fog. Someone was hiding among the stark black trees.

He spun around, reaching unconsciously for the nylon holster at the small of his back.

"Buddy, you look like you seen a ghost," the fat man said. Nick noticed there wasn't a smile on his face anymore and his piggish eyes had turned hard and bright. The overweight man lumbered to his feet, started moving toward Nick.

"Back off." There was steel in Nick's voice and the fat man stood still.

It's a trap, Nick thought. *There's a second one —*

He came out of the trees. A goth maniac with

a face like a hatchet. He charged out of the fog, howling, and Nick checked him with a forearm across the chest that sent his attacker crashing to the ground.

The freak scrabbled to his feet with the quickness of a cat. He's fast, Nick thought. Be careful. Then he noticed the black device in his attacker's hand. A stun gun.

"Don't just stand there, Fatso!" the freak hissed at the jogger. "Grab him."

Nick had slipped up by forgetting the fat man. Both men came at him from different sides. He knew he'd be in trouble if the fat one pinned his arms long enough for the freak to zap him with the stun gun.

Nick started to move but lost his footing on the slick wet path. The fat man caught him from behind in a bear hug. The goth came at him, his lips curled back from yellowed teeth. Nick couldn't take his eyes off the stun gun in his hand. The freakish one was cackling and the noise made Nick's blood run cold.

Nick curled up from the waist and kicked out with both legs, catching the freak in the chest. Nick could hear the wind go out of him. The stun gun slipped to the ground.

"Grubb, hurry up, get him!" the fat one squealed. The freak was down on one knee in the dirt, gasping to get his breath back.

The fat one's arms were mostly blubber and

Nick broke the bear hug like a wrestler would, grabbing the hands that held him and peeling them away. The fat man backed off, his palms held up flat and uselessly in defense. Nick nailed him in the nose with a left and threw a right uppercut that crashed against the fat man's jaw so hard his eyes rolled back white in his head. Then Nick grabbed two handfuls of hair and yanked the fat face down to meet his knee coming up the other way.

He turned back to meet his other attacker. The freak was grabbing for the stun gun again and Nick let him. He had the Beretta out of its holster and pointed it at the one called Grubb.

"I'm the police," Nick said.

"That makes it even better," Grubb answered, sneering. In one swift motion he snatched up the stun gun and fired. Nick ducked just in time and the prongs of the electrical probe just missed him. Nick brought his own weapon up as Grubb ran for the safety of the woods. The front sight was settled on a spot between the freak's shoulder blades when something exploded against the side of his head. Nick saw stars. He staggered sideways. His ears rang and his head buzzed.

"Wait for me!"

The fat one was retreating into the woods after the freak. He held a thick, broken tree limb in one hand.

"Hold it!" Nick yelled, trying to focus enough to aim his .45.

"I should've hit you harder, you son of a bitch!" the fat one yelled. Tree branches and underbrush swayed as he rammed his huge form deeper into the woods. It was like some great big animal getting under cover—a bear or a water buffalo. Even after he was out of sight Nick could still hear branches cracking.

The side of his face felt wet. Blood. Quickly, Nick searched for the damage with his fingertips. If it was bad, he didn't want to black out in the woods with those two goons on the prowl or where the local marsh rats might start gnawing on his soft parts if he passed out.

The fat one's makeshift club had left a deep gash just above and behind his ear. The tip of his ear stung and his fingers came away bloody. He was beginning to feel seriously pissed off. He forced himself to stay cool, but a thought nagged at him.

His attackers were getting away.

Nick started after them. The wet branches slashed at his face and in the fog he quickly became disoriented. *Just where I don't want to be,* he thought. *Alone in the woods with a couple of real psychopaths.* If they were laying up for him somewhere, he was in real trouble, because moving quietly in the underbrush was impossible. He glanced around. He was surrounded by fog-shrouded woods, and all the black tree trunks and underbrush looked the same to him. He had no idea how to get back to the trail. Too bad he had never been a Boy Scout. He kept the Beretta out in front of him at the ready, but out here in the woods the weapon had come to feel small and useless in his hand. He wished he had a shotgun, or maybe even a spear with a nice, sharp point.

He stopped and listened for any sound other than the ringing in his head. Nothing. Either the fat one had gotten so far away that Nick couldn't hear the brush snapping or they were waiting to ambush him. His head hurt like hell thanks to those bastards. If he caught them in the woods, he would save the taxpayers a bundle by making sure there would be no trial.

Nick forced his way through the dense underbrush, the leaves licking at him like so many wet tongues. Goddamn, but his head hurt. Something was running down his sides under his sweatshirt, and he wasn't sure if it was sweat or blood from his head wound. He really didn't want to find out.

Chunk. Nick swung the gun toward the noise. Sounded like a car door slamming in the fog ahead. Another *chunk.* An engine churned, died away. He started running toward the noise, tripped and fell headlong in the underbrush. The motor turned over again and caught.

Nick got to his feet and lurched through the

trees in time to see brake lights wink around a bend in the gravel road that cut through the woods. He caught a glimpse of a van before it disappeared around the curve. He didn't bother to chase it. No way he could have caught it on foot.

He looked around. Just beyond him were the ruins of an old artillery bunker. This area had been heavily fortified during World War II to keep German U-boats from launching any surprise attacks. Vandals had smashed bottles against the concrete sides, littering the floor of the bunker with shards of glass. The yawning black slit that had once housed a big gun looked vaguely like a giant gap-toothed smile. Nick shook his head to get the fuzz out of it. Was he beginning to hallucinate? Maybe he was hurt worse than he thought.

He started back through the fog-shrouded woods, making his way toward the jogging path. It probably wasn't as far as it seemed, but if he missed it somehow he didn't want to wander around the woods until the fog burned off and he find his way. Nick turned and began following the tire tracks up the gravel road. It had to come out on a paved road somewhere because that van didn't resemble an off-road vehicle. He'd stop by the state park office later and get a map.

Something caught his eye. He stooped and picked up a candy bar wrapper. It hadn't been lying there long and he thought he knew who had left it. That fat slob. Nick folded the paper into his holster. Maybe the lab would be able to lift some prints off it.

Nick hoped to hell his legs would carry him down the dirt lane to a main road before he passed out. His head was beginning to feel as foggy as the woods looked. He started walking.

CHAPTER 22

Since retiring from the federal government, Burt Pennington spent most of his days surf fishing. After spending thirty years in a cubicle in some damned federal office building he loved being outside in the salt air, and it got him the hell away from his wife. Marriage didn't come with a retirement plan except death or divorce, and Burt wasn't ready to embrace either of those options, so he went surf fishing instead.

His wife's idea of a big catch was a sale at the outlets on Route 1 and a trunk filled with shopping bags. She couldn't understand that he didn't mind coming home with an empty cooler.

Burt liked to point out to his wife that every day was a fishing day, but not every day was a catching day. That usually made her roll her eyes before she put a couple of TV dinners in the microwave. This day looked to be different. He had just hooked one hell of a big fish. He pulled mightily on his surf rod, then reeled frantically to take in the slack. Yep, today was shaping up to be a catching day.

He hoped it was a striper. He had seen thirty-pounders come out of the water here. A fish that size could fill the freezer and give them a break from TV dinners.

This was a good spot, right at what the locals called "the point." It was where the Delaware Bay met the Atlantic Ocean, and big fish liked to come in close to shore to eat what got churned up in the mix of currents. A lot of days it got crowded with retired guys like Burt who drove four-wheel trucks rigged with rod holders and cooler racks right out on the beach, then set up lawn chairs, maybe a radio, and spent the day fishing and drinking the occasional beer.

A couple months ago the News Journal had done a story about how the fish were polluted. They had chemicals in them from the factories along the Delaware River closer to Philadelphia. Eating those big bluefish could give you cancer. The fishermen had thinned out pretty good after that.

Burt thought it was a questionable piece of journalism, considering that the reporter had relied on reports downloaded from the Internet without bothering to talk to anyone who went fishing, but that was the media for you. He didn't put much stock in the idea of fish giving anybody cancer. Microwaved dinners, maybe. But fish? Hell, there were plenty of old guys here, some of 'em close to eighty, who'd been eating fish out of this very spot their whole lives. Maybe they'd all get cancer. But when you were eighty years old, you had to die of something, right? By then, a lot of things besides fish could kill you, like maybe two packs of cigarettes a day for sixty years or bacon and eggs every morning for breakfast.

He pulled on the rod, reeled in the slack. What the hell was on the line? Sometimes it fought back, other times like now it was like a dead weight on the line. He began to think maybe it wasn't a striper. Sometimes a snag would bounce along the bottom, eddy in the currents, make you think it was fighting. Then you hauled it up and you had landed yourself an old chunk of wood or a plastic garbage bag. One time he even reeled in the grate from an old fireplace. Thought he'd had a real lunker on the line.

He tugged and reeled, tugged and reeled. Whatever it was, it was beginning to seem like it was not a fish.

Another old guy wandered over to see what he was reeling in. "What you got on there?"

"I ain't got shit," Burt said. "Just some trash on

the line."

"Damn. Let's see what's on there."

He had to agree. He was curious. What the hell was it? Pure dead weight. He tugged and reeled. Something began to be visible just under the surface of the green-blue water.

"What the —"

A face. Legs. Arms.

"Sweet mother of Jesus," Burt said.

"Well, huh," the other fisherman said. "I'd like to know what you used for bait."

• • •

When Nick got to the beach, it was already crowded with rubberneckers and police.

"What the hell happened to you?" Grabowski wanted to know. "Don't tell me those thugs in the park did that. Or did you get smart with that pretty partner of yours and she smacked you upside the head?"

Nick scowled, touched the gauze pad on the side of his head. "I almost had them."

"I heard."

"Two guys, Bob. That's who we're looking for."

"A fat one and a skinny one, right?" Grabowski asked.

"Yeah, why?"

"Well, that's exactly how one of the uniforms described the two medics who picked up one of our disappeared accident victims who later turned up kidney-less in the bay. A fat one and a goth-looking dude."

"It's got to be the same guys. What the hell are they up to?"

Grabowski shrugged. "Beats me. By the way, where is your oh-so-attractive partner?"

"Hawley's got her busy writing press releases. Between the abductions and the bodies from the bay and the fire bombings, there's quite a demand."

"Two months in the department and she's already Hawley's pet, huh?"

It was Nick's turn to shrug. He wasn't interested in gossiping about Sarah. Unlike Grabowski, he didn't have a horse running in the office politics race. "I should have nailed those two bastards, Bob. Damn. This whole mess would be over already."

Grabowski fixed him with an appraising eye. "From the looks of it, you're lucky they didn't nail you. In case you haven't noticed, Nick, you're not superhuman. Where was Detective Monahan when all this was going on?"

"Patrolling the trail about a quarter mile ahead of me."

"On her own?"

"Well, yeah."

"Great. That's really smart of the two of you, Nick. So she could've been the one who ran into these psychos. How did they miss her, anyhow?"

"I don't know for sure. Maybe they weren't ready to go yet, or they got into position after she went by."

"It's a good thing they ran into you instead of your partner," Grabowski said. "You're an ass-kicker and from the sounds of it you barely got away. I have a hard time believing Sarah would have done as well."

"She can take care of herself," Nick said defensively. "She might not have been sucked in by them in the first place."

They were interrupted by a commotion just beyond the yellow crime scene tape. Someone was calling his name.

"Hey, Logan! Detective Logan!"

Jorge Alvarez, the News Journal reporter, was trying to duck under the tape. A cop stood squarely in front of Alvarez, blocking his path. The uniform glanced toward Nick, caught his nod, and stepped aside so Alvarez could slip under the barrier.

The reporter wore a windbreaker that was a couple sizes too big for him and looked as if it had been liberated from a thrift shop, baggy khaki pants, and surf fishing boots. Alvarez couldn't have been more than thirty and yet he was going bald. His hair, what was left of it, refused to conform to and stuck up in random directions. He dropped his notebook, picked it up, hurried a few more steps and dropped his pen, which he promptly lost in the wet sand. Nick suppressed a smile. He loved the thought of an old-fashioned reporter who took notes with a pen on paper, then wrote an article that was printed in an actual newspaper. Nick handed him a new pen.

"George," Grabowski said. "What a displeasure to see you. I suppose this will be all over the front page now."

"Man, I could use a front page story. We've got another round of layoffs coming up at the paper. I hope you got a good story for me or I could be taking your next order at a drive-through window. Would that happen to be Doug Keller, jogger who disappeared from the trail?"

Both Nick and Grabowski exchanged a look.

"I thought so. I've heard the talk around town." The reporter nodded at the body, looking pleased with himself. He waggled the pen Nick had given him. "I may actually have to take notes for this one."

"We can't identify the victim at this time," Grabowski said. "Next of kin —"

"Cut the crap, Grabowski," Alvarez said. "I just need to know by 10 p.m. My absolute deadline. Think we can work that out? Um, please?"

As head of the investigation, Grabowski was also in charge of handling the media. He shrugged.

The fact that Grabowski hadn't said "no" seemed good enough for Alvarez. He asked a few questions about when the body was found, who found it, and whether there was any evidence of how the man had died.

"Have you checked to see if any of the local hospitals are selling organs on Craigslist?" he asked.

"Very funny."

Then Alvarez was stuffing his notebook and pen away, dropping them once or twice on the sand in the process. "I'm gonna go over here to this fisherman," he said, jerking his head toward a knot of onlookers by the water. "See what he can tell me."

"Good riddance," Grabowski said under his breath as Alvarez walked off.

"He's not so bad," Nick said. "He won't screw you over like some of the TV people. Besides, you can use him."

"Yeah?"

"You know how it goes. We help him and he helps us."

Grabowski shook his head. "I'd sooner walk through a pit of leeches than deal with the media." There was a stirring among the Sussex County cops and state troopers parked along the dirt road leading to the fishing spot. Nick thought at first that TV crews were arriving. It was even worse than that. A black Lexus SUV churned to a stop and Mayor Edward Gates stepped out and started down the gravel beach, looking rather excited. The visit was a surprise considering this area was far beyond Rehoboth Beach city limits. But Gates would be one to know bad publicity didn't end at the city line. He liked to say that the beach was the beach was the beach. People on vacation didn't think in terms of town limits.

Nick watched him coming. Gates stopped long enough to take a look at the lumpy bundle the body made on the beach, but made no attempt to lift the tarp. Then he stormed toward Grabowski and Nick, walking so fast his aides had to trot to keep up with him.

"Who is terrorizing my city?" he demanded. He stopped just short of the two detectives and glared at them with flinty eyes. Nick had never seen him so enraged. A vein throbbed in the mayor's temple.

"Well, sir, we uh —"

"Who, damnit! Who? And why are they doing this? The firebombings would be bad enough, but now we've got bodies washing up on the beach! We're talking millions of dollars in damage at the boardwalk and now this. A lot of those merchants aren't coming back."

"The state fire marshal's office is investigating —"

"I know that, detective!" Gates turned and stabbed his hand toward the body at the water's edge. "But you are investigating *that.*."

"The county police asked us to come down after taking a look at the victim's, uh, injuries."

"Who is it?"

"His name is Doug Keller. He's the vacationer who disappeared from the breakwater trail. At least, he's wearing the same clothes Keller's wife described him as wearing when he went out running."

The News Journal reporter had seen the mayor's arrival and was edging closer to hear what they were saying.

"Beat it, George," Nick said, waving him off. Alvarez shrugged and walked away.

Gates was fuming. "This is just wonderful. Arsonists firebombing police cars and the boardwalk, fake ambulances abducting people, and now some maniac is killing people on the Junction and Breakwater Trail."

"One more thing, sir," Grabowski said. "About his injuries. His kidneys have been surgically removed. Just like those people who were picked up by the fake ambulance and who we consequently found floating in the Delaware Bay."

Gates couldn't have looked any more shocked if Grabowski had sucker punched him.

"You mean to say that someone *stole his*

organs?" Gates asked. He made a face like someone watching a scary movie. "My God!"

"That's how it looks to us, sir."

"What are you going to do about it?"

"We are investigating," Grabowski mumbled.

"I almost had them this morning, sir," Nick said.

"What's that?"

"I almost had them," Nick repeated. "The guys who killed that guy over there. They jumped me in the park and did this." He pointed to the gash above his ear. "It's only a matter of time before I run across them again. End of problem."

Gates studied Nick's face uncertainly. Finally he looked away, his anger gone. "You do what you have to do, detective. Stop whoever's doing the killings. As for the arsonists, we'll just have to see what the state fire marshal's office comes up with."

"We'll get them," Nick said. "Like I said, it's only a matter of time before they slip up."

"We haven't got time," Gates snapped at him. "It's the middle of summer! Rehoboth Beach is gonna be a ghost town! If Chief Hawley doesn't come up with some results, there will be some changes around here, believe me. I may have to make Councilman Jenkins the interim chief. We sure as hell won't need so many detectives. So unless you want a bright new career writing parking tickets, go catch these goddman killers."

CHAPTER 23

The text from Nick was to the point. *Chinese. My place. Thirty minutes.* Sarah thought of a dozen reasons not to go. It was already after 9 o'clock, for one thing. But Nick had almost gotten killed today. They could talk about the body found on the beach. And she was hungry. The low-fat frozen dinner she had nuked hours ago had been too disappointing to eat. She texted back. *OK.* Sarah put on a patterned blouse and a pair of yoga pants, then took a look in the full-length mirror on the back of the bedroom door. Too dressy, she thought. She pulled off the clothes and shrugged her way into a pair of jeans and an old linen shirt that was downy soft to the touch.

"Hey, Cagney, what do you think?" Sarah asked

her cat. Cagney was busy rubbing up against her ankles and meowing, as if warning her this was a bad idea. "If you were human, you'd understand. Besides, I've seen how you act when that tomcat comes around."

She checked the mirror again and tugged the shirt tail out so that it hung down over the jeans. Casual. And unlike the yoga pants it showed off less of, well, it wasn't like Nick hadn't noticed her ass before. He wasn't shy about where his eyes wandered.

And why should he be? *Because we're partners working a case together. We have to keep our relationship on a professional level.* Dating your partner only brought trouble. She had heard all the horror stories. She told herself she was only going to see Nick because the two of them had business about the case to discuss. *Yeah, right,* another part of her said. *Then why are you so worried about what you're wearing?*

She wondered if she should bring along a bottle of wine to go with the Chinese carryout. She didn't want to give him the idea that she was trying to fit together something besides the puzzle pieces of the case. She decided on a six pack.

A few minutes later she was standing on the front porch of his beach house. Sarah tugged at her denim shirt again. Tucked or untucked? Untucked. Through the window, she saw Nick kick a pair of running shoes lying on the floor under the couch as he walked over to answer the door.

"Hello, Detective Monahan."

"You look like hell," she said. She tried without success to hide her smile.

"I'm glad you find that so amusing."

"Sorry."

Nick's ear was still cut and bruised from the blow he'd taken during the fight with the two thugs in the park. His face was shadowed with two days of beard and she could have sworn he was wearing the same clothes he'd had on the day before. Nick was one of those men who looked stylishly rumpled and didn't even try, she thought.

"So this is where you live, huh?" Sarah asked, looking around. "Pretty sweet."

"Yeah, I get the place for free all summer. The one catch is that I have to feed their cat."

She looked around and noticed a cat hiding beneath a chair, not quite sure what to make of the stranger in the house. Sarah scooped her up and stroked her head. "Awww. Aren't you a cutie. I hope this big guy is being nice to you."

"We used to have a cat, Karen and I," Nick said, quickly adding an explanation, "My old girlfriend."

"Oh." Sarah wasn't ready yet to let him know Nick Grabowski had told her all about Karen Richardson and Nick's act of revenge against her killer. Instead she asked, "What happened to the cat?"

"I wasn't around enough to take care of him. So I gave him away to some friends."

She stood up. "Where's that Chinese?" she said. "I'm starved."

"I was thinking we might walk out and eat on the beach. It's a beautiful summer night."

Nick was right—it was a great night. The beach right out in front of the house had a million dollar view of the stars and a waxing moon, plus the lights of some ships moving through the channel toward Philadelphia. They spread out a blanket and dove right in. The moonlight was all the light they needed.

With a pair of chopsticks, Nick deftly picked shrimp and broccoli off his plate, bending toward the food in the Asian manner. "A fork?" he asked incredulously, watching her eat. She had been hoping he'd be too hungry to notice.

"I'm more of a Pennsylvania Dutch girl," she explained. "It's hard to eat shoo fly pie with chopsticks."

Nick was such a puzzle, she thought. Just when he seemed to be the biggest oaf on the East Coast he did something like use chopsticks to eat his Chinese food. He was full of surprises.

"Mmm." Nick couldn't wolf it down fast enough. Between bites he managed to steal glances at his partner. Her long blond hair was undone and on one side it was pushed back behind her ear to fall to her shoulder blades, while on the other it spilled down the front of the old denim shirt she wore. Her hair was still damp from the shower and the scent of some fragrant soap clung to her. Until now he hadn't seen Sarah let her hair down. He liked it.

"Did you come up with anything useful today from your sources?" she asked.

He told her about the fingerprints on the candy bar wrapper one of his attackers had left behind. The prints hadn't turned up in any databases.

"If we lift prints from any eventual crime scenes those prints might help us nail the fat one, whoever he is," she said.

"Exactly. Until then, they really don't do us much good. One thing I did find out today is that our friends from the park may be doing some extracurricular work."

She paused between bites of lo mein. "What do you mean?"

"I did some asking around today. I've been hearing how a skinny cop with black hair and a fat cop were rounding up homeless people last winter." Nick had been surprised at first that a beach resort had homeless people.

She nearly dropped her fork. "What?"

"Yep. I was told they were loading these people into a white van, never to return. Nobody questioned it because they were cops. At least, they were dressed as cops."

"Maybe that worked so well that they tried a phony ambulance next."

"Bingo."

"My God. If it's those same two guys who attacked you in the park, there's no telling how many people they've killed."

"Exactly."

She thought about it.

"Cops?"

"Yeah. The weird thing is that nobody questioned it."

They finished eating and Nick handed Sarah her fortune cookie. "Don't forget to add 'in bed' at the end of your fortune."

" 'He who is generous will always have many friends ... in bed.' "

"Mine says, 'You are very creative ... in bed.' Now that's a good fortune. Who writes these things?"

"Old Chinese philosophers. They're very wise ... in bed."

He settled back on the blanket and closed his eyes. Full now of food and a couple of beers, he had a chance to feel just how wiped out he was.

"Tired?" Sarah asked.

"Yeah. I don't think either one of us has been sleeping much lately. I'm also a little sore from my slugfest with those creeps."

His eyes were still closed, but he opened them when he felt her weight settle beside him. "Maybe I can help," she said. "Lean forward." Her hands began to knead the knotted muscles in his shoulders.

Uh oh. You know where this is going, warned a little voice inside his head. He ignored it.

"How does that feel?" she asked.

"Good. Very, very good."

After a while she stopped. Nick felt light as a bag of feathers. He turned around and gave her a quick kiss on the lips. "Thanks," he said.

Double uh oh, that little voice said. Why did you have to go and do that?

She was staring into his eyes. They drew closer and kissed again, long and deep this time.

Stop it right now. You'd better stop, you idiot —

He kissed her throat, then the lobes of her ears. His lips tasted the milky whiteness of her throat. Her hands slid up beneath his T-shirt and caressed his chest.

Stop —

His breath was ragged and quick as his fingers fumbled with the buttons of her old shirt.

"I don't know about this, Nick," Sarah whispered.

"I've never had sex on the beach, either. But nobody's around."

"That's not what I mean. Jobs and relationships don't mix. I think this is going to be a mistake."

"It's too late." His lips moved lower and a delicious shudder ran through her. "That ship has sailed."

• • •

"She ain't got no clothes on," Mike said, killing the engine and tugging his helmet off.

"Bullshit," said the other boy, Willy. Like he was supposed to believe there was a woman lying outside tonight with no clothes on. But he didn't like the look on his friend's face. Even in the moonlight he could see that his friend was scared. "What the hell is wrong with you, dude?"

"Take a look," Mike said.

Willy got off his own bike and moved closer to where his friend was pointing. This was private property out here, but it was a great place to ride. He saw the pale white body outlined against the muddy shore of the saltwater creek.

He didn't have to go any nearer to know she was dead. And naked.

There was nothing sexy about it. Just gross. Her skin looked like bread that had been soaking in a pan of water too long. Her eyes were open, staring sightlessly at the sky. An old tire lay near her head, the blackness of it contrasting against her white flesh.

"At first I thought she was swimming or

something," the other boy said.

"She's dead," Willy announced, as if he were an expert on judging corpses.

"What should we do?" Mike asked.

"Call the police."

"If we do that, they'll ask what we were doing out here. We're trespassing, you know. There are about a million signs that say no dirt bikes."

Willy hadn't thought about that. "I think the cops will give us immunity," he said. "What do they call it — diplomatic immunity or something? I mean, it is a dead body."

"Yeah, maybe they'll give us diplomatic immunity," the other boy said. "She looks totally gross."

Then without getting off his dirt bike he leaned over and vomited on the sand.

• • •

Sarah took a few extra minutes in the shower, letting the water run over her as she got a good steam going. It helped that the fancy beach house had a deluxe shower. She wasn't in any hurry to get out and face Nick. *Oh boy, did we really do that last night?*

People always made a big deal out of sex on the beach. Well, it *was* sexy. What nobody talked about was the sand. It had gotten into some interesting places. She turned up the shower.

When she got out, Nick was just getting off the phone.

"That was Grabowski checking in," he said. "Good morning, Sunshine." Sarah was wrapped in nothing more than a towel, and he took his time looking her up and down.

"What's the matter, didn't you see enough last night?"

To her surprise, Nick came over and hugged her. "The best part was waking up this morning and having you here."

Sarah blushed. "Thank you, I guess." It didn't say much for her love life that Nick's words were some of the most romantic that anyone had said to her.

She pulled open a drawer. The beach house was completely stocked right down to clean T shirts in the dresser drawers. Fortunately, the lady of the house was just her size. "Out. I'm getting dressed."

Nick went out, but came rushing in a minute later.

"That was Grabowski again. Some kids on dirt bikes just found Tara Conrad's body. The chief is calling a press conference. Guess who he wants up there at the mic?"

"Great. I guess I need to find a nicer T shirt."

CHAPTER 24

Later that morning, Grubb drove the white van like a maniac down Route 1 on their way back into Rehoboth. From the passenger seat, Fat Boy watched as Grubb cut off a gray-haired old dude in a Cadillac. The old guy laid on the horn. Grubb flipped him off. "Better watch it, buddy!" Grubb shouted. "Your organs are dry rotted, but we could still turn you into beef jerky!"

"You could slow down a little, Grubb," Fat Boy pleaded. His stomach felt as if a small tropical storm was churning inside. Too many Moon Pies, he thought. He had shoplifted several boxes of them from a gas station while Grubb flirted with the girl at the counter—more like *scared* the girl at the counter. Grubb's driving didn't help his stomach any. "Hey, Grubb, slow down, man."

"I'm driving here, Fat Boy. You can shut up or roll out and waddle."

No use arguing when Grubb was in one of his moods, which was nearly all the time now.

Right after Doc Kreeger cut out Tara Conrad's kidneys, they had dumped the body into the Lewes-Rehoboth Canal. They were in a hurry to get the organs to the Philadelphia airport and hadn't taken the time to weigh her down with chain. Already, Doc Kreeger had called to chew them out for being sloppy because some kids on dirt bikes had found the body washed up. He said it had been on the news. He and Grubb had just driven to the airport and back, so he was too tired to worry about Kreeger not being happy.

Fat Boy sighed, fished under the seat, and grabbed the last of the Moon Pies. Behind him in the van, several milk crates held empty booze bottles. The "empty" part helped explain Grubb's erratic driving.

"Grubb, what are you going to use all those bottles for?" Fat Boy asked, chewing his Moon Pie.

"Unless you're in the band, I can't tell you," Grubb said. He was driving fast, knuckles white on the steering wheel. Wired. "This is strictly Dog Smell's business."

"Are you going to breathe fire on stage or something?"

"Dog Smell doesn't need cheap tricks like that, Fatty. We let the music speak."

"Sure." Fat Boy thought a minute. He wasn't the sharpest tack in the box, but he wasn't a complete idiot. A band of arsonists had been running around the city. He had seen on TV where they had used Molotov cocktails to set part of the boardwalk on fire.

Fat Boy glanced over a Grubb, who was staring intently at the road with eyes that burned with a crazed blue light. He decided he didn't really want to know anything about Grubb's plans.

"Don't worry about the bottles," Grubb said, as if reading Fat Boy's mind. "They won't be there by tomorrow morning."

"Whatever," Fat Boy said. He sighed. What he really needed now was a chocolate milkshake to settle his stomach.

• • •

Nick decided to hang at the back of the room during the press conference. Most of the media people there were from out-of-town, drawn to the story like moths to a flame. A reign of terror was great news fodder, and a trip to the beach was just an added bonus. They herded into the room, angling for the best position while trying not to mess up their hair. A cameraman shoved Nick while forcing his way toward the front.

Nick shot an elbow into the man's ribs. The cameraman turned angrily, took one look at Nick, and melted away into the crowd.

"This should be something," said a small, birdlike woman with a reporter's notebook who had appeared at Nick's side. "I can't believe that cult of devil worshippers is killing people. This is amazing."

"Devil worshippers? Huh. I heard from a reliable source that a gang has been stealing sexual organs, drying them, and shipping them to Asia for use as aphrodisiacs."

"Wow, I haven't heard that one, although I've heard just about everything else," she said. The woman extended her hand and Nick shook it. "I'm Marcia Powers from the Dover Patch. Who are you with?"

Nick was about to say, *I'm a cop*, but thought better of it. "I'm with The New York Times."

"Oh!" she said, her eyes sparkling in a flirtatious way. Had he said something sexy? "This story is really getting big."

"There's a guy here from National Geographic, too," Nick said. "I think he's doing a story on the, uh, environmental impact this is having."

"Ohh," she exclaimed, looking around. "Where is he?"

Nick pointed out Bob Grabowski, who was standing a few feet away beside the door.

"Maybe I'll just say hello," the woman said.

"Find out what angle he's taking. National Geographic? Amazing." She moved off and started chatting with Grabowski, who looked puzzled as hell.

The room quieted as Mayor Gates walked in, followed by Chief Hawley and Detective Monahan, all three of them solemn as priests in the harsh glow of TV lights.

"Good afternoon," Mayor Gates began, and introduced himself to the crowd. Out of the corner of his eye, Nick could see the woman from the Dover Patch had stopped talking with Grabowski and was already busy scribbling notes. "As you know, there have been several abductions reported from the area, with the bodies of the victims consequently turning up . . . "

Nick watched Sarah as she stood calmly at Mayor Gates' elbow, waiting for her turn at the podium. He knew from experience that she was going to have the hardest job, because it would be up to her to answer questions from this pack of news hounds. No wonder Grabowski had looked relieved when Chief Hawley appointed her to the task instead of him.

Nick watched her with pride. She was waiting calmly, her blond hair pulled back into a business-like style. She wore a dark blazer and tan slacks, thanks to the owner's wardrobe at the beach house. Her white blouse was open at the top, right about where Nick had been running his tongue last night.

She saw him watching her and gave him a small smile. He knew without a doubt that he was becoming awfully fond of Detective Sarah Monahan.

Now Hawley was talking, saying something about how every effort was being made to catch the perpetrators. No mention yet of bodies with their organs carved out. The press could hardly wait, their light stands and camera tripods clicking together like gnashing teeth.

"— our department has focused its attention —"

Nick was mulling over what Alvarez had said out on the beach about checking the hospitals to see if they were selling organs online. The reporter had been kidding, but Alvarez had a point. If someone really was carving people up for their organs, there had to be fairly sophisticated surgical machinery and skill being used. Cutting out a kidney wasn't quite the same as stripping a car on the shoulder of Route 1.

How did the goth and his fat sidekick fit in if this truly was a sophisticated scheme to steal organs? The goth handled himself well in a fight, but Nick couldn't picture him with a scalpel. It could be those two were only being used to bring in the victims.

If this truly was a human chop shop ring, whoever was in charge wasn't looking at long-term profits. Anyone could see the police would eventually figure out what was happening. How many bodies might there have been before the last four? What about the street people who had been rounded up? None of their bodies had been discovered. Nick felt a chill. The chop shop might have been going on for months beforehand. No telling how many people had fallen victim to the organ thief's scalpel. Anyone headed to the beach had a whole lot more to worry about now than sunburn, no matter what the mayor and police chief said.

"— let me introduce Detective Sarah Monahan," Hawley was saying. Nick perked up. He wished he could help her somehow, but here at the rear of the conference room all he could do was glare at the backs of the reporters' heads. "She will do her best to answer any questions you have about the investigation."

Hawley was sly. He liked the TV cameras and the publicity to a point. But he didn't want this mess. Turn it over to Sarah and let her do the hard part.

The press corps surged forward as a mass and started shouting questions. Nick had to resist the urge to bull through the crowd and wring the necks of a couple of the pushiest TV reporters at the front of the room.

Nonplussed, Detective Monahan spoke calmly but firmly into the microphone, "One at a time, people. You'll all have an opportunity to have your questions answered." She pointed out the woman from the Dover Patch, who was standing on her tip toes, waving her notebook in the air. "What's your question, please?"

The reporter said shouted across the room: "Can you tell us anything about the possibility that gangs are stealing human reproductive organs and drying them for export to Asia?"

A murmur ran through the crowd. To Nick's dismay, the other reporters didn't appear amused by her outlandish question. Instead, they acted as if they were concerned because they had missed something.

Sarah blinked a couple of times before she could answer.

"We aren't considering any such theories at this time," she said, already picking another reporter out of the crowd. "Next question, please."

"Detective, is it true that an undercover agent on the bicycle path had to fight off the abductors to avoid becoming a victim himself?"

Nick bridled at the question. He'd been trying to capture the bad guys, not keep himself from becoming an involuntary organ donor.

"There was contact between an undercover officer and two potential suspects," Sarah said slowly, picking her words. "I would not characterize it as the officer 'fighting off' the suspects —"

"Why weren't there more officers present to assist him?"

"The officer was on routine patrol," Sarah said. "Since that incident, procedures have been taken to ensure that if these same suspects make contact again —"

"Who was the officer involved?" someone shouted.

"We cannot divulge —"

"Was it Detective Nick Logan?"

"As I said, we cannot divulge —"

"Why was an officer who was investigated for murder assigned as a decoy?"

"There was no decoy situation involved in the incident," Sarah went on calmly, returning order to the press conference.

Nick knew Sarah wasn't telling the whole truth, but she was lying effortlessly. Only he and Sarah knew the real story, which was that they had taken a chance, hoping to lead the abductors out on their own. Whether he wanted to admit it or not, deep down Nick knew it had nearly gotten him killed. It wasn't up to Sarah to announce such things at a press conference. At a time like this, the public needed to have faith in the police, not doubts.

He noticed the woman from the Dover Patch was still scribbling. She stopped now and then to do some filming with her iPad.

Nick couldn't handle any more. He shoved his way out of the room. He stood out in the empty hallway.

"Tough crowd, huh?"

Nick whirled around at the voice. It was only Grabowski. He must have slipped out when Nick wasn't looking. He was leaning against the wall, his ear to a crack in the doorway to hear what was happening in the conference room.

"I want to catch those bastards," Nick said. "That's all. Those people in that room want to make me out to be some kind of incompetent cop."

Grabowski pushed off from the wall and laid a hand on his shoulder. "Screw 'em. What I want to know is, why did that girl think I worked for National Geographic, and what's a Dover Patch? It sounds like something a stripper would wear to cover up the illegal parts."

Located as it was near the Air Force Base, Dover had a few topless bars.

"The Dover Patch is a hyperlocal news site."

"You don't say. Huh. I like my definition better. It leaves more to the imagination."

• • •

Kreeger had the suitcase open on the bed and was tossing clothes inside. Calvin Klein briefs to impress the ladies, socks, jeans, a few T-shirts and a couple pairs of shorts. Where he was going he wouldn't need much.

In the background the TV was on, tuned to the live press conference at police headquarters. He could hear the blond policewoman saying, "We do have a description of two possible suspects in the abductions, but we don't want to disclose at this time what they look like."

He was a little distracted from his packing by the fact that she was attractive for a cop. Then he shook his head to clear it, and went back to filling his suitcase. How many pairs of socks should you bring when going on the run in a foreign country?

Kreeger could have told the sexy cop who the police were looking for: a crazy goth kid and a fat, candy bar-eating slob. If the police picked up Grubb and Fat Boy, Kreeger knew his own arrest would soon follow. Which was why he was packing the suitcase. He planned on being someplace where the long arm of the law wouldn't reach. He tossed in a bottle of sunscreen. Despite living at Rehoboth Beach, Kreeger had never much liked the sun, but spending the rest of his life in Costa Rica was better than spending it in, say, Serbia. Of course, even Serbia would be better than a prison cell.

Or the electric chair. Did they still do that in Delaware? He vaguely recalled his grandfather talking about going to see the last public hanging in Harrington, way out in the middle of the

Delmarva Peninsula. Whole families went to see the hanging. They brought picnic baskets and blankets. You could still find postcards of the scaffolding in some of the local antique shops. Kreeger gulped.

"— we are trying to determine a motive for the organs being taken," the policewoman was saying on TV, answering a reporter's question. "We do not have one at this time."

Kreeger walked out of the bedroom and stood for a moment in front of the television, transfixed. It gave him a weird feeling of unreality to be watching a press conference about crimes he had committed. He tried to assess how it made him feel, what emotions or moral chords had been plucked. Nothing resonated. He didn't feel any guilt about harvesting the organs from the people Grubb and Fat Boy had brought him. By the time they were on the operating table, they were no longer real people to him. Some switch flipped in his brain and professional interest took over. The victims became mere collections of flesh and bone, blood and tissue, and of course, kidneys, livers, corneas and so forth, which all had their value in the marketplace.

As Kreeger watched the live press conference, the camera man panned slowly around the conference room at the crowd of media people who had come to grill the police. The steel double doors at the back of the room opened just wide enough for a man to slip inside. Kreeger's breath caught in his chest. It was that big, tough-looking cop whose picture had been in the Cape Gazette for catching those muggers on the Junction and Breakwater Trail. His eyes flicked up and locked with the camera, so that Kreeger was caught by the man's stare.

I'm coming to get you, those eyes said. I know you're watching this, asshole, and I'm gonna nail you.

Kreeger took an involuntary step back from the TV, but the camera had already swung past the cop. He hurried to finish packing.

He had to be ready. Everything would come crashing down at once, he knew. When it happened, he'd be on a plane out of the country.

But first there were a few more organs to harvest. Just a few more. Life as an exile would be expensive. As valuable as the organs were, it meant the difference between spending the rest of his days in a grass shack on the beach, or in an oceanfront villa.

It was a chance he had to take, but that big cop worried him.

He shut the suitcase and fastened the various zippers and straps. Just a couple more harvests to go—maybe three or four—then nothing but sunshine and pina coladas all day. His only regret was that he'd have to leave the Aston Martin behind. If things worked out in his new life, he might be able to hire someone to drive him around.

CHAPTER 25

"We're going to stick out like nuns at a biker convention," Sarah insisted.

They cruised past the Cracked Saloon, and Nick had to admit he felt uneasy, watching all these kids paying their cover at the door so they could enter the club and see Dog Smell play.

Thanks to one of the younger summer cops, they'd heard about the Cracked Saloon. It had a rep for hard core music. You weren't going to find any tourists there sipping tropical drinks and listening to Jimmy Buffet tribute bands. But there was a good chance you could find a goth there. Maybe even the one they were looking for.

"It's dark inside," Nick said. "Nobody will even know we're there."

"I'm not sure about this, Nick. If this is the same goth we're looking for, he's going to spot us."

"That's the idea," Nick said. "I want him scared. He starts getting scared and he starts screwing up."

Nick had decided against a full court press for tonight. If he recognized the rocker as the same man who had attacked him in the park, it would be sufficient grounds for arresting him. On the other hand, Nick would look like a fool if he had a whole team of officers come in to arrest the wrong guy. That's why he had talked Sarah into going to the club with him. He wanted to see for himself first.

The thing about beach real estate is that it's so valuable that there really aren't any bad neighborhoods. The area around the Cracked Saloon came close. There were warehouses, pawn shops and rundown houses. That didn't keep the crowd away, because for a two-block radius around the Cracked Saloon there wasn't a parking space to be found. To Nick's surprise, the cars were mostly second-hand Hondas with a few older European imports mixed in. Mom and dad's hand-me-down cars. It seemed to Nick that these alternative music fans were just suburban kids playing dress up.

Nick dumped his pickup in an alley behind the club.

"You can't park here," Sarah said.

"Watch me," Nick said. The only vehicle in the alley was one of those Japanese crotch-rocket motorcycles and it was small enough to squeeze around the truck if whoever owned it needed to get out.

Nick had on jeans, boots and a black T-shirt— just what he might have worn splitting firewood. Sarah wore a slinky black outfit more suited to a nightclub, but at least the color was right. This was not a pastels kind of crowd.

They flashed their shields at a fat man in a biker jacket who was working the door. He nodded and they were inside.

It was like walking into a vortex. Smoke filled the air and tracers of red and blue light cut through it. Music so loud it shook Nick's teeth. Dark as a cave. The leather-clad kids around them may as well have been bats. He just prayed his niece hadn't picked this night to go club hopping.

Nick stood for a moment until the sensory overload went away and he could get his bearings. He grabbed Sarah's hand — she didn't resist — and worked his way toward the bar through a sea of punk rock fans. In the flash of multi-colored strobe lights he glimpsed what could have been a sideshow of carnival freaks. He saw earrings, nose rings, purple lipstick, a tattoo of a lizard on the back of a hand, a choker necklace of what looked like human teeth. He reached the bar and put a hand on it, like a swimmer coming to a diving raft.

"What a place!" Sarah shouted into his ear. Even then he could barely hear her.

Safe by the bar, Nick peered toward the stage. It was so smoky and dark the band was hard to see. The singer finally stepped into a pool of light and Nick tensed. *Bingo*.

He bent down to Sarah's ear. "That's him on stage. That's the son-of-a-bitch jumped me."

The goth's black hair was stringy with sweat and when he whipped his head droplets of moisture flew into the crowd. He was stray-cat thin so that his bony shoulder blades and even the points of his rib cage protruded through the sleeveless white T-shirt he wore. At the same time, he projected a wiry strength. This guy was all sinew and bone. He had on black leather pants and enormous engineer boots. There was no mistaking him.

Nick grabbed the bartender. "What's the name of that guy up on stage?"

"Grubb."

"Grubb what?"

"Just Grubb."

Up on stage, the goth was wringing the microphone and singing so hard flecks of spit sprayed from his twisted, angry mouth.

Producer said he didn't like our sound,
Tonight I'll put him six feet in the ground.
Light a pyre to his bad taste,
Use the fire, lay it all to waste!

It's all about money, all about greed
You see, it ain't good music that you need
Dye your hair purple, jump up and down,
Burn the producers who wanna own this sound.

"His lyrics are incendiary," Sarah shouted into his ear.

"Ha, ha."

Nick had never heard music quite like it. To his way of thinking there were four categories of music: country, rap, rock and classical. This wasn't any of the above.

It didn't seem to him that Dog Smell was very good, and the goth kid wasn't much of a singer. Basically, the band was good at being loud. Grubb was a screamer, a shouter, an angry, juiced-up half-assed poet.

The audience loved it. Up close to the stage, kids danced wildly in the cramped space, jarring against each other, bumping and grinding as the goth on stage screeched out his songs. Along the edges of the room tables had been set up, and groups huddled around them, smoking cigarettes, drinking beer. Nick had the feeling they were less into the music than the scene.

Nick still hadn't seen the fat guy. Where was he? Maybe Dog Smell wasn't his favorite band, either.

Grubb gnawed at the microphone like a rabid animal and his face contorted as he sang:

The mayor he's got a little project
Doesn't want the city to be a reject
This weekend he'll open the new storefront
On TV that day they'll see it all burnt.

It's got plate glass windows and brass rails
When he sees all the ashes he'll shit nails.
Inside those shops there's gonna be a bomb
What a fire sale they'll have when I'm done!

We want anarchy! Not a tourist factory!
Burn it all! Bomb it all! Spread the misery!

"This guy is spooky," Sarah said.

Nick nodded. He had to agree that the lyrics were unsettling, and seeing this crazy singer screaming the words made it that much worse. The time had come to put the fear of God into this kid. "Come on," he said. "Let's go squeeze his nuts a little."

They worked their way to the edge of the room, then began to weave through the row of tables toward the stage. Nick was sure they stuck out in the crowd, but it didn't worry him. It was about to work in their favor. Grubb was too wrapped up in shrieking out his songs, and the stage lights shining up at him must have been blinding.

Nobody seemed to pay them much attention. In a couple of minutes they had worked their way to the edge of the stage, between the speakers and the wall. From where they stood they could feel the heat and energy radiating off the dance floor a few feet away.

Grubb had his eyes shut and was nodding his head in time to the music—if you could call it that—as the guitarist played a few chords warming up into the next song. He was so close Nick could have lunged out and grabbed one of Grubb's ankles.

"Hey, Grubb!" Nick shouted. No reaction, just that too-thin face with the eyes screwed shut nodding in time to the beat. "Grubb!"

Finally, Dog Smell's lead singer opened his eyes, swung round to Nick. Blinking, nothing registering.

"Remember me?" Nick shouted, his heavy voice edging out the music.

Grubb turned even paler, if that was possible for a guy who lived at the beach.

"Shit!" he howled directly into the microphone, and took off running. He made it beyond the stage lights and disappeared into the darkness. Nick and Sarah swarmed up on stage and went after him. Beyond the bright lights of the stage was a dark vacuum that Nick couldn't see into.

"Where did he go?" Nick demanded of the remaining members of Dog Smell. The band stared blankly at them, hands drooping on their instruments. Feedback screeched in the background.

"Who?" one of the musicians asked. Nick couldn't tell if he was stupid or monumentally stoned.

"Grubb!"

"I guess he ran out the back." He stared at Nick, not seeming to see him.

The crowd had spotted Nick, all right, and was shouting that he had interrupted the show. Things were about to get ugly. He could see a couple of bouncers moving toward the stage. "C'mon," he said to Sarah, and darted toward the darkness beyond the lights.

Couldn't see a damn thing. His hands touched a block wall, he felt along it, located a door, shoved down on the latch bar —

He bulled out the door with his head down and fists up, half expecting Grubb to be out there with a baseball bat or a broken beer bottle or a knife. Sarah was right behind him, her gun out. She was backing him up, doing this by the book.

It didn't matter. Grubb was gone. Vanished into thin night air.

Nick looked up and down the alley. Nothing.

"Where the hell —"

The motorcycle. He remembered that a bike had been parked in the alley. It was gone.

"Son of a bitch!" Nick shouted.

The two bouncers crowded their way through the door. They were big, ugly guys, one of them the biker-type who had let them into the club.

Their eyes went to Sarah's drawn gun, then to Nick, who had his feet planted, ready to swing.

"We're cops," Nick said.

"Look, just 'cuz you guys are cops," one of the bouncers started to say. "That don't mean —"

"Shut up," Nick said coldly. The man fell silent. "You know Grubb? Does he come around here a lot?"

"Sometimes. He's in the band, you know."

"Give him a message from me. Tell him I'm going to cut out his kidneys, pack them in ice, and send them to some more deserving human being."

Sarah was staring at him like she thought he'd gone nuts. Completely off the rails. Maybe he had.

"Who should we say the message is from?" the bouncer asked.

"He'll know," Nick said. "I'm one of his biggest fans."

• • •

Ron Rodale thought he smelled gasoline, which was strange, because the only place it could have been coming from was his car. But it was parked thirty feet down the street. He opened the front door and looked out at his shiny black Lexus, just to check on it. Huh. The street lights shone down on the car, which was undisturbed. He shut the door, sniffed. There it was again. A whiff of gasoline. Strange, considering he didn't own anything else that used gas, not even a lawnmower.

His postage stamp sized backyard didn't require much mowing. Rodale and his wife lived in a new beachfront townhouse built to look rustic, right down to the weathered cedar shake siding. Character with all the modern amenities. And priced accordingly.

Rodale sniffed at his shirt sleeves. Had he spilled some gasoline on himself filling up the car? But that had been yesterday . . .

• • •

Outside in the dark, Grubb was hiding in the shrubs. He felt surprisingly calm, considering that crazy cop had flushed him out of the Cracked Saloon just an hour ago. A more rational person would have laid low after that, but Grubb wasn't going to change his plans for tonight on account of what had happened. He was looking forward to roasting Rodale too much.

He had seen the record producer open the front door and look out, as if the man sensed something. Detected the danger. But the door closed and after a moment Grubb's worry was replaced by a sense of glee and he had to fight the urge to cackle wildly at the joke he was about to play on Ron Rodale. Maybe Dog Smell wasn't good enough for Rodale Records, but the band's lead singer wasn't one not to take it personally. He planned to light up Rodale's house like one giant flaming G chord. End of song. End of story.

He worked his way out from behind the bushes, being careful not to make them rustle. Damn, but he felt like Davy Crockett. Grubb hustled up the front steps and dribbled gasoline over Rodale's front door and on the stair landing.

Make it a good show, he told himself.

Tonight it was strictly a one-man show. He had planned to bring the whole band along, but after what had happened back at the Cracked Saloon, he decided against it. How the hell had that cop from the park found him? Grubb could deal with him later. He'd whip up a grilled cop sandwich, then barbecue that bitch he was with.

He crept around the side of the house, being careful not to let the liter bottles in his rucksack clank together. He opened another bottle and poured gasoline on the shrubs, splashed some at the windows. Everything had to burn! Giggles escaped his lips and Grubb had to put a hand over his own mouth to stifle the noise. Roasted record producer, coming right up! Hot hits, baby!

• • •

There it was again, Rodale thought. He smelled gasoline. Very strange.

Alarm systems were standard in houses in this neighborhood, and Rodale walked over to the control panel and checked his. The red light was on, indicating the system was armed. He wasn't sure what burglars had to do with gasoline, but he was beginning to feel uneasy. His wife was upstairs sleeping and he was half tempted to wake her up, ask if she'd spilled gasoline cleaning a paint brush or something. It was driving him nuts.

Rodale decided to shrug it off. He went into his home office and sorted through a pile of demo CDs. He liked to do this, bring music to his weekend home and listen to it all the way through, the way he didn't have time to do during the week at the office. Bands sometimes hid a gem of a song behind a lot of bad music just because they weren't good judges of their best work.

He picked up a demo CD by that band called Dog Smell, popped it into the player.

Set this city on fire! Pour the gasoline, yeah!
This place must burn. Burn it down, yeah!

Rodale hit the stop button, popped the CD out. Truly bad music. That screwy band member who had dropped the demo off left his poor secretary with jittery nerves the rest of the day. Really creeped her out. Most musicians had egos the size of Mt. Everest and they could be haughty or even downright rude, but they weren't dangerous. That guy from Dog Smell was another story. He looked nuts. Rodale tossed the CD into the trash and selected another.

But he couldn't concentrate. He kept hearing the lyrics from the Dog Smell song in his head: *Pour the gasoline, yeah!* Just then something hit his front door.

And exploded.

• • •

Grubb stood in the small front yard with a Molotov cocktail in one hand and a lighter in the other. Anyone passing in the street or looking out a window could have seen him, but he was beyond caring. In thirty seconds it would be too late to stop him.

The strip of rag stuffed into the bottle was damp with gasoline and Grubb held it carefully away from himself as he flicked the lighter and lit the fuse. The rag caught instantly, flared, and Grubb let loose with a wild cackle as he pulled back his arm to hurl the bomb.

"You should have signed us, asshole!" he shouted.

The flaming cocktail crashed against the door. Fire filled the porch and spread through the gasoline-drenched shrubbery beds, then licked up the walls. In seconds the house was a fireball.

Grubb had wanted the band here for this. He had planned on having everyone stand out on the lawn as the house burned and sing, just like kids around a campfire. *Kumbaya, baby!* That damn cop had ruined his plans. So Grubb stood alone and shrieked out a solitary song as people began appearing in doorways, shouting about the fire.

Set this city on fire! Pour the gasoline, yeah!
This place must burn. Burn it down, yeah!
It's the only way those drones will ever learn.
Set it on fire! Yeah! Make it burn, make it burn!

"Get him!" Grubb heard someone shouting. "He set the house on fire. Somebody get him!"

In the firelight he could see people running toward him. He backed away from the flames, which were beginning to sear his face and his bare hands with their intense heat. Then Grubb turned and ran for his motorcycle. Before anyone could catch him he was down the street, rolling the accelerator forward and laughing like a madman.

CHAPTER 26

Nick showed up at her door with a pizza.

"Some girls get flowers," Sarah said as she unlocked the door to her apartment. "I get pepperoni and mushroom."

"The florist shop was closed but Grottos was open. It's the least I could do for the night we've had. I can't believe that freak got away. I'm losing my touch."

"You had a little help losing him," she pointed out. "I was there, too."

"Yeah, but you haven't let him get away twice like I have. First on the trail, then tonight at that goddamn club. I can't believe that guy."

"He won't get far." Sarah forced a smile. "Let's eat this before it gets cold. I've got some leftover salad in the fridge we can have with it."

"I don't suppose you have any cold beer?"

"I may have a couple of bottles in the fridge for emergency purposes."

"Me stopping by with a pizza is an emergency."

He sighed, plunked the pizza box down on Sarah's kitchen table. "I could get used to this," he said. "I like the idea of having someone around to make sure I eat my salad."

"Then maybe you should move back in with your mother."

Sarah was busy taking things out of the refrigerator. Nick opened the beers. Dogfish Head IPA, which was growing on him.

"Mmmm."

"Mmm mmm."

Aside from that, neither of them spoke for a minute. They were too busy eating. In the night's excitement, Nick had forgotten just how hungry he was.

He finished his first slice, grabbed another. Sarah was doing the same. He watched her secretly as she closed her eyes to take a bite of the crust. What a beautiful woman. He could hardly believe she was having a late-night pizza with him.

"Let's try either Cape Henlopen or the beach trail again tomorrow," she said. "I can play decoy."

Nick shook his head. "Too dangerous. Besides, he might know what you look like. You were at the club tonight, and you were all over TV today."

"Grubb didn't get a good look at me, and he doesn't seem like the type who watches the TV news or reads the paper. I think he'd have all the more reason to come after me if he knows I'm a cop. It gives him a chance to thumb his nose in our face."

"That's what I'm afraid of," Nick said. "He's a maniac —"

"It's worth a shot."

"I don't know . . . "

"Do you have any better ideas?"

"Not really."

"Besides, it won't just be the two of us. We'll have teams throughout the park."

"If you're willing to do it."

Sarah smiled. "Nick, you're worried about me, aren't you?"

"Hell, yes. You should be worried about you, too. Grubb is bad news."

"You're sweet."

"Thank you."

"If I didn't have a mouthful of pizza, I'd kiss you."

"Save me for dessert," he said. Nick grabbed another slice of pizza. "God, Sarah. What are we doing? I mean, where are we heading with this?"

"With the pizza? You're right, we'll have to run a couple extra miles to work it off."

He laughed. "You know what I mean."

She took a sip of beer. "Let's just see what happens, Nick. One day at a time. For instance, I haven't even invited you to stay over tonight."

Nick blanched. "Oh."

"I know it's not the smartest thing, sleeping with your partner. That's all you hear, how dumb it is. It probably won't help either of our careers."

"We won't have careers if we don't catch those two assholes, Grubb and Fat Boy," Nick reminded her.

"True. What I'm trying to say is that sometimes you can't play by the rules. You of all people should know that. And while we're on the topic of rules, my biggest one is not to have any secrets. No skeletons in the closet." She paused. "From what I understand, you have something you should tell me."

Nick looked past her at the kitchen wall. Of course she had heard by now. "What do you mean?"

"Tell me about Karen."

Nick gulped, kept staring at the kitchen wall. There was a fork in his hand and he began toying with it, tapping it against the open palm of his other hand. In the silence of the kitchen it sounded like a drum.

He wasn't sure he could do this. "If you already know, then why are you asking me?"

"Because I want to hear it from you, Nick. First hand. We can't have secrets. Not ones this big, at least."

He nodded, brought his gaze from the wall back to Sarah's face. And he began to tell her about Karen. How they had been in love and she had been murdered when she walked in on a burglary at their home. He began slowly, but the past began to rush out, all coming back to him at once. Nick had never told anyone what had truly happened, and as the story came out he felt a huge pressure seep from his mind, another weight being slowly lifted from his chest.

Then he got to the part about finding Wallace Green. "Not long after I got there, he jumped out the window," Nick said.

When he finished his story, Sarah held out her open hand and said, "I'll take that."

"What?" Then he realized she was talking about the fork in his hands. He had somehow twisted it as he spoke. Nick handed it over.

"I don't know what to say," Sarah said. "So I guess I'm not going to say anything. Thank you for telling me, Nick. I know it wasn't easy."

"I feel better now. And thank you for not asking if Karen's killer really committed suicide."

"If you say he jumped out a window, that's good enough for me. If you told me that you threw him out the window, that would be okay, too."

"Yes," he said. "Thank you for listening. You know, I guess I'm not much better than the bad guys we're trying to catch."

"No, don't tell yourself that, Nick. The circumstances are different. It's not the same at all. Sometimes the bad guys have it coming."

They both sat quietly, staring at the remains of their dinner. Finally Sarah spoke up, "Let's go into the living room."

"Why?"

She began to pull off her T-shirt. "Dessert," she said.

•••

"One more time," Dr. Kreeger said. "That's all you've got to do it. One more time. Then we're out of this for good."

Grubb shrugged. "Hey, why stop? I'll get you as many donors as you need."

"I don't know," Fat Boy said. "This isn't too smart, going to the same place all the time. It's a sure way to get caught."

"You two need to stop being such a buzz kill. The cops couldn't catch the clap in a whorehouse," Grubb said, cackling at his own joke. True, they had tracked him to the Cracked Saloon last night, but he hadn't told Fat Boy or Dr. Kreeger yet. He was still feeling too good after turning that record producer into a crispy critter. No need to spoil the mood.

"They're going to catch on," Fat Boy insisted.

His voice was whiny, like a little boy. A *fat* little boy. "Why don't we just round you up more street people?"

Kreeger shook his head. "No good. We cut half of them open and then find out we can't use them because their organs are pickled or diseased. We need quality."

"Prime beef," Grubb said. "We need some health nuts cruising the Junction and Breakwater Trail or Cape Henlopen State Park."

"This is crazy."

"I've got a plan to get around any surveillance they have," Grubb said.

Kreeger looked up. "What's that?"

"It's called a canoe."

"I'm not getting in any tippy canoes," Fat Boy said.

"Shut up, Fatty Face, or we'll cut you up instead," Grubb hissed. "How about it, Doc?"

Kreeger was half tempted. All they needed was one more. He looked Fat Boy over, then shook his head. "No. He's one of us. It wouldn't be right."

The truth that Kreeger didn't want to carve through all those layers of fatty tissue. It made the surgery too difficult.

"Oh, I get it," Fat Boy said. "Ha, ha. It was a joke."

"I wasn't joking, Fat Man," Grubb said. "Lucky for you the Doc here has morals."

"What's that I keep smelling?" Kreeger asked. He sniffed. "Smoke. Has one of you been around a fire or something?"

"A friend of mine was burning garbage," Grubb said casually. The truth was, he hadn't changed his clothes or showered since setting Ron Rodale's house ablaze. He kind of liked the smell. He liked to think of it as *l'eau de Molotov*.

"Is that what you wanted all those bottles of gasoline for, Grubb?" Fat Boy asked.

"Shut up, Fatso."

"I was just asking. Geez."

"Both of you shut up and get out of here," Kreeger said. "I have work to do. And I believe you do, too."

Grubb and Fat Boy left the cramped office in the hospital basement and climbed into the van parked just outside.

"I'm surprised you take that off him, Grubb," Fat Boy said. "You let the Doc just push you around."

"We need him, Fattoroni. Are you going to remove people's organs?"

"It can't be that hard. I could do it."

"With what, a butcher knife and a spoon? You've got to be handy with a scalpel. The Doc needs us and we need him. It's what's called a symbiotic relationship."

Just beyond the next traffic light was a convenience store and gas station. "Pull over, will you, Grubb? Let's get some breakfast."

"Does it look to you like they serve ham and eggs?"

"No, but I'll bet they've got Moon Pies."

Grubb pulled into the lot. He hadn't eaten in nearly twenty-four hours, and the mere mention of food reminded him of the rumbling cavern of his belly. They locked the van and Grubb quickly checked the ropes holding the canoe onto the top of the vehicle.

"I still think you're paranoid, Grubb, bringing that canoe along."

"They'll have all the entrances to the trail watched, Fathead. You'll see. But nobody's going to be watching the water."

They walked into the store. Both of them hungrily prowled the aisles, Grubb pulling bags of potato chips and packages of beef jerky off the shelves. Fat Boy went for the Moon Pies, filling his hands with them.

The old woman behind the cash register was so obese she could have been Fat Boy's mother. "That ain't much of a breakfast," she chastised them.

"Unless you want to whip us up some pancakes then I guess it'll have to do," Grubb said.

Her laugh had a lot of phlegm in it. "I ain't gonna make you boys no pancakes. Sorry. Hey, you want a kitten?"

Fat Boy blinked. "You cook kittens?"

"Not usually," she said, giving him a look. "What I've got are some free kittens, if you want one." She bent down and lifted a cardboard box onto the counter. Three small gray kittens were inside, meowing.

"We'll take one," Grubb said.

"Wha —" Fat Boy started to say something but Grubb cut him off.

"Pick one out, Fat Cat."

Fat Boy reached inside the box and grabbed a kitten. Grubb paid the old lady for the junk food.

"Take good care of him," she said.

"We will," Grubb said. "For a couple of hours or so. Then he goes for a swim. How long do you think a cat can tread water?"

"If you're serious, you'd better give him back."

"What do you care, lady?"

The fat old lady scowled. "Them that harm helpless creatures will come to a bad end," she said. "The kitten comes with that warning."

Grubb walked out, cackling. Fat Boy carried the kitten snuggled in his thick arms. The little thing was purring. "Aw, Grubb, he's cute."

"That's just what we want. That kitten is perfect. You'll see what I mean."

They climbed into the van, Fat Boy holding the kitten in his lap and feeding it bits of Moon Pie, and headed toward the public boat launch along the Lewes-Rehoboth Canal.

• • •

Nick was working up a sweat. It was early even for the health and fitness nuts, so the trail wasn't very busy. After yesterday's press conference, only fools or those who scoffed at danger would be taking to the path. Exercising was usually a good way to stay healthy, but with two maniacs on the loose in the park, chances were good of losing more than a few pounds. You might lose your kidneys.

As if the murders weren't enough, he had caught the morning news on the car radio. Last night there had been a firebombing that left a well-known music producer injured and his beachfront home severely damaged. The resort city of Rehoboth Beach really was going to hell.

He had gotten up before Sarah was awake, changed into his running gear at headquarters, and headed over to the trail. He was hoping the goth and his fat sidekick would set their trap early, if they came back at all after the publicity. Nick wanted another crack at them. Maybe he'd get lucky this morning and arrest them both before reinforcements arrived.

His stride was long and easy as he ate up the mulched path along the Lewes-Rehoboth Canal. Funny how easy it now seemed, considering the pain he had been in when he first started running. His joints had loosened up. Of course, maybe it wasn't just the exercise that put a spring in his step. A night with Sarah probably could have made anyone feel great.

Sarah. He didn't like the idea of using her as bait for a trap later today. Grubb was a nutcase, and a dangerous one at that. Nick remembered some of the lyrics Grubb had shrieked on stage the night before.

Set this town on fire! Pour the gasoline, yeah!
This place must burn. Burn it down, yeah!
It's the only way those drones will ever learn.
Set it on fire! Yeah! Make it burn, make it burn!

Chilling lyrics, when you thought about them. What else had Grubb been singing last night? Something about it nagged at Nick. As he ran, he tried to get the beat in his head and then the words finally followed:

Producer said he didn't like our sound,
Tonight I'll put him six feet in the ground.
Light a pyre to his bad taste,
Use the fire, lay it all to waste!

Nick ran along with the music in his head, making his feet move to the beat and doing a good job even though the music was kind of fast. Then he came to a dead stop and stood there panting, having come to a realization.

Grubb was also the mad bomber. It made sense. He shook his head to clear it. Started running again. He needed to make a call and tell the state fire marshal's office about his theory regarding Grubb. They might think it was a fantasy, but the song lyrics were more of a lead than they had at the moment.

Pour the gasoline, yeah!

The crazy goth was a one-man crime spree.

CHAPTER 27

"Good luck," Nick said. "And for Christ's sake, be careful."

If anybody noticed something more than professional concern in his voice, they didn't say a word. Their team this morning consisted of nine police officers: Sarah, Nick, a K-9 squad, a couple of detectives Nick didn't know very well, and four cops wearing running outfits. Grabowski was due momentarily. It was the largest contingent yet that had worked together in the park, all of it assembled with the hope of nailing Grubb and his chubby accomplice if they were stupid enough to return. For once, they would even be using state-of-the-art radios to stay in touch. Delaware state police had loaned them the equipment.

They had it covered, or so Nick thought. Still, there were miles of paths through the woods and dunes. That was a lot of ground to cover.

Sarah was all business. "Everyone's in position?" she asked.

"Yeah," one of the officers said. "If they try anything, we'll nail them."

"Okay," she said. Her eyes swept the knot of officers, found Nick, and they traded a glance. He just hoped they were doing the right thing. He had a bad feeling about sending Sarah out into the park, but he couldn't tell if it was intuition or emotion that was setting off those warning bells in his head.

Sarah went through the last of her stretching routine as Nick went through the plan with the team.

"All right, let's go over it one more time. Detective Monahan will be in constant touch with us over the air. If she spots anything, we move in. It's that simple. Jones and Martinez will be right behind her. The K-9 stays here with the rest of us. I want you two —" Nick pointed out the two uniformed officers "— to take your radio cars out and circle around through the state park. If Grubb and his sidekick try taking that old road into the Cape Henlopen State Park again, we cut them off. Any questions?" He waited a moment. "Then let's do it."

Without another word, Sarah headed out on

the path, running smoothly.

Nick spoke into his microphone. "Monahan, do you read?"

"Loud and clear," she answered.

He watched her cross the footbridge and run out of sight into the woods. As soon as she disappeared he felt a knot begin to form in his belly. That bad feeling was back again. He tried to tell himself he was being overanxious, considering that Grubb and the other thug were probably nowhere near the park this morning.

He turned in time to see Grabowski hurrying over. The detective jogged up, puffing even after the short run from the parking lot.

"You're late," Nick snapped. He was more edgy than he thought.

"Yeah, yeah, I was busy," Grabowski huffed, trying to catch his breath. "You'll never believe this. The mad bomber that's been torching the boardwalk and the music producer's house —"

"It's Grubb."

"Jesus, Logan, you're no fun. You stole my thunder. How did you figure it out?"

"I saw him sing at a club last night. He's in this band called Dog Smell. He was singing about torching music producers. It was Ron Rodale, owner of Rodale Records, who got hit last night."

"Bingo," Grabowski said. "Rodale's secretary was questioned this morning about any threats her boss received, any enemies, you know how it goes. Well, she remembered this goth-looking guy named Grubb who gave her the creeps. Who else could it be?"

"He's definitely number one on Santa's naughty list," Nick said. "We've got to nail his ass."

"We can start by catching him." Grabowski nodded off toward the woods. "She's in there?"

"Yeah."

"You worried?"

"Of course I am. She's my partner."

"From what I hear, she's a little more than that."

"What the hell are you talking about, Grabowski?"

He laughed. "Hey, I'm just getting some of my thunder back. Besides, you don't have to be Sherlock Holmes to figure out what's going on between you two. For what it's worth, I think you make a good couple. Opposites attract, right?"

Nick grunted in reply. He didn't especially feel like discussing his love life while Sarah was playing decoy to catch a couple of psychopaths. "What else is going on with the case this morning over at headquarters?" he asked, hoping to change the subject.

"I'm having some people call around to see if they can figure out where the organs have been going. They're checking with all the major transplant centers around the country and asking them what their source for kidneys is and whether they've had an unusual number of them come from Delaware. That way we can pinpoint the hospital and bring down whoever else is in on this."

"Good," Nick said, turning to look at the woods. "Meanwhile, let's hope Sarah has some luck out there.

• • •

On any other morning, the rhythm of her feet hitting the path would have lulled Sarah into a daydream, but not today. She was all nerves as she ran the trail waiting for something to happen.

Even though she had a radio transmitter, a handgun, and a team waiting to back her up, Sarah wasn't so sure she was ready. She felt kind of like a giant piece of cheese being used to bait a rat trap. But if it helped catch the two psychos who had been preying on people in the park, it would be worth the ordeal.

She felt somewhat safer on this part of the trail that followed the tidal Lewes-Rehoboth Canal. There were no roads nearby, just the waterway, so it was doubtful the two thugs would try anything without transportation. The plan banked on Grubb using the roads on the western side of the park, because that was where the radio cars were stationed to pick them up if they made it out of the police net. The ocean hemmed them in on the western side.

Sarah was replaying the plan in her mind when on the path up ahead she spotted something moving. Her heart instantly hammered inside her chest as if she had been sprinting this whole time. But what she had seen couldn't have been Grubb and his henchman because it was only a tiny gray and white blur, obviously an animal of some kind. A squirrel? A rabbit? Whatever it was, the creature crouched in the underbrush at the side of the trail, but didn't run away.

Sarah slowed down to get a look. She considered radioing about the animal, but they might think she was paranoid. Her feet carried her a few yards closer and she saw that it was a kitten.

Sarah stopped, breathing hard as much from adrenalin as from running, and bent down to examine the kitten. The tiny creature meowed, and Sarah smiled. Somebody must have dumped the kitten at the park when they couldn't find a home for it. It happened all the time, but that didn't make it right. What kind of mean bastard abandoned a kitten?

"Hey, little fella."

The kitten meowed bravely at her, standing its ground. It must be used to people. Sarah crouched beside the kitten, picked it up, and wondered if her cat would mind sharing the apartment.

"Are you lost, kitty? Aww. What's your name?"

"Grubb," said a voice behind her.

Stupid, stupid, she wanted to scream at herself, fear running over her like ice water. A trick. She started to turn, going for her gun, but something heavy knocked against the side of her head and Sarah slipped into darkness.

• • •

Grubb stood over her slumped form as Fat Boy shrugged his way out of the mountain laurel lining the path. "Let's move," he said.

"What about the kitten?" Fat Boy asked. The tiny creature had jumped safely out of the way as Sarah slumped over and was off to one side now, mewling.

"Oh yeah," Grubb said. "We don't want to leave any evidence, do we?" He grabbed the kitten by the back of the neck and flung it toward the canal, where it landed with a splash. The current rippled over the disturbance in the surface of the water and all was still again.

Fat Boy gulped back his protest and grabbed the woman's feet as Grubb picked up her shoulders and started hustling down the steep incline toward the water.

• • •

Nick was on the radio again.

"Monahan, do you copy? Monahan?"

One of the undercover officers on the path behind her broke in. "We don't have a visual on her, Logan."

"Where the hell is she? See if you can catch up with her."

"That might give us away."

"I don't give a damn. We might already be given away."

Nick paced outside the unmarked car where Grabowski and the other homicide detective sat.

"Maybe her radio went on the fritz," Grabowski said. "It happens."

"Not in the middle of the dance it doesn't," Nick said. "Something's wrong."

Nick was wearing running clothes and he thought about going into the park after her. But there were already two armed cops right behind Sarah, though they had somehow lost sight of her.

"Come on Sarah," he said, silently praying for the sound of her voice through the transmitter in his ear. "Don't let this turn into a nightmare."

• • •

"Come on, Lardo, pick up her feet," Grubb snarled. "We don't want to damage the goods."

Fat Boy was panting from the effort. He slipped and Sarah's legs dragged through fallen leaves as Grubb rushed her toward the water's edge. Fat Boy hurried, caught her feet, and helped lift her down the steep bank.

"Move it, move it," Grubb said. "We've got to get out on the water before the cops figure out what happened."

"She's wearing a radio or something," Fat Boy said. There was a tiny plastic receiver in her ear that fell out as they moved down the canal bank. "Holy crap, I'll bet she's a cop."

Grubb took a closer look at the woman's face. He'd seen her somewhere, maybe on TV. "Yeah, she's a cop, all right. The whole damn park is probably full of cops."

The canoe was shoved up onto the canal bank, halfway out of the water. Overhanging branches nearly hid it from view.

Grubb and Fat Boy dumped her unconscious form into the center of the canoe. Grubb jumped into the stern and grabbed a paddle.

"How come I'm the one who has to get his feet wet?" Fat Boy said.

"Shut up and push us off."

On the trail above them they could hear footsteps. It sounded like at least a couple of runners. The woods were thick, but if someone glanced toward the water, they might spot the canoe and its cargo.

"Cops," Grubb hissed, digging his paddle into the mud and raising swirls of muck as he tried to urge the canoe into deeper water.

Without another word, Fat Boy grabbed the bow and gave it a tremendous shove that sent the canoe sliding into the canal. Then he scrambled aboard, accidentally banging the aluminum hull so that it rang out like a drum.

"Oops.

"Hey, why don't I give you my phone so you can call 911," Grubb said. "Or you can just keeping banging on that canoe."

He took two quick steps into the water and jumped into the bow. Fat Boy piled into the stern. In a few quick strokes of their paddles, the canoe shot toward the center of the canal, headed toward Rehoboth.

• • •

"What was that?" one of the cops on the path asked. He stopped and spoke into the radio. "Logan, I heard something and I'm stopping to check it out."

"What?" Nick demanded. "What did you hear?"

"Something banging. Like something metal."

His partner spotted it first. A couple of guys in a canoe were heading down the canal.

"We found it," the first cop said into the radio.

"Just some people canoeing. I think they banged an oar against the side."

"A paddle," his partner said.

"Whatever."

"Okay, okay," Nick said. "Keep going. Hurry up, damn it. Keep an eye out for Sarah."

• • •

"Jesus, what the hell is going on?" Nick wondered out loud.

"She disappeared?" Grabowski asked.

"Gone."

"Better tell the radio cars to watch the roads out of the park. That's our safety net."

"We're watching all the roads in or out. How did we not see them? Tell your guys to keep their eyes open."

Grabowski considered reminding Nick he wasn't in charge, but Logan had that look in his eye like he was about to swing his splitting maul into a chunk of wood. Grabowski knew it was best to stay out of his way. Besides, Grabowski was just as worried as Nick was about Sarah.

"I'll get the word out."

Nick hardly heard him. He was pressing his head between his hands, and hissing between his teeth, "Think, think, think!" He moaned. "What the hell's going on?"

Grabowski watched, hoping Logan wouldn't

squeeze too hard.

Nick went on the radio. "What's the situation?"

"No sign of her," the runners radioed.

"Nothing here," reported one of the cars watching the northern roads.

"Zilch," said the uniformed officer in the second car.

"This is crazy," Nick fumed. He wanted to go in, comb the trail, find out what the hell was going on. Give it a minute, he told himself. He half expected Sarah to come on the air or for the other runners to catch up with her.

"I don't get it. Where is she?"

Grabowski and the other detective got out of the car. "You want me to call backup?" Grabowski asked.

"Yeah, and see if they can get a helicopter out here. I want those bastards."

"Roger."

"I'm going in," Nick said. "I can't wait any more."

He started running, thinking, *How? How did they do it? If they got Sarah, they slipped right past us.*

Nick rounded a bend in the trail. Down the canal, he watched a canoe pull ashore, moving fast. What was their hurry? They grabbed something long and heavy from the belly of the canoe. One of the paddlers was tall and lanky. The other resembled Jabba the Hut.

Son of a bitch!

Fear rushed through Nick. Then he felt an angry bile rise in his throat, raging. He started running.

Grabowski was out of the car, moving toward ¨the woods. He didn't have a radio, so Nick waved him back, shouting and pointing across the canal. They had to get in the car and go after them. Grubb and the fat guy tossed the bundle into the back of a white van, slammed the doors shut.

Nick ran back the way he had come. Grabowski had his hand to his ear, signaling Nick he hadn't heard. Nick sprinted toward Grabowski, back toward the parking lot. He watched gravel spit from under the tires of the white van. Grabowski saw the van, understood at once what was going on, then turned and started running toward the car.

"They've got Sarah," Nick shouted into his radio. "Everybody get back in here. We're going after them."

This was crazy. This couldn't be happening. That psycho Grubb had outsmarted them with a goddamn canoe.

And he now had Sarah.

CHAPTER 28

"You cops think you're so smart," Grubb said. "But look who's got who. I've got *you*, babe."

He laughed and the sound made Sarah shiver. He was a total creep, a complete psychopath. Her next thought was, *How do I get out of this?*

Fat Boy was too busy sulking to gloat. "I can't believe you threw that kitten in the canal."

"Shut up about the kitten, Fat Boy! So what? I'll get you another one."

"It doesn't work like that, Grubb." He shook his head. "You are one sick dude."

While they bickered, Sarah rolled onto her belly on the gritty metal floor of the van. It smelled like oil and rust and garbage. Out the front windows she saw buildings and trees whip past, but nothing she recognized. Wherever they were going, it was in a hurry. The van's motor strained to push them down the road.

She tried to get her bearings and take stock of the damage. Her head throbbed, and she wondered what Grubb had hit her with. There didn't seem to be any blood, which was a good sign. Her wrists were bound together behind her with Duct tape, which was not a good sign.

Even if she could free her hands, there was nothing to use as a weapon. Where was her gun? She rolled slightly, hoping to feel its pressure against the small of her back. Nothing there.

If you can't shoot them, talk to them. She wasn't about to go all Stockholm Syndrome, but if she made herself seem human to them, they might not kill her. Forcing her fear back down her throat, she managed to ask, "Where are we going?"

"Don't you worry your pretty little aching head about that," Grubb said.

She tried a different approach. "You really threw that poor little kitten into the water?"

"Splash."

"You are one sick motherfucker," she said. "Fat Boy, how could you let him?"

"Are you kidding me? Grubb does what he does," Fat Boy said. "I'm not gonna stop him."

"He's the perfect sidekick," Grubb said. "He doesn't question my authority. You Tonto, me

Kimosabe."

"I liked your band," Sarah said. "You ought to try singing more, though, instead of screaming everything."

"What were you doing watching my band?"

"We got a tip that you were the one who had taken the girl off the trail. We wanted to check you out."

Fat Boy spoke up. "The cops came to see you play? They knew it was you? Why didn't you tell me that!"

"What, like it did them any good?" Grubb said to his partner. "We got the bacon right here, and they don't got us."

Sarah asked again, "Where are we going?"

Grubb took his eyes off the road long enough to look over his shoulder at Sarah. That look alone made it feel like his hands were all over her. "You'll find out where we're going when we get there, and I'm sure you won't like it. Maybe we can take a detour first and find a quiet spot to spend some quality time together, if you know what I mean. That is, babe, unless you're in a hurry to die."

• • •

Nick gunned the car down the road, keeping an eye out for the van. They didn't have much of a head start, but they could have disappeared at any point down a side road. He was starting to think maybe that's what had happened, because they were nowhere in sight.

Each minute mattered. It was like one of those word problems from math class. In thirty minutes, a van traveling at fifty miles per hour could be twenty-five miles away. In any direction. He didn't even want to think about where it could be in an hour.

What they needed were some eyes in the air.

He grabbed the mic, called for a state police chopper.

"It's fifteen minutes out," the dispatcher said.

"We don't have that much time. We need it now."

"It's not like ordering a taxi."

Nick kept driving. Where the hell was that van headed? *Think, think.* He worried that Sarah, like the other victims, was just going to disappear for a while until her body washed up on some tidal creek in the marshes. Nick knew he couldn't let that happen.

He keyed the mic again. "Any luck with determining which hospital sent the organs to the transplant centers."

"Negative." This time, it was Chief Hawley on the radio. "But there's only one hospital around here. Southern Delaware General. Listen, I lit a fire under the state police. That chopper ought to be overhead any minute. Meanwhile, I've got everybody on the road. We'll find her, Nick."

"I'm headed for that hospital. I got a hunch."

"Wait for backup."

"Right," he said. Like hell.

• • •

"Forget it, Grubb, no fun and games," Fat Boy said. "The Doc wouldn't be happy about that. We need to get her to the hospital."

"So that's where we're going," Sarah said. Nobody answered. Several bumpy minutes later, she felt the van slow and make a couple of turns. Then they stopped. She felt a growing sense of dread.

Grubb came into the back of the van with a roll of duct tape. He ripped off a piece and slapped it over her mouth. She tried to kick him, but Grubb shot a couple of vicious punches to her ribs in return. She scrunched up in pain.

"Now you've got it," he said, twisting more tape around her ankles. "No kickee, no punchee."

Fat Boy lumbered back, and the two men rolled her inside an old piece of stinking carpet. She felt herself being lifted. *Where's the cavalry? Oh my God. This can't be happening! Nick, where the hell are you?*

• • •

Nick drove toward the hospital. There was a lot more traffic as he approached Route 1, and he began to realize that there were about a million white vans on the road. Every contractor had one. A chopper in the air wasn't going to do them much good. His best hope was getting to that hospital. There was always a chance that they had taken her somewhere else. If that was the case, then Grubb had outsmarted them. Again.

If Sarah died because he had screwed up, Nick knew he could never forgive himself. He had already let Karen down. Being a cop hadn't done anything to protect her. That crackhead burglar had murdered her, and nothing he had done to Wallace Green could change that fact or bring Karen back.

Pushing those thoughts from his mind, he pressed down on the gas pedal. The unmarked vehicle plunged through the beach traffic. Horns honked at him. He ran a red light, narrowly missing a minivan coming the other way. He glimpsed a young mother behind the wheel, her eyes wide in terror. He punched the accelerator and steered around them, not even so much as slowing down, heading toward Southern Delaware General.

• • •

The carpet unrolled enough for Sarah to look out

and see pipes and exposed wires overhead as Grubb and Fat Boy carried her into a building. Clearly they were in some kind of basement in an industrial-type of setting. That was a puzzle, because it's not like there were a lot of industrial buildings at the beach. She tried to kick her way free, but Fat Boy had a firm lock on her legs. At the end of the hallway, an unmarked door opened and a man in a green surgical smock appeared. He held the door open for them.

"Here she is, Doc," Grubb said. "One feisty pair of kidneys to go."

"She'll do nicely," the man in the green smock said.

It came as a shock that they were talking about *her*. Sarah tried to scream through the duct tape, but it was like trying to force her breath through a wall. They unwrapped her and set her down on a table. Holy crap. An operating table! She wriggled like a worm on a hook. Fat Boy held her down as Grubb secured nylon straps across her arms and legs. He ripped off the duct tape covering her mouth.

That hurt like hell, but Sarah didn't waste a second. She started talking, thinking this was her last chance.

"Please don't do this," she said. "It's just not worth it."

"Actually, it's worth tens of thousands of dollars," Grubb said.

"No conversing with the donor, please," the man in the green smock said.

"Who are you?"

"Dr. Kreeger." He studied her face a moment. Where had he seen her before? "You're a police officer. You're the one who was on TV, aren't you?"

"Yes, that was me," Sarah said, her hopes rising. She strained without success against the straps binding her to the table. If only she could convince these thugs that she was a real person, not a faceless victim. "I spoke at the press conference about the abductions."

Dr. Kreeger looked at Grubb. "You must be even dumber than you look. You abducted a cop?"

"Gimme a break, Doc. She had it coming."

"I watched the entire press conference," Kreeger said. His face mask and surgical cap were already on, as well as the magnifying glasses that surgeons wore. He looked more like something out of a horror movie than a normal human being. "Needless to say, I was fascinated by what you had to say."

"I really sweated through that one," she said. "Those media people are like sharks."

"I would imagine," Kreeger said. "Well, your worries are over. Grubb, give her the anesthesia, will you?"

"No, wait—"

But the doctor was already cutting away her

light running top to expose her abdomen. He squirted antiseptic solution from a plastic squeeze bottle over her skin and she felt the cold liquid running down her sides. A needle went into her arm and she flinched. Moments later, the world began to blur. A mask went over her face. She kept fighting it, fighting it, but from a long place away she saw the scalpel in Doc Kreeger's hand, poised over her belly.

• • •

Nick dumped the car near the hospital entrance and raced inside.

"Police!" he shouted. "I need to find a woman who is undergoing surgery to have her kidneys removed."

The woman at the front desk stood up, looking at him like he was crazy. "Officer? If you remove someone's kidneys ... oh. Let me call administration for you."

"There's no time for that!" Nick spotted a sign behind the desk. *Surgery, third floor.* He ran for the elevator.

An older man in a maintenance uniform was already there, waiting for the elevator. He pushed a cart loaded with mops and brooms. "Nobody is up in surgery getting their kidneys removed. You best try the basement," the maintenance man said. "Take the elevator all the way down, turn left, go to the end of the hall. There's an old operating room down there that nobody is supposed to use, but there's been something going on down there lately."

Nick got in the elevator, punched the B button. It seemed to take hours to reach the basement.

• • •

Kreeger paused with the razor sharp blade of the scalpel just touching Sarah's skin. Under anesthesia, she was beyond noticing.

"You two have to leave now," Kreeger said. "You're not scrubbed up and I can't have you in the OR."

"Aw, Doc, we never get to watch."

"Maybe next time."

"I didn't think there was going to be a next time," Fat Boy said.

"We need to take a break for a while," Kreeger agreed. "I'm leaving for an extended vacation in Germany. I've always wanted to drive on the autobahn, you know. When I get back I may hang out my shingle again."

"Look us up when you get back, Doc."

"You know I will. Listen, these organs will be ready shortly. Grubb, you'd better go bring the van around. They're going to BWI, and then on to Atlanta. I'll tissue type them while their en route."

"You got it, Doc." Grubb went out the door.

Kreeger turned to Fat Boy. "You. Out. Go find a snack machine or something."

Fat Boy turned and opened the door to the hallway. He was startled to find the big cop from the trail standing there.

"Uh oh," Fat Boy said. "You again."

Nick slugged him in the face and he went down.

Then Nick stepped into the room. He took his gun out. "Police," he said to the figure in green surgical scrubs. The doctor's eyes, already magnified by the ocular glasses, got even wider at the sight of a .45 muzzle pointed at him.

Nick, though, wasn't really watching him. He saw Sarah's motionless body on the operating table. Was he too late? Had he already cut Sarah? The doctor—or whatever he was—held a scalpel with a single drop of blood on it. Sarah's blood. His finger got tense on the trigger.

"Put it down," Nick said.

The doctor sighed and set the scalpel down on the operating tray with the other surgical instruments. "Should I put my hands up?"

"What have you done to her?"

"Nothing yet. I haven't really started."

"Good." Nick looked down at Fat Boy, moaning on the floor. "Where's Grubb?"

"He went to get the van. If he's got half a

brain, he'll figure out what's going on and he won't come back."

"Too bad." Nick took two steps toward the doctor, twisted the man's right arm behind him, and ran him face first into the nearest cinder block wall. The doctor slid to the floor like a sack of potatoes.

Nick used the scalpel to cut Sarah's restraints, then took her hand. It felt frighteningly cold. He shook her gently, but she was out. He wanted her to wake up so she could talk to him and reassure him that she was okay.

There was shouting in the hallway, and Bob Grabowski came barreling through the door, gun out, followed by a couple of uniformed officers.

Grabowski scanned the room, took note of the three bodies, and asked, "Nobody's dead, are they?"

"No."

"Thank God. How's Sarah doing?"

"They knocked her out. We'd better call an ambulance."

"In case you haven't noticed, we're already in a hospital."

"I want her out of this place."

Grabowski holstered his weapon and nodded at one of the officers, who went out to make the call. An ambulance could take Sarah to the regional hospital in Dover.

"Where's the goth?" Grabowski asked.

"He got away."

"Not good."

"Exactly."

CHAPTER 29

He was going to burn them all this time and nobody could stop him.

Grubb combed the alleys, looking for empty liquor bottles. No way he could drink enough to come up with all the empties he needed for Dog Smell's next work of anarchy, although he would have liked to try. He just didn't have time. Or an iron liver.

He kicked an empty can, sending it clattering down the alley. No sense being quiet, he thought, even if every cop in Rehoboth Beach—maybe even every cop on the East Coast—was looking for him. After he made this final performance, Grubb was going to blow this town and lose himself and the band in New York. They would be an outlaw band. *Real* outlaws. He had enough money to get started up there, and he even had a new name picked out for the band: Charred Dog.

He hadn't even known the Doc and Fat Boy had been arrested until he went into the Popeye's on Route 1 about five o'clock and some people in line were talking about it. They'd seen it on TV. Grubb didn't bother to find out any details. It was all part of his past now. One more arson gig, and he was out of there. RIP, Rehoboth Beach.

Wandering the back streets of town, Grubb was thinking so hard he nearly tripped over a pair of legs sticking out from under a sheet of cardboard. Even the beach had homeless.

"Hey . . . " a voice complained, then fell off into muttering.

Grubb flung back the cardboard and saw an old wino looking up at him. The man had a nearly empty bottle of wine in his filthy hand.

"Gimme that," Grubb said, grabbing the bottle.

"Don't take my bottle, you son of a bitch," the bum complained, starting to lurch to his feet.

Grubb stomped the man's chest and put him back on the ground. Then he kept stomping and kicking savagely until the man stopped cursing and groaning and there was only the sound of Grubb's boot thudding against the thin flesh and bones. He upended the bottle and poured the last of the booze on the man's head. One more bottle for his final show in town.

Too bad the Doc was locked up, Grubb thought. He could have hauled in the bum and made a little money off the man's kidneys, or what was left of them inside that rotting body.

Grubb walked off, blowing air through his teeth in time to the song playing through his head. He sang out loud, not caring who heard: "Pour the gasoline, yeah!"

• • •

"It's not your fault," Sarah said over the phone.

"I shouldn't have let this happen," Nick said. "It was stupid. Using you as a decoy, then letting those assholes grab you —"

"Nick, they used a canoe on the canal, for God's sake. Nobody ever thought about that."

Someone tapped him on the shoulder.

"Look, I gotta go," he said. "We're having another pow wow here to figure out what the hell to do next."

"Grubb's still on the loose?" Nervousness in her voice. Sarah was home resting after the day's ordeal. The doctor had pushed to keep her overnight for observation, but after her experience earlier in the day she wanted to be as far as possible from any hospitals.

"Yeah. Listen, if you want I can send someone over there."

"I'm fine, Nick. Just come and see me as soon as you can."

He hung up and hurried down to Chief Hawley's office. Hawley waited for Nick to find a chair, then cleared his throat.

"What next?" Hawley asked. "We've still got two guys on the loose."

In questioning Dr. Kreeger, they had learned that the hospital administrator, Roger Cramer, was an accomplice. Both he and Grubb had made clean getaways.

"We need to focus on Grubb. He's the one who's going to cause problems for us. Cramer isn't going around setting fires. It's only a matter of time before he turns up."

"Then where the hell do we find Grubb?"

Grabowski shrugged. "Who the hell knows?"

Nick unfolded a scrap of paper he had been fiddling with all day. On it he had written the lyrics to one of the songs Grubb screeched out on stage. The problem was not whether he had the words right, because they had burned into his brain like everything else about the goth rocker. Nick just wasn't sure he believed the lyrics.

"What's that?" Hawley asked, seeing Nick studying the sheet.

"It's something Grubb sang when I saw him at the Cracked Saloon." Nick explained that in another song that night Grubb had promised to burn the home of Ron Rodale, the music producer. "From his song lyrics, I think it's clear what he's going to do next."

"Sing it baby, sing it," Grabowski said.

"I'll do the words," Nick said. "You can just hum along." He read out loud:

The mayor he's got a little project.
Doesn't want the city to be a reject.
This weekend he'll open the waterfront.
On TV that day they'll see it burnt.

It's got plate glass windows and brass rails
When he sees all the ashes he'll shit nails
Inside those shops there's gonna be a bomb
Better plan a fire sale for when I'm all done.

"I like the part about the mayor shitting nails," Grabowski said. "I think that's exactly what he'll do if Grubb burns down the entire boardwalk."

"Sweet Jesus," Hawley said. "This is not good. The grand opening ceremony for the Mermaid Zone Shops is set for tomorrow morning."

"I don't think we can take it lightly," Nick said. "Not after what he sang about torching the music producer. This is the real deal. Here's our chance to keep him from doing it again."

"Better call the state fire marshal's office and have them get a K-9 in there to start sniffing for bombs."

"I don't think Grubb will do it that way," Nick

said. "Frankly, he's not sophisticated enough to rig explosives. The scenario I see is Grubb roaring up on his motorcycle, tossing a few Molotov cocktails, then hightailing it out of there."

"Either way, people could get hurt," Hawley said. "And there's going to be a lot of media there covering the opening of those new shops. Whatever happens is going to be very public."

"We've got trouble," Grabowski agreed.

They sat there, thinking it over. All of them had been through a lot the past few days and they were feeling tired and burned out. After nailing Fat Boy and Dr. Kreeger at the hospital, it seemed as if the case should have been over. But neither of the two suspects they had in custody knew anything about Grubb, other than that he was crazy. He was mostly a mystery to them.

Finally, Hawley broke the quiet to ask, "Nick, how's Sarah doing?"

"Fine," he said. "I just talked to her."

Nick knew Hawley hadn't asked him about Sarah just because they were partners. There were no secrets at headquarters. He supposed when this mess was over, Hawley would take him and Sarah aside and give them a talk on maintaining professionalism, doing his best not to look embarrassed. Hawley usually steered clear of words like "relationship," but as the police chief he would have to say something.

Of course, if Grubb managed to firebomb the Rehoboth Beach boardwalk on live TV, there would be a new chief and several new detectives. Mayor Gates would clean house. Nick doubted if he and Hawley would make the cut.

• • •

"Want another?" Sarah asked.

"I'll get it," Nick said, shoving himself up from the couch. He grabbed another beer from the refrigerator, then settled back down beside Sarah.

"How are you feeling?" he asked again.

"Lucky to be alive. And mad as hell. So you're going to get him tomorrow?"

"Yep," Nick said. "We're going to nail his bony ass."

"I think I'll sit this one out," she said.

"I don't blame you," he said. He was quiet a moment, running his thumbs over the cold, smooth skin of the beer can. He put the beer on the coffee table, unopened. "I've been thinking. After all this is over, I may head back to the mountains."

"And do what? Split more firewood?"

"I guess so."

"Don't quit the job, Nick. You love it too much."

"I just don't think I could handle another situation like today," he said. "Putting you in danger like that—"

"Will you stop beating yourself up over that?" she said. "You won't fix it by moving back to the mountains. By moving away from me. I'm the only one to blame. I fell for their stupid trick. A kitten, for God's sake."

"Yeah. Well, I would have fallen for it, too. We've just got big hearts."

"Hold me, will you Nick? Just give me a big hug."

He put his arms around her and they snuggled together on the couch. What the hell was he thinking, moving back to the mountains? In a moment they were both asleep.

• • •

"I can't believe we're out here because of a song," Grabowski said. "I mean, I could understand if it was Frank Sinatra we were talking about, or even Elvis. But this is a song by some band called Dog Smell. Jesus. I hope we're not going out on a limb on this one."

"We'll find out soon enough," Nick said. "I hope to God that Grubb does show up. I want to even the score with that asshole."

Nick looked out over the crowd. Maybe five hundred people were crowded onto the new section of boardwalk that had been replaced since the fire. Balloons bobbed up and down, bright pennants snapped in the breeze off the ocean, and off to one side a jazz band was playing. There was a wonderful sweet-salty smell of french fries, pizza and taffy all mixed together. Up front, a handful of media people camped out near the podium where Mayor Gates would make his speech. They looked jaded if not exactly bored— this was the kind of assignment that reporters hated but that publishers loved because it made the advertisers happy to see pictures in the paper of their new businesses opening. It wasn't exactly news, but it brought in new advertising that helped pay the bills.

Nick could just make out Jorge Alvarez, looking out of place in his rumpled khakis and oxford shirt, considering that most of the crowd was wearing shorts and T-shirts—even bikinis. People stopped just to see what all the excitement was about, while others came for the free hot dogs and sodas promised in the newspaper ads. Nick had tipped Bernie off that he might want to be there, although covering ribbon cuttings was not what he usually did as the police reporter for the state's largest daily.

Behind the podium, a large red, white and blue ribbon was stretched in front of the row of glass doors leading to the boardwalks new Mermaid Zone shops. After the mayor's speech, he and other dignitaries were scheduled to cut the ribbon and open the shops for the very first time.

Nick's hand slid inside his cream-colored sports jacket and felt the reassuring cold metal of the gun in a speed holster under his arm. He then took a phone out of his jacket pocket, put it back.

"Quit fidgeting," Grabowski complained. "You're making me nervous."

"I just want to be ready."

The band stopped playing and Mayor Gates walked from the dignitaries' row of chairs to the podium. Nick held his breath, scanning the crowd. If Grubb was going to make his move, he couldn't pick a better time.

They had done their best to anticipate him. Patrol cars were stationed on Rehoboth Avenue and at each of the streets leading to the boardwalk. The crowd streaming in this morning hadn't given the officers a second glance, figuring they were there just in case the line for the free hot dogs got rowdy.

What today's spectators didn't know was that each officer was watching people carefully as they arrived, on the lookout for a black-haired freak who wanted to crash the party in a very nasty way.

Mayor Gates began speaking. He was using a microphone, which crackled a bit as it caught the sea breeze.

"Welcome, friends, to a great day for the City of Rehoboth Beach —"

Where the hell was Grubb? Nick's eyes darted around the crowd of spectators. Chief Hawley had pulled out the stops on security for this event based on Nick's theory. If Grubb didn't show, Hawley wasn't going to be happy about the overtime.

"— and it's a great day for shoppers." Mayor Gates smiled like a conspirator, letting everyone in on a secret. "In fact, my wife, Lucille, is right over there warming up her credit card." Laughter rolled out from the crowd. "She has on her shopping shoes today, and you'll have to be quick to beat her inside the new Mermaid Zone shops, let me tell you." More laughter. "Today, like many days to follow, is going to be great for the merchants here. It's going to be great for you, the people of Rehoboth Beach —"

There. Nick picked Grubb out at the edge of the crowd, a tall, gaunt young man in an old military overcoat, mirrored sunglasses, a hat pulled down over his black hair, and a rucksack hanging from one shoulder. The hat and sunglasses did a good job of disguising him, and Nick might not have picked him out of the crowd, except for the fact that he looked very out of place in that coat. It was at least eight-five degrees in the sun.

Nick felt hot and itchy in his summer sports coat, so Grubb had to be sweating rivers. Grubb seemed to be listening intently to the mayor's speech, and Nick had to wonder what he was planning.

He nudged Grabowski. "Ten o'clock. The dude in the military overcoat."

"Got him," Grabowski said. "What the hell? He's just standing there listening to Gates."

"Yeah. But what do you think he's got in that rucksack?"

"It ain't salt water taffy." Grabowski paused. "I'll be he's got a whole bag full of Molotov cocktails. Oh, shit! I think I know what he's going to do. He'll get inside the Mermaid Zone after they cut the ribbon and open the doors, then start lobbing those babies. We've got trouble."

"Let's grab him." Nick went on the radio, told everyone the situation. Undercover officers were stationed in the crowd, and they would all try to converge on Grubb. "C'mon, let's move."

He and Grabowski began walking behind the crowd, skirting the group of onlookers. No way they could have cut in front, although it would have been shorter, because Grubb would have spotted them.

"Hope he doesn't wander off," Grabowski said, already huffing as they walked quickly around the rear of the spectators.

"You're in terrible shape, Bob, you know that?"

"It's not like I ever have to chase anybody," Grabowski said. "You know how it is in being a detective. You make phone calls and you drive around."

"You should get in shape just for your health," Nick said. "Lose a few pounds. You'll feel better."

"That new girlfriend of yours really converted you," Grabowski said. "If I remember correctly, you were a firm believer in a strict diet of jelly doughnuts and cheap beer just a few years ago."

"Just try to keep up," Nick said. He broke into a jog, trying to cover the distance to where Grubb was standing.

At the edges of the crowd, a few people saw them running and cast curious glances their way. They had to dodge kids and senior citizens who had come by to see what all the commotion was about on the boardwalk. Nick began to gain on Grabowski, then slowed down enough for him to catch up. He wanted both of them there when they took Grubb down.

They reached the other side of the crowd and pushed their way toward Grubb. Nick could see movement in other parts of the crowd as the three undercover officers moved to surround him.

Slow down, slow down, warned a voice in Nick's head. *If you can see what's going on, so can Grubb.* The guy lived on nerves. They didn't want to push him. Nick was just reaching for his radio to tell everyone to take it easy when somebody shoved past him, going the other way as fast as he could ram through the crowd. Too late, he realized it was Grubb—he had tricked them by shedding his overcoat. Around him, Nick could hear people grumbling and swearing, looking after Grubb, wondering where he was going in such a hurry.

"He'd better not even think about butting ahead of me for the hot dogs," somebody muttered.

Behind Nick, Grabowski had been looking up and he saw Grubb coming. Something gave Grabowski away—maybe it was the fact that like Nick he was also wearing a sport coat to hide his gun—or maybe Grubb just saw something in the man's eyes. Grubb threw a punch at the detective. Grabowski went down. A woman screamed.

"He's out, he's behind the crowd," Nick blurted into the radio as he shoved his way toward the rear. "He's coming out near the edge of the building."

People were shouting now, trying to figure out what was going on as uniformed police officers moved purposefully through the crowd. So much for the mayor's speech, Nick thought. A man tried to block his path. "Hey you, what the hell's —"

"Police," Nick said, shoving him aside to get to Grabowski. He reached down to help the detective to his feet. "You okay?"

"Son of a bitch slugged me good," Grabowski said, swiping at his bloody nose with the back of his hand.

"C'mon, c'mon," Nick said, shoving

Grabowski ahead of him.

"Jesus, take it easy, Nick, I think I got a broken nose."

They burst free of the crowd. Grubb was running down the boardwalk, out in the open, not a cop in sight. If this had been a football game the announcer would already have been yelling "Touchdown!" Except that the boardwalk was still crowded with tourists of every variety. Grubb shoved a woman and she went down. He upended a baby stroller. The mother screamed.

"Get him, Nick," Grabowski said. He was hunched over, his nose bleeding badly. "Don't wait for me. I can't keep up."

Nick started sprinting. Amazingly, most of the crowd at the Mermaid Zone grand opening hadn't noticed the commotion, and was still listening calmly to Mayor Gates or waiting patiently for a hot dog. Nick quickly lost the sounds of the speech in his ears. He was up on his toes, pumping his arms, running flat out after the crazy goth.

Grubb was still lugging the haversack, and it was slowing him down. Nick could hear bottles clinking. As if sensing Nick was gaining on him, Grubb let it slip off his shoulder. Nick hopped over it, smelling the gasoline. If Grubb had gotten inside the new shops—

No time to think about that. Grubb went down an alley, running wildly, his feet skidding out from under him as he took the corner. Nick was maybe fifty feet behind him but Grubb was momentarily out of sight. Where the hell was his backup?

The next sound Nick heard was a motorcycle engine. *Damn.*. Grubb was one step ahead of them, ditching his bike here to make his getaway. Nick remembered the bike that had been behind the Cracked Saloon. Once Grubb was on that thing, they'd never catch him.

Nick went around the corner and only had time to jump out of the way as Grubb gunned the bike toward the street. Grubb roared past, his black hair whipping, whooping insanely. The guy wasn't scared, Nick thought. He was getting a rush out of this. Grubb was nuts. They were dealing with a psychopath.

Nick went for his gun, then dropped his hand. He couldn't shoot a fleeing suspect in the back, and if he missed, there was no telling who he might hit on that busy street.

He had to watch helplessly as Grubb disappeared down the street on the motorcycle. *Think, Logan, think.* He watched a couple with a small child walk up to their Chevy Tahoe parked on the street. Dad fiddled with the keys, started to open the door for the kid.

Seeing that big SUV, Nick figured there could still be a chance to stop Grubb.

Grabowski came running up. "I've been on the

radio. We've got the road shut down. He's not going anywhere. Just like shooting fish in the barrel."

"I wish I felt sure about that.

"He's not getting past us."

"He's on a bike, for God's sake. He can go anywhere he damn well pleases. But I've got an idea."

He walked up to the couple that was putting the stroller into the Tahoe. The woman saw him coming and eyed him suspiciously, nudging her husband.

"Police," he said, opening his jacket so that they could see the badge clipped to his belt and get a glimpse of the shoulder holster. "I need to use your vehicle."

"I don't think so," dad said.

Somewhere a siren was blaring. Nick heard Grubb's motorcycle revving in the distance, echoing off the fronts of the shops on Rehoboth Avenue, racing through town. Unless his ears were playing tricks on him, Grubb was coming back this way.

"You know what, honey, I think this is for real," the woman said to her husband.

"They don't really do this," the husband said. "That's all stuff on TV —"

The whine of the motorcycle was louder, like a giant mosquito.

"I need your vehicle *now*." Nick grabbed the

keys out of the door, jumped for the driver's seat. Dad didn't try to stop him, only said, "Hey —"

Nick gunned it around the loop by the bandshell where the DART bus let people out on the boardwalk. The street was one-way down to the traffic circle just before the Lewes-Delaware Canal bridge.

Here came Grubb up the wrong side of the street, trench coat flapping in the wind like wings. A patrol car was in pursuit, but the bike was absolutely flying. No way was anybody going to catch Grubb. If he got to the top of Rehoboth Avenue he could get out onto the boardwalk, maybe even out onto the beach. If that happened, a lot of people could get hurt.

Nick stood on the gas, not backing off as Grubb zoomed closer. At the last instant Nick yanked the steering wheel to the left, hit the brake with one foot and the gas with the other as he worked the wheel, swinging the big Tahoe like a two-ton baseball bat.

Grubb came on like a fastball. He was going sixty, maybe seventy on the motorcycle. Nothing he could do. The bike smashed into the side of the Tahoe and Grubb flew through the air like a big awkward stork. He sailed fifty feet before he nailed a light post, then hit the pavement and tumbled, his arms and legs limp like a rag doll.

Nick backed up, dragging the motorcycle that had caught in the bumper, and stopped the Tahoe a few feet away. He got out, then walked over to the crowd gathering around Grubb.

Nick looked down at Grubb's body. When Nick was a little kid, he used to play with a GI Joe doll, twisting the arms and legs into impossible positions. That's how Grubb looked now. Blood and some sort of clear fluid leaked out of his ears.

"Is he dead?" somebody asked.

I sure as hell hope so, Nick thought.

A man had his phone in hand. "I'll call an ambulance."

Grabowski walked around, gripped Nick's elbow.

"You got him."

"Yeah, I guess I did." He took a closer look at Grabowski. "Hey, your nose is still bleeding."

Grabowski swiped at it again with the back of his hand. "You got a handkerchief or anything?"

"Nah. Wait, hold on. I'll be right back." Nick walked over to the Tahoe, took out a package of tissues he remembered seeing on the dashboard. By the time he reached the crowd around Grubb again the ambulance crew was there.

It looked to Nick like they were just going through the motions for the benefit of the spectators. Grubb was still breathing, but he overhead one of the medics say the words "brain dead."

Nick stepped forward. "I'm his uncle," he said

to one of the medics. "My nephew's last wish was that his organs be donated."

"You hear that?" the medic called to his partner. "Radio the hospital and tell them we've got a donor coming in. There might be time if we hurry. It's a quick run down to Southern Delaware General." The medic looked back at Nick. "I'm sorry about your nephew."

"I know you tried," Nick said.

"Maybe some good will come of this," the medic said. "His organs could really help someone."

Nick grinned. "I certainly hope so."

CHAPTER 30

Hawley's office felt like a locker room right after the team won a big game. They had good reason to feel like all was right with the universe. Fat Boy and Dr. Kreeger were behind bars. Hospital administrator Roger Cramer had been picked up trying to board a plane to Costa Rica. Grubb's organs were on a plane to help someone who needed a transplant.

To put the icing on the cake, it was a beautiful blue sky day at the beach, with a pleasant salty breeze off the Atlantic. Life was good, if you didn't dwell too much on those who would never enjoy another day like this. The good news was that the bastards who had turned so many beach vacations into a nightmare were permanently out of business. Nick preferred to see the tide as coming in, not going out.

"Hey, Logan, I hope you clipped out some of those newspaper stories and put them in your scrapbook," said Grabowski, whose nose was now about the shape and color of a plum. He had gauze and a metal splint taped over it. For a skinny guy, Grubb had landed a solid punch.

"Is that why you bought a dozen copies of the News Journal this morning?" Sarah asked, ribbing him.

"I just wish somebody had quoted Logan saying, 'I'm his uncle,' " Grabowski said. "That was rich. I love the idea of Grubb getting parted out like a stolen Honda Civic."

They had a right to feel good, Nick thought. Their lives had been pure hell the last few days as they ate, worked and slept with this case. Closing it out was like walking out of a cave they had been lost in.

Chief Hawley walked in with Councilman Jenkins and everyone quieted down. Nick flicked his eyes at Sarah, then at Grabowski. They nodded back.

"Okay, okay, great job everybody," Hawley said, looking pleased, his round face bright. "Before you get to feeling too good, don't forget there's still a lot of bad guys out there."

"C'mon, chief," Grabowski said. "This is Rehoboth Beach. Is somebody double parked?"

"In case you haven't noticed, we've had quite the body count around here."

"We just want to savor the moment."

"Well, go ahead and savor it. You can savor it the rest of today and even this evening, but tomorrow let's get back to work," Hawley said, not sounding as annoyed as he wanted to. He was obviously pleased, too, with visions of a secure retirement on the horizon, or perhaps because of a possible hefty pay raise courtesy of a deeply grateful city council. Two days ago he'd been on the verge of being forced to resign in disgrace.

Now, he was the police chief who had saved summer.

Nick spoke up. "Like the chief said, there are a lot of bad guys still out there. Some of them are right here in this room."

Hawley stared at him, looking puzzled. "Nick, what the hell are you talking about?"

"Really, detective," Jenkins said. "All of you have done a fine job. The mayor is very happy."

"There's still one small loose end in the case," insisted Detective Monahan.

"Go on and tell the chief," Grabowski urged. "He needs to hear this."

"We know the people abducted from the trail had their organs removed," she said. "So did the victims hauled away by that ambulance. And some homeless people were rounded up and taken to the hospital, too."

"Sure," Hawley said. "We know that. Grubb and Fat Boy dressed as cops and picked them up, back in the winter."

"Somebody knew what Grubb and Fat Boy were doing," Nick said. "Somebody on the inside was covering for them."

"Don't go stepping on any land mines," Hawley warned, looking concerned.

"Something funny has been going on the whole time we've been on this case," Nick said. "It all started with the victims hauled off in that fake ambulance. One night Frank Wilson's wife came in to check whether we'd learned anything. I couldn't even find the missing person's report, even though she swore she'd been in to fill one out."

"What are you getting at?"

"I'll come back to that," Nick said. "Remember the first abduction? It happened when Sarah and I were *not* patrolling the trail."

"Someone tipped off Grub and Fat Boy that we wouldn't be there," Sarah said.

"After that, Grubb did as he pleased," Nick said. "I think he decided there was no way we would ever catch him. Not while he had someone on the inside feeding the bad guys information."

"Grubb's luck ran out," Grabowski said.

Nick smirked at Grabowski's comment, then continued. Hawley was still staring at him with his mouth half open, as if he was watching a train wreck, but was helpless to stop it. "The person who helped protect Grubb and Fatboy wasn't someone who knew everything about the investigation," he said. "For instance, he didn't tip off Grubb that we'd be staking out the ribbon-cutting ceremony at the boardwalk yesterday. But he knew enough to give information to the bad guys."

"Nick, you're not making much sense," Hawley said. "I don't think you've got much going on here beyond a wild idea."

"I'm getting to the proof," Nick said. "I'll admit that not too long ago all I had was this nutty idea that someone was helping these assholes steal organs."

"What proof?" the chief asked.

"Your police dispatchers were told that there would be a special detail rounding up those street people to make sure they received medical care," Nick said. "When some concerned citizens called, that's as far as they got."

"Who told the dispatchers that?" Hawley asked, looking genuinely mystified. "It would have to come from me, and I sure as hell didn't tell them that."

"What if the order came from a city councilman?" Nick said. "Ask Mr. Jenkins about it."

Jenkins stood up. "This is all ridiculous," he said, laughing nervously. "I don't know what you're talking about."

"Are you sure? You went around the chief here and gave the order directly to the dispatchers that let Fat Boy and Grubb have a free hand," Nick said. "You personally told those dispatchers not to concern themselves with any complaints coming in. They told me all about it."

"As a member of the city council I observe police operations and make recommendations to the mayor of this city regarding operational procedures. I don't give direct orders to police officers—or dispatchers."

"That's not what the dispatch shift supervisor told me," Nick said. "According to her, you put out the word that Grubb and Fat Boy were on special assignment and to leave them alone. Of course, you didn't identify them by name. You told the shift supervisor that it was a city hall project. She couldn't have known, of course, that those two thugs weren't actual police officers but were wearing uniforms you obtained for them. She didn't question it, Councilman Jenkins, because it came directly from you."

"I don't know what you're talking —"

"Don't try to deny it," Nick said. "The street people rounded up were taken to Southern Delaware General Hospital where their organs were harvested and sold. You just happen to be on the hospital's board, don't you, Mr. Jenkins?"

"I belong to a number of boards and

committees," Jenkins said. He sniffed and puffed up visibly, playing the offended do-gooder. "I volunteer for everything from the Pumpkin' Chunkin' Festival to the Lewes Historical Society to the Boy Scouts."

"How many of them run facilities that make lots of money selling people's organs?"

"I'm leaving," Jenkins said. "I don't have to listen to this."

Grabowski stood and blocked his path. "You're not going anywhere," he said quietly.

Jenkins turned to Nick. "You son of a bitch! This is all your fault."

"What's my fault? That you're going to jail as an accessory to murder? You wouldn't have gotten away with it. That loopy surgeon Kreeger didn't know you personally, but the hospital administrator did. When we picked him up last night he told us everything. The thought of going to Gander Hill prison had him scared witless. He was the one who was fixing the books to feed money to you, Kreeger and himself. You were getting thousands of dollars to run interference for him because he needed a safety net. He needed inside information that you could provide."

"That's preposterous!"

"Is it? You told him when we'd be on the Breakwater Trail so that Grubb and Fat Boy knew to avoid us. You even snooped around here until you found Frank Wilson's missing person's report, and then you removed it. Because you were in here all the time, no one suspected anything when you started going through the files. You completely abused your privileges as a councilman. We only know there *was* a report because of Wilson's widow."

Jenkins shook his head. He took a long time answering. When he did speak, it was in a quiet, defeated voice. "I didn't know anybody was going to get hurt. I wouldn't have done it if I'd known that. That guy Frank Wilson was already dead and gone. I was just passing along information. It was easy money."

"Then I hope the money was worth it. I'm sure ten to twenty years in the Delaware state prison isn't going to be easy time." Nick turned to Chief Hawley, who sat behind his desk, looking stunned. "*Now* we've got all the bad guys."

• • •

"This is how we celebrate?" Sarah said in disbelief. "With fish and chips?"

"My treat."

"You really know how to spoil a girl."

"I was thinking about putting some vinegar on my chips," Nick said. "You might want to try a little gratitude on yours."

They were in line at the Go Brit! take-out window on Rehoboth Avenue. It was shaping up to be a lovely day, hot and sunny, but with that fresh breeze coming in off the ocean. Nick breathed deeply, feeling his chest swell and the air expand inside him. The breeze had a salty tang. He kept catching whiffs of sunscreen and banana-flavored taffy.

The case had worn them all down, but at the same time it had done his body a lot of good. He was in better condition than he'd been in for years from all that running. Now if he could just get a load of wood to split out at the beach house, his workout would be complete.

"I wonder if today's meeting was the best time to bring up Jenkins," Sarah said. "You do realize that once Hawley gets over the shock, he's going to chew us out for not letting him know our suspicions sooner."

"And we'll tell him we had to be sure. These aren't allegations you make lightly about someone in Jenkins' position. Besides, we took him by surprise. The dumb bastard admitted it."

"I'm not looking forward to the rest of the day," Sarah said. "I don't know if I can face all that paperwork."

"Get used to it," Nick said. "Catching the bad guys is fun. The hard part is filling out forms in triplicate."

"They'll be wondering where we are down at

headquarters," Sarah said.

"Who cares? We're entitled to a two-hour lunch after what we've been through. After this, I'm thinking about a slice of the bacon and sausage."

"Is food all you ever think about?"

Nick looked at her. "No," he said. "As a matter of fact, it's not. I was also thinking about what a great job you did catching these bad guys. I was thinking about what a great cop you are."

"I'd say the same about you, Nick. You've got to admit, we make a good team. Are you still thinking about going back to the mountains?"

"I'm not in any hurry," Nick said, and raised his soda in a toast. They tapped their paper cups together. All around them, throngs of vacationers went about their business, lugging towels and blankets and kids on the way to the beach like happy sun-drenched lemmings.

"Ching, ching," Sarah said.

Then they walked down the boardwalk, soaking up some sun of their own, munching on fish and chips. Partners.

ABOUT THE AUTHOR

David Healey has been a journalist, librarian and teacher. He has written several novels, including the Civil War novel *Sharpshooter* and a mystery, *The House that Went Down with the Ship*. His nonfiction books include *Great Storms of the Chesapeake*, *Delmarva Legends & Lore*, and *1812: Rediscovering Chesapeake Bay's Forgotten War*. His articles and essays have been published in many magazines, including American History, The Washington Times, Blue & Gray, Running Times and Maryland Life. When not writing, he enjoys hiking, working on his old house, and driving his family crazy by pulling over to the side of the road to read historical markers. Visit him online at www.davidhealey.net

CPSIA information can be obtained at www.ICGtesting.com
Printed in the USA
LVOW11s1908240315

431820LV00005B/605/P